ACKNOWLEDGMENTS

This book was written with a fervor I'd never imagined myself to have. Only because of my family's encouragement was I able to scribble with abandon. Kaela, Ava, Isla Belle and Damon—because of you, I get to be me.

Behind the pages of every book is a quiet village made up of authors clapping, cheering and consoling each other—and for the lucky ones, there's another level of commitment—babysitting. A big shout-out to Esther Hatch and Melanie Jacobson for keeping me on task and my butt in the chair.

Adam Berg and Connie Williams, I am continually apologizing. You both have the horrible task of seeing the roughest of drafts (how we're still friends is beyond me).

Ranée and Kaylee, you're everything this girl could ask for—and more.

And to my ARC readers, Sarah Reynolds, Mandy Biesinger, Loretta Porter, Jess Heileman, Shelley Strong, Chantell Farley, and Jill Warner. Without you, I would hang my head in shame. Thank you for catching my errors and plot holes—I absolutely appreciate all that you do.

OF INK AND SEA

CLARISSA KAE

CARPE VITAM
PRESS LLC

To Damon...
If fate hadn't stepped in, I cannot imagine how our lives would be.

※ I ※

S ienna
   Los Angeles, California: Present Day

THE POLICE STATION HAD UNDERGONE A RECENT REMODEL SINCE MY last arrest. The sickly pink walls and baby blue linoleum was replaced with neutral, off-white paint and gray tiled floors. Old or new, neither version had quality lighting, giving everyone—officer or visitor alike— an unhealthy pallor.

I waited until my camera was safely handed over by the clerk before breathing a sigh of relief. Being arrested at a protest wasn't uncommon—an occupational hazard for some photographers, a badge of honor for others. It didn't matter how eager the magazine or news outlet was for pictures. No media house, and I mean *no media house* reimbursed for a broken camera.

Inspecting the lens, I double checked the flash bulb, ignoring the officer's grunt of disapproval. Before I could respond, my cousin cleared her throat.

"Thank you for taking care of her." Hugging the camera to my chest, I purposely batted my eyes at the clerk, *not* the brooding police officer. It was childish, but his brutish behavior hours before begged me to retaliate.

Lacy smiled sweetly to the police officer, apologizing on my behalf. She ushered me out the door, her high heels clicking along the floor. Lacy kept her face neutral and her mouth shut. Being my older cousin by several years, she was my self-appointed caretaker. Lacy caught my smirk and frowned. She motioned to her car with a slight shake of the head.

I tossed a wink over my shoulder at the frustrated police officer exiting the building. He folded his arms across his puffed-up chest. He'd ignored my media badge last night at the university protest, and with the help of my cousin, had a meeting with his superiors. It wasn't the first time we'd locked horns. Waving my fingers at the officer, I assured him it wouldn't be the last.

Sliding into the passenger seat, I caught Lacy's searching gaze. She waited until we were on the freeway before she gave her practiced sigh. This time however, she shook her head instead of launching into her hour-long dissertation on my careless behavior.

She said nothing. Tension filled the silence.

I fidgeted when she didn't take the exit to my hotel. "Lacy?"

She gave a curt shake of her head, her dark hair sliding forward on her shoulder. She hadn't curled it, nor had she styled it. She must have heard about my arrest and drove straight to the station. "You're lucky they dropped the charges."

"They wouldn't have stuck." This wasn't my first rodeo. My arrest had been recorded and spread by protestors greedy for a viral video. There were several photographers, but I was the only one greeted by name—it was media gold.

"It's getting harder, Sienna."

"Thank you for getting me." Guilt wiggled in. I could almost hear my parents—and her parents—lowering their voices, whispering their justifications for my behavior. With only a bachelor's degree, I was the odd one. My conversations and friends were light on cerebral and heavy on passion.

"Which time?" Her tone was light but her lips were taut.

"I did show him my badge." I sounded half my age and by the way Lacy was treating me, I deserved every bit of it. At twenty-seven, I still hadn't found my rhythm.

"You defied his orders, Sienna. Plain and simple." She mumbled something else. I wasn't dumb enough to ask.

She must not have seen the video yet. My favorite police frenemy yelled for me to move while grabbing me, making it impossible to comply. Granted, the students I photographed were completely out of control—throwing bottles and insults. The poor officer was walking a tight rope, keeping the peace in one hand and not losing his temper in the other.

Lacy combed her hair with her hand—a giant sparkler winked from that all-important finger.

"You're engaged."

A stiff smile pulled at Lacy's lips. "Yes. I am."

I'd missed it—Brian's proposal. He'd been waiting for the right moment for weeks. Curling into the seat of her car, I was seven years old again, waiting to be scolded for stealing the pie to feed the neighbor's hamster—or rushing through the house with muddy shoes, a dying baby bird clutched in my hands. My intentions were always noble. The timing, however, was horribly wrong.

"I interrupted it, didn't I?" Shame pierced me, quick and fierce. I was forever in the way. If I could have hung my head or tucked my tail, I'd do it. But the moment was already stolen. For eternity their proposal would be marred by my selfish behavior.

Lacy reached over and squeezed my hand. "No, you didn't interrupt it."

"You're a terrible liar."

She eyed me. "Thanks for helping him."

"He didn't need much help." Brian was anxious to get her the perfect ring. He was a man in love, eager to please Lacy, no matter the cost or inconvenience.

Warmth spread through my chest. The guilt was still very much alive, but its bite was less severe. Lacy had been a sister to me, a lifeline to a girl with only brothers, two older and one younger. Several years older than me, she'd somehow pitied me enough to become my biggest champion. In my family of brains and bank accounts, I was blessed with neither.

She flicked her hand, a smile spreading. "You did a good job."

"I *am* sorry."

"I know, Sienna." It came more as a sigh than a sentence. "Then you can start by forgiving me for checking you out of your hotel. I had Brian grab your stuff and take it to the house."

The image of Brian grimacing while collecting my clothes made me wince. "Please tell me you didn't."

She arched an eyebrow. "You ain't got nothing he hasn't seen before."

I smirked. Her fiancé's kids had rubbed off on her. She'd spoken like a California girl instead of the aristocrat her English parents insisted she was. Every Rothesay—save me—was born in the states. Everyone held a pure, unadulterated American accents. That was the beginning and end of my family's love affair with America. Our British roots were a matter of boasting—a belief beat into our psyche since infancy. My family memorized our genealogy, which helped doctors predict our unusually high penchant for Alzheimer's.

"Brian invited everyone to dinner tonight." The hesitancy in her voice told me all I needed to know.

Her tentative gaze divulged even more. I groaned and turned to the window. My parents had gathered from their Atherton compound—I refused to call it a mansion—and if they'd deigned to leave their granite columns, my brothers would be arriving as well.

"I had Brian bring your clothes because it might look better if you were back home." Lacy glanced over her shoulder, checking the lanes. A few years earlier, my brother had noticed my clothes in her guest room. When my family assumed we'd become roommates, we didn't correct them. They would be properly mortified if they knew I was essentially homeless, skipping from one news story to the next—often in different states. Every generation had a *Lost Rothesay,* and I played my part well.

"Thank you." There, in my cousin's car, I felt the beginning of farewell. Brian had pulled me aside a month before, confessing his impending proposal. He was a decade older than her but loved Lacy for who *she* was instead of her family's prestige. My parents believed he'd retired early due to his financial success connecting investors to aspiring app developers. In reality, he'd been gutted by his divorce and wanted his kids to know their father. Not even Lacy, the serial dater, could withstand Brian's tender devotion to those he loved. I'd told him as much—and found myself smashed against his chest in an eager bear hug. They would marry and their joy would overflow, leaving little room for the baby cousin who'd never found her way.

It was ridiculous how I felt both ecstatic for her and sorry for myself but emotions were something I had in spades. Controlling them was where I needed help. My mile-long arrest record was evidence enough—although, Lacy had managed to extricate me from each and every hiccup.

Like the PR champ she was, Lacy began her instructions with a low, calming voice and exited the freeway. "Only Brian knows where I went, and we are going to keep it that way, especially if you leave."

"Leave?" There was another protestor rally scheduled for next weekend right here in Los Angeles. Lacy was the one who'd told me about it, potentially the biggest protest of my career. "I can't go anywhere."

She stopped at the red light, her head pivoting. "Ioan called—"

"Who's Ioan?"

"Grandad's Ioan." Lacy looked me dead in the eyes as if I'd lost my mind. "Ioan said he was worried and did a little research, found you'd been—"

"Wait, what?" I held up a hand. She was talking about someone I'd never met. And in the same sentence as our grandfather. Grandad was more than just a grandparent to me. "Who called you?"

"I just told you, Ioan." She shrugged. "The neighbor. Come on, Sienna. It's Lydcombe."

Grandad lived thousands of miles away in Lydcombe, a small town in Cornwall, England. He hadn't so much as turned on a television—or telly, if you asked him—or touched a phone in at least a decade. He hadn't even recognized me the last time I visited. A blow I'd yet to recover from.

"And just how often does this stranger call you?" I pinched the bridge of my nose. There was something completely wrong with this scenario. Grandad's longtime housekeeper normally called my father with health updates. Not the nurses or whoever this person was. Another emotion crept in. Lacy had kept information from me. Not just idle gossip, but information on my grandfather. Something was— or had—shifted between us.

"Every month or so." She let her foot off the brake and started driving again. I swallowed the hurt, the shift widening to a canyon. She hadn't given the slightest thought to how eerie this situation was becoming. "He calls, checks in on you. Nothing untoward."

"There." I pointed at her. She'd gone formal—which meant she was maneuvering into position. My heart ached. We were normally on the same team, moving in tandem. "You just pulled a Rothesay. You said *untoward.*"

Lacy rolled her eyes. "You didn't seem to mind when I said it to your police friend."

"You don't think it's odd that a strange man calls about me? He could be just a creeper. We don't even know if he works for Grandad."

"You're assuming it's a strange man."

"Please tell me you haven't told my parents about him."

"Sienna, it's *Ioan.*" She waited, her eyes expectant. "Ioan. Lydcome Ioan."

"It doesn't matter how many times you say that name. I still have no idea who you're talking about." Groaning, I closed my eyes for a brief second. It wasn't her fault. She was getting married and shouldn't have to orchestrate my affairs. "How did he get in contact with you?"

She hesitated. "Your parents sort of talked to my parents. Then called me. And I called him."

"This is getting better and better."

"Would you rather have them calling you?" She sighed. "Your parents would have been all over you, peppering you with questions." She wasn't wrong. My parents were funny about Grandad. They wanted to dictate his diet and social calendar but they rarely spent actual time with him.

"Do my parents know he's asking about me—do they know I'm involved in any way?"

Lacy fished her phone out of the console and let her Face ID unlock the screen. "Read it."

Despite the benign texts about my grandfather, the hairs on my neck stood on end. "I don't know about this." There was something unsettling about this Ioan person. It bothered me that Lacy seemed so *un*bothered by him.

She shrugged. "Sienna, anything to do with Grandad involves you."

"Have you spoken to him on the phone? What if he's just a bot or something?"

"Yes, Sienna." She turned into her subdivision. We had five minutes before our family would make this conversation even more difficult. "Just an FYI, you're going to want to communicate via text. His accent is way stronger through the phone. In person it's a little easier."

Way stronger was about as Californian as *yeah, no*. Lacy was shedding her stiff upper lip. She caught my smirk and shook her head. "Sienna Rothesay, I swear to you. This is not your parents doing their little puppet string stuff. But Ioan does need help. So does Grandad. Your parents think you should go over and help out. They're not too keen on letting a neighbor into the house. But just know this isn't a Rothesay thing. Ioan is just a Good Samaritan here. Not a creeper. He's the same boy who dragged you from the sea. He's the same boy who listened to you prattle on and on—"

"The sea ..." A faded memory flickered in my head. I'd always had an obsession with the Bristol Channel. "I don't think I remember him."

"I do. Your brothers certainly do. He was fuming, yelling at them for letting you come down the trail." Her eyes lit with mischief. "They couldn't understand a word. He'd gone nuts, swearing at them in Cornish. Or something like that."

Eying her, I swatted her shoulder. "Like my brothers had any idea I was there."

She scoffed. "Of course not. Neither did I."

My parents said I was born with a fury, smack in the middle of a wicked storm, indicative of my personality. Curious and quiet could have been strengths if I had a healthy dose of fear. Fourteen broken bones and a dozen hospital stays had given me a reputation I couldn't quite shake.

Lacy frowned, her car slowing. I followed her gaze to the row of expensive cars lining Lacy's street. "If only Ioan were here to drag you from these waters."

❧ 2 ❧

S ienna
　　Los Angeles, California: Present Day

MY NIECES AND NEPHEWS SAT WITH PERFECT DECORUM ON THE bench, a breeze playfully pulling the branch of a jacaranda tree just above them. Their dark hair and soft, gray eyes tugged at my heart. I didn't remember their names and would have to dance around that fact. It was my own fault. I dashed from city to city with my camera in hand, my family never on my mind.

"Catherine, James and Diana," Brian whispered over my shoulder. "And over there ..." He stepped forward and gave the subtlest of nods to the chubby baby laughing in Lacy's arms. "That's Matthew's baby."

Chuckling, I looped my arm in Brian's. My younger brother had been married a couple years and, like clockwork, delivered a baby at the two year mark. "Is Matthew's baby a boy or a girl?"

Before he answered, Lacy turned, revealing the baby's adorable pink dress. Brian grinned, mischief in his eyes. "A boy. Definitely a boy."

9

"Ah, plain as day." I felt the twinge of farewell again. Brian had filled in nicely as the older brother. He laughed instead of frowned at my antics.

"Is there a reason you're sad?" He didn't look at me. His gaze was on the joy written in Lacy's face. She'd pivoted from swearing off babies to cooing at them all—fur and human alike.

"She's going to be a wonderful mother."

His gaze snapped to mine. "Do you know something I don't?"

"Oh." My face went hot. "I didn't mean that. No, I don't think she's pregnant. No, sorry."

His lips tugged to a wide smile. "She already is a wonderful mother. I guess she's technically a step mother, but it's the same to me." His face relaxed to one of contentment. "And hopefully she'll be a mother in her own right."

With the tender look in his eye, I was intruding on an intimate moment. As if on cue, Brian's daughter came to Lacy, begging for her turn with the baby. Lacy bent to hear the request but our view was blocked by my parents entering the backyard, their gazes searching. I flinched, knowing their destination.

"It's good they came." Brian's voice was low, almost apologetic. "This way you can tell them goodbye *before* you take off."

"I've repented of my bad habit." Not entirely. Instead of calling my parents to let them know where my next assignment was, I'd send a text and then shut off my phone. "Besides, there's another protest in L.A."

The upcoming protest was too good to pass up. Opposing sides were both right—local judge caught red-handed aiding refugees after their status was revoked by the ever-changing administration. Like the sea crashing against rugged cliffs, nothing was more breath-taking than an equally matched argument. Protests like this made for beautiful photos—humanity in all its glory.

He shot me an arched eyebrow. "You're not taking their offer?"

Before I could answer, my parents were congratulating Brian on the engagement. Dad's skin was peeling. He'd begun a new skin treatment to *stay relevant* as my mother called it. Apparently the job description of a consultant included never aging.

Dad and Mom were showering Brian with praise. I nodded along in all the right places and slowly inched backward. If I stayed around long enough, I'd be trapped into another one of their *time to grow up* lectures. I had a sneaky suspicion they were going to push an agenda. They'd given up on any postgraduate program.

Brian set an arm around my shoulders, preventing my escape. He turned to me and said, "I couldn't have done it without Sienna."

"Yes, she's definitely in her element." My mother smiled, her hand gesturing to the lights strung across the backyard. One party—I went to *one* college party and my parents believed I was the All-American-Sorority girl. If they only knew what their sons had done, I'd be painted the saint, not the sinner. It didn't help that my one party landed me in the hospital with a broken arm.

With a twinkle in his eye, Dad squeezed my hand. "I'm proud of you too. It's a good move."

And there it was—the agenda. With my striking features, I was the pretty princess who chased after sparkly trinkets and stories. I might not be the brains of the family but I wasn't stupid. The awkward silence in our little circle said otherwise.

"I haven't decided." I didn't know the details, nor did I feel comfortable that Lacy had kept information from me. But right now, I was grateful she'd given me a heads up. "I still have a lot of work left to do here."

"Of course you do." Dad's eyes crinkled, his smile growing. He leaned forward—if he patted me on the head, I was going to lose it.

I took a step back and felt the tension rise. We were talking about Grandad, my favorite person in the entire world. There was no reason for me not to jump at the chance to be with him. And yet that childish, rebellious side of me had me digging in my heels. For once, I wanted to be taken seriously. Just once.

Mom arched an eyebrow. "You can leave when you're done with your little project, right?"

Disappointment fell heavy on my shoulders. My work, my *little project* meant nothing to her. I wasn't a professor, a lawyer—my career wasn't important. It didn't matter that I'd won the National Humanity

Award every year for the last three. No, my work was just a *little* hobby I dabbled in until I could find myself.

"I think Sienna needs a vacation. If she goes, she should go to relax. Not work." Brian dropped his hand. "Don't worry, Sienna. Lacy's in good hands, you don't have to take care of her anymore."

My parents stifled a chuckle. They didn't believe Brian's interference anymore than I did. Lacy had always taken care of me. She'd taught me the art of verbal self defense and thought my inability to stay put was a strength, not a weakness.

"I'm going to miss her," I whispered, watching her greet Brian's parents. Guilt tugged at my heart. I should be congratulating Lacy, not pining for her.

My parents followed my gaze, my mother's face softening. "You two have been more like sisters than cousins."

"You will be missed." Brian elbowed me. "Please know that."

"I'm not going anywhere."

My parents' answering smiles made me question my own future. Everyone in this circle thought I was leaving—when was the only mystery.

"It'll be good to have you in Lydcombe. My father needs a family member, not that neighbor." Dad caught Brian's gesture. "You've done much for this family, Brian."

Another subtle blow. I shrank in size. Brian was given credit for our bond, not me. And in truth, he deserved it. He'd continued to stretch out his hand when I doubted his concern. When I was in trouble—which was often—Brian and Lacy were the ones I'd call. Not my brothers. Not my parents.

"Thank you for your influence." Mom blinked and glanced at my dad. She blinked again, seemingly surprised at the emotion she felt.

My gut twisted while I fidgeted next to Brian. I'd kept my future plans close, mostly because there was freedom to change if no one knew the details.

"The entire family appreciates your example of loyalty. No one more than my father." Dad offered his hand to Brian. Dad was giving the credit for my impending move to England to Brian. I hadn't even decided to go yet. Lacy's mother descended the porch steps, drawing the focus of my parents. Their attention—thankfully—would be gone for the evening.

Turning to Brian, I folded my arms and pierced him with a look. He rubbed his neck before holding up his hands. "How angry are you?"

"Why did Lacy keep it from me? She *just* told me in the car." Holding up my phone, I said, "They've been texting for months."

He stepped back and motioned to house. "She wanted to talk in person. No offense, you're not exactly easy to pin down."

We smiled and nodded to people streaming in and out of the house. No one needed to hear our conversation. I followed him into the kitchen. "My work is important."

Brian nodded, his face guarded. "I believe you. Lacy believes you. No one's disputing that." I pointed to my parents in the backyard. He shook his head. "They don't count. I mean, come on, they don't have a clue what you really do and it's not all their fault. You do as much damage by not explaining yourself than by their assumptions." Only Brian could give me a set-down with a twinkle in his eye.

I felt the frustration fall away. "I'm not sure if I'm supposed to be angry with you or thanking you."

"How about you just take the offer?" He grabbed Lacy's phone and plugged it into the charger on the counter. "Ioan's wanting to make sure you're compensated for helping out. He seems to know how much photography means to you and what it'd mean to leave it behind." Brian tapped out a passcode but then shook his head, doubting the code.

"Lacy already showed me the texts. They won't change my mind."

"Let's be honest, capturing your grandfather's old things isn't going to hold your interest for long."

His words pricked my heart. Brian was everything I could want in a brother but he was dead wrong. Grandad's things had always held my interest. There was magic in the walls of his home, the subtle creaking of the ancient home and the whispers of the Bristol Sea. But most of all, I loved his sketches and his family heirlooms. There was a comfort in Lydcombe I'd not felt anywhere else.

Or with anyone else.

Ioan was a stranger. He'd texted Lacy about hiring me to document

Grandad's things. The offer felt hollow. How would a stranger like Ioan have a clue about my grandfather's house or his family's history? The idea didn't make sense.

"How does Ioan have that kind of authority?" There were too many loose ends but in the safety of Brian's kitchen I felt a growing curiosity. "Wouldn't my dad and his siblings have the final say? And for the love, why am I the only one suspicious?"

"Your parents are."

"That does not make me feel any better." I'd rather not be on the same page with them.

"Lacy never mentioned Ioan?" Brian at least appeared to be confused at her secrecy.

"Only that he calls once in a while." My phone lay next to hers. Grabbing mine, I turned it on. A thought wiggled in. "My phone died before the officers rounded up the media. How did she know I was there?"

Brian held out his arms. "That's what I'm trying to tell you. *Ioan.* He knows you and your grandfather are close. He follows your career and supposedly keeps your grandfather up to date."

I doubted Grandad was *up to date* on anything, let alone his forgotten granddaughter. "Some random guy that lives near my grandfather in England calls up your fiancée. Does anyone else have a problem with that?" It was a cheap shot but the smile on his face meant I'd missed the point.

"He calls to check up on you. Not Lacy."

"That's a little convenient." My phone's screen lit up, beeping with all the missed notifications. "He's never once called me."

"Ioan's been a help." Brian tossed a bag of chips toward me and pulled out two bowls. He opened another bag and started filling one. "Your grandfather isn't doing well."

"He hasn't been doing well for a decade." I winced, realizing how crass I sounded. Most of my family avoided talking about Grandad around me. "That's not what I meant."

Brian shrugged. "He responds to Ioan."

With both hands on the chip bag, I paused, my heart racing. That was a blow I wasn't ready for. "Are you telling me my grandfather responds to Ioan but not his own family?"

"I'm not saying anything." Brian's eyes were wary. He'd touched a nerve. I had little doubt Lacy had already warned him. I was a bit touchy when the topic turned to Grandad.

Aside from Lacy, Grandad was the only one who'd truly understood me. With one look we could unite against our family's arrogance. I was the only one who'd sit in his kitchen and beg for another story, another myth. Anything to hear about the people I'd never meet. Perhaps, I did the same thing with the camera—captured stories of strangers.

"Then what are you saying?" My grandfather served his country, traveling the world before settling down in his ancestral home. His progeny—my father included—were born and raised far from the warm waters and black rocks of Lydcombe, a small town in Cornwall, England.

Except me. I'd come six weeks early in the middle of a raging storm. Not only was I the first girl born to a Rothesay son in generations, I was born in the ambulance. My first breath was the mist of the sea. From that moment, I was the darling of my grandfather's life. No sin was too great —until seven years ago, when Alzheimer's wiped me from his memory. My greatest cheerleader was ripped from me. I'd been untethered since.

I dropped the bag of chips and braced myself against the counter. Emotions were never something I could hide. My relationship with Lacy was changing—she'd been talking to a stranger about me—about Grandad. Betrayal, anger and hurt fought for dominance. My face flushed. This party wasn't about me. Brian should be outside celebrating, not confessing another trap my family had laid.

"I'm sorry," I finally whispered.

"Sienna..." He reached for me, his expression unsure. I shook my head. He pushed the bowl I was supposed to be filling aside. "Lacy loves you."

"I'm not questioning that."

"Ioan asked if you'd be open to staying with your grandad. He was hoping you'd be able to see him, maybe talk to him." Brian lowered his head. "Lacy said you two always had a connection. Something special."

"We do." I shook my head. "I mean, we did. But he doesn't remember me."

Like an old wound, the ache in my chest reopened. Jumping from story to story, kept the hurt of my grandfather's illness at bay. If I stopped—or if I returned—would it consume me?

"Maybe Ioan reminds your grandfather of himself. Ioan could be the bridge for you." Brian went back to loading the chips in the bowl. "You spend your life capturing moments that will be marked in history. What if you could capture the moments of your own history?"

"Like what?" There was no history of little ol' me. I didn't live anywhere long enough to put down roots. Although, just the idea of Grandad's history lulled the anger to a simple rolling wave.

"Ioan thought you could photograph your grandfather's pictures and things. He seems to think documenting his history will trigger his memories. You'll be paid by the estate." Brian slid my empty bowl from me and began filling it.

I blinked at the bowl, realizing I'd never filled, or fulfilled, anything. I'd bounced from one university to the next and barely graduated with a photography degree. I was twenty-seven years old and never once signed a lease. "Does this Ioan know about me?"

"You mean, did your parents strong-arm him?"

"They seemed pretty certain." I might have asked the question, but I didn't want the answer. Leaving for Cornwall was out of the question. My heart shriveled at the mere thought. It wasn't just that I was a coward of the first order, but my grandfather's Alzheimer's had hurt more than I cared to admit. Cornwall was where I was Sienna Rothesay, the pride and joy of Sir Liam Rothesay. The sweet shop down the way from my grandfather's house carried tart lemon drops just for me. The doctor up the hill would chuckle while setting my bones after another spill. There was magic in Cornwall as if everything I touched became softer, more colorful instead of the black and white, the good and bad of the world. Or maybe Cornwall was gray, a blend of both. The last time I visited, the joy had been sucked from the small town—everyone looked at me with pity instead of pride.

"Your parents, well ..." Brian's voice pulled me from my thoughts.

"Lacy let the idea of you going to Cornwall slip so they'd stop pestering her."

"What were they saying?" My heart warmed. Lacy had never stopped defending me, even when I didn't deserve it.

"They kept thanking her for taking such good care of you." Brian pulled the chopped vegetables from the fridge. There wasn't a need to refill the platters but he must have wanted something to do. "She told them you helped her see what was most important. Said that because of you, she realized she wanted a family."

"That's not true."

"She told them you were thinking of heading back to Cornwall to visit him." He stopped and faced me, his eyes full of brotherly affection. "I don't know if it's the right move. I'll support whatever decision you make but..." He looked away.

"What?" I hated that I asked. Whatever he was about to say felt weighted.

"Your parents, shoot, even Lacy's parents, well ..." He rubbed his neck. The internal debate was written on his face. "They're good people."

"I'm not questioning your love for my family," I said softly.

He smiled ruefully. "Sienna, they're good people, but I sometimes wonder if they're good for you. They mean well, I know they do, but you can't shove a circle into a square hole."

"I've always known I don't fit in." I'd hoped it alleviated his guilt but his frown deepened.

"Just because you're a different shape doesn't mean you don't fit." He gathered both bowls of chips in his arms. "I don't like that idea at all. It implies you're wrong because you're different. Maybe they're wrong. I guess what I'm saying is this, instead of searching—instead of capturing protests or other points of history—why not make your own? And why not make it with people who see you as you are. If you're a circle, be a circle."

His brow furrowed up in frustration. He'd never been eloquent, his talent lay in numbers, not emotions. But the message came across all the same. My bond with Grandad was based on acceptance, a foundation of love I could not break. I could not sink low enough or behave badly enough to earn his ire. My grandfather loved me—whether I was a circle or not. My heart softened. Maybe it was time to return to Lydcombe.

Brian sighed and turned to go.

"Thank you, but I'm not going to document my own history. Or my grandfather's things." When he paused, I added, "I'm going to document him. The great Sir Liam Rothesay." I blinked, hating the fact that just an idea could bring me to tears. "I'll go ... but not for my parents. Not for Ioan. I'll go for myself. I'll go to take pictures of the Grandad I knew. The grandfather I miss."

3

enan
Coch Bay, South Wales: 1606

In the early afternoon light, Morgannwg Castle stood before Kenan, its walls overlooking the Bristol Channel between Wales and Cornwall. For the hundredth time, Kenan questioned his father James' ambition. James Rothesay was the baron of Lydcombe not the king of England. Even from Kenan's hidden position, the Welsh castle appeared to sigh. No flags adorned the towers, the drawbridge was down, only the metal gate closed for protection. The occupants seemed to have abandoned the sad stone walls, not a soul in sight. Kenan's father had a ruthless reputation, his strategy never wrong—and yet he'd sent his son, Kenan, to extract a heavy debt payment from a derelict castle. The last time James Rothesay had been this hungry for restitution was before Kenan's birth—and over a woman.

Kenan placed a calming hand on the muscled neck of his nervous horse. The men fidgeted behind him, hiding in the cracks and low hedges. The woodland surrounding the castle was recently felled.

Abandoned tree stumps dotted the small clearing between the army and the stone walls, like the gravestones of a cemetery. The lack of cover altered Kenan's plan. With the earl's ground cover immediately surrounding the castle now gone—Kenan could not take the castle by force. He would have to use strategy. He eyed his friend Jowan. Both men were homesick, eager for their farms on the island. Kenan was well versed in Welsh warfare. They laid traps in the forest, hiding their mercenaries in the cracks of their bloody country. Kenan would know —he was both Welsh and Cornish. If he were English, he'd pray to their God, hoping the rumors of the foolish earl in the castle were true, that the man's mind was as dim as the weather.

Kenan held up four fingers, signaling his most trusted men to follow, Jowan included. Kenan had already donned the clothes of a plain soldier and instructed his men to do the same. Without a word, the men mounted their horses and left the canopy of beech and hawthorn.

Within moments of leaving their hiding places, Kenan noticed men running from the front tower. They would notify the earl of Kenan's approach. He would keep his speech to a minimum, his accent a mixture of Welsh and Cornish nobility. He'd already hidden his ring engraved with his family crest—only his mother's side. He'd never worn his father's.

He slid from his mount and approached the guard with the missive. "I come from Lydcombe. I'm to speak with the Earl of Morgannwg."

The guard blinked, his eyes scanning the missive from right to left. He couldn't read. The man nodded to the tower. The metal gate lifted, the gears creaking in protest. The guard's eyes flicked to Kenan's pistol and sword, his brow furrowing. Kenan kept his expression blank. He'd forgotten to switch his weapons for a musket and knife, evidence of a soldier instead of a highly ranked officer.

Their horses were taken to the stable while the men filed into the great hall. The earl sat at the end of the table, his eyes drooped in boredom. His servants bustled about, placing steaming platters on the table. The plates were chipped and covered with bread and vegetables —no meat for the earl. The tenant farms must not have paid their rent.

The nobleman either hadn't noticed Kenan and his men or he was ignoring them. Morgannwg huffed and perched his chin on the top of his hand. The chair next to him was empty, his wife long passed.

Kenan waited for the guard to return to his post before stepping forward. "Lord Morgannwg, I've come from Lydcombe."

"Lydcombe?" Morgannwg glanced at them, his face screwed up in confusion. "I've never been."

The sound of approaching feminine boots echoed into the room.

Kenan felt the curious stares from his men. "Ay, my lord, tis true. But we're on an errand—"

"To rob my son blind." The shrill voice of Morgannwg's mother pierced Kenan.

She approached from the corridor, her back curved at the neck, the sign of a dowager. Her gown's bodice was low, a round neckline and tight sleeves. A matching emerald petticoat was pinned into flounces on a drum, like a stick stuck in the middle of a wheel. It would be deucedly hard to wear while riding—not at all practical wear for movement. The woman must never venture far from the castle walls.

The pieces fell into place in Kenan's mind. She was the castle's authority.

Lady Morgannwg straightened her posture, hiding the curve of her back. If not for her gray hair, she'd pass for half her age. "I've asked the almighty Baron of Lydcombe for evidence of this supposed debt. Lord Rothesay has yet to deliver anything of the sort."

Kenan bowed, his gaze flicking to the young beauty at her side. She wore a gown the color of sapphire, her neckline modest and her skirt plain. The hem was worn—this woman spent her days walking. Her chin was lifted, her eyes dark and proud. Her auburn hair was the color of tree bark after a storm. She was undoubtedly Lady Morgannwg's lady in waiting.

He straightened his stance and addressed the older woman. "I've brought a missive."

"You've not read it?" Lady Morgannwg arched an eyebrow as if to say, *can you read?* Without a sound, she stepped to her son, her hand on the back of his chair. He glanced up at her, adoration in his eyes. He blinked and glanced around happily, like an innocent child.

"I'll read it." The younger woman extended her slender hand, her gaze boring into Kenan's. She couldn't be the lady's companion, not with her pride and forward manner.

Kenan hesitated, not missing the furtive looks between the women. They were playing Kenan for a fool. He'd seen this before—he could taste the desperation in the air. He'd known Morgannwg was a simpleton but Kenan's father had made it clear, Morgannwg was deeply in debt. After numerous attempts, the poor fool had avoided payment. Kenan now wondered who'd signed the document, the earl or his mother. "I was given orders to deliver this to Morgannwg."

"As his daughter, I assure you, I can handle the task." Her lips turned to a disarming smile.

He hadn't known about a daughter or her widow status. Details his father had not mentioned. Had Kenan not spent his life in strategy and warfare, temptation would have him. Her face was warm but her eyes were hard.

Warning rang in Kenan's head but he held his ground. The servants had left; only the earl's family and Kenan's men were witnesses to the repayment—or lack thereof. "I'm sorry, Miss—?"

"Under this roof, I still am addressed as Miss Morgannwg." Her smile was forced.

There was a reason she'd not given her married name. Two could play this game of distrust. "I am but a soldier. My orders were clear."

"Will tragedy befall this document in the few steps it takes to my father?" Miss Morgannwg stepped closer. Her scent of rosewater tickled Kenan's nose. A thin Celtic ring adorned her finger.

Feigning humility, Kenan let his shoulders sink. He dropped his gaze and fidgeted like the servants in his father's castle. "I'm to witness your father reading it. I'm to testify that he understands the written word."

The ladies exchanged a worried glance. And there was the truth. If Morgannwg was too dull to understand the law, he was too simple to stand as earl. As the nearest male relative, Kenan's father, Rothesay, would inherit the land and titles. The women would be cast aside, both widows—dowager Lady Morgannwg *and* Miss Morgannwg. Kenan's father would be delighted to hear of Miss Morgannwg's predicament.

Whispers of the earl's madness must have kept his daughter out of sight and without a second match. Lord Rothesay had asked for female collateral in his missive. Kenan assumed he meant Lady Morgannwg, unaware of the daughter. The realization made Kenan's throat dry. He knew exactly how his father would twist this bit of fate.

"His eyesight has dimmed." Lady Morgannwg nodded to her granddaughter. "I've been his eyes for some time now."

Kenan folded his arms, the missive tucked safely back in his hands. The earl was looking at the food on the table—a feat for a supposed blind man. Losing sight would allow the earl to keep his title. His mind would no longer be questioned. Kenan felt a bit of pride at the woman's attempt to outwit his father. "Has he seen a physician?"

"Of course." Lady Morgannwg's tone was clipped. She pulled her son to a stand.

The earl balked, his eyes wide. "I've not eaten yet."

"I believe he sees his dinner." Kenan took in the scene, the fidgeting servants and pensive stares.

Lady Morgannwg narrowed her gaze. "He is not completely without sight."

Kenan pulled a chair from the dining table and sat, the room filling with tension. He would play their game. "When did the physician expect his sight to fully return?"

"Not for weeks, sir. If at all." Miss Morgannwg sat next to Kenan, her voice soft. Inviting.

"Then we shall accommodate." Kenan motioned to his men. They sat at the table, chairs scraping and grunts included.

Her color paled. She sent a pleading glance to her grandmother. "We were not expecting company."

"To be true, Miss, we'd rather not stay," Kenan whispered. He nodded to Lady Morgannwg who led a pouting earl from the dining room. "This isn't the first time we've come to collect what was owed. I've just been given orders that this will be the last."

"Might I have a word?" Miss Morgannwg walked slowly, gracefully —fully aware that her audience was male.

One of Kenan's men hissed. Another murmured, "Don't be a fool."

Kenan gave a subtle nod to his men and followed the beauty to the corridor, the missive in his hand. He leaned against the door frame, keeping his back visible to his men. He'd not be alone with the pretending nymph. Kenan was not like his father; he would not be enticed by a woman.

"Shall I send for some ale?" Miss Morgannwg blinked innocently. "Wine?"

"None, my lady. I am on an errand."

"And yet we just entertained the priest. He declared spirits the blood of the Almighty." She spoke over her shoulder, her walk even and smooth, as if her feet never touched the stone floor. She was practiced in her art of ensnaring men. This was why Rothesay's debt collectors would return empty handed—or not return at all. She paused at the end of the corridor, her hand on the door.

"This is as far as I go." Kenan stood his ground. He'd not take another step toward temptation.

"And nothing could sway your decision?" Keeping her hand on the door, she pivoted, her other hand touching the top of her hair. The soft light from the corridor's window accentuated her silhouette. She plucked a pin from her hair. "Nothing?"

"I'll not move from the view of my men." He didn't miss the fleeting panic crossing her face. "I don't know what you're planning but I'll not partake."

Her hand dropped, her face hardening. "Are you made of stone?"

"I know the look in your eye. You were keen on deception, not passion." Kenan had only guessed. The way her jaw set and her hands clenched, he'd hit his mark. "How many of Rothesay's men did you blackmail?"

Her mouth fell open. "I've done nothing of the sort."

"Maybe not." Kenan shrugged. "But you've done something with them. Half of the men never returned. You're playing us false. You're hiding something."

"I am but a woman." She lifted her chin, her tone imitating Kenan's earlier declaration.

"I beg to differ, my lady."

"Are you confessing to being more than a mere soldier?" The gleam in her eye returned.

Kenan pulled out the document. "The roof over your head is about to be ripped away. I'd not risk the ire of Rothesay. Your father owes him a great deal."

"My father—"

"Is a simpleton." He held up a hand, halting the storm building in her eyes. "You've a choice to make. He's either incapable of running the earldom, or he's swindled a small fortune from Rothesay."

Miss Morgannwg's gaze flicked to the door where her father and grandmother had gone. Her dark eyes were drenched in fury. Kenan felt a brief twinge of guilt. He was grateful this was his last errand for his father. She lifted her chin. "A small fortune? Is that your way of being kind? Telling me I've no choice in my father's future?"

"I'm only telling you the truth."

"The truth? Can you hear yourself?" She marched toward him, her finger aimed at his chest. "How can a man be a simpleton and still be enslaved to Rothesay? How does that happen? He cannot swindle if he cannot think. It's one way or the other. And you—" She pierced the air between them with her finger. "You say you're but a soldier but your speech is fine—and you wear the sword of an officer."

Kenan held out his palm, giving her finger a mark. "What I am does not change your situation."

"Rothesay is a snake." She pursed her lips, her nostrils flaring. Her anger touched her cheek, the blush red and becoming. "And who keeps company with a snake?"

He enclosed his hand around her finger, ignoring the softness of her skin. "Other snakes?"

"Prey." She stepped back, her eyes flicking from her hand to his. "He keeps company with his own prey. Perhaps, it is you who needs the warning. Not me."

4

Sienna
Heathrow Airport, London: Present Day

GRIPPING MY ARMREST, I STRUGGLED TO KEEP MY STOMACH FROM twisting. Despite my years of traveling in the states, I never got used to flying. No matter how skilled the pilot, I hated the landing—almost as much as the take-off. Traveling to London was an entirely different animal, especially from California—a solid eleven hour flight. It didn't help that the enormous time change would have me wide awake and dead asleep in all the wrong places.

The airplane hiccupped, its tires skidding to a stop while I held my breath. I fished out my phone and turned it on, anxious for a text from Lacy. She'd visited a local church in California for a possible wedding venue and was recording snippets. I wanted to be a part of her planning—and yet, secretly every word she spoke about her upcoming wedding felt like a knife to my heart. She wasn't my mother or even my true cousin. Her stepdad was my uncle. She was a toddler when he married Lacey's mother. She wasn't biologically mine. And yet it felt like I was losing a piece of me with each step she took toward marriage.

Only one text lit my screen. Ioan had sent, *Emergency came up. Sending William. Text when you land.*

I'd spoken to Ioan exactly twice and still couldn't remember a thing about him. His accent wasn't English but it wasn't like my grandfather's either. Everything about him bothered me—even though I knew I was being petty. He'd booked my flight—giving me my favorite window seat. Views of the ocean calmed me, whether I was flying or driving. I should have felt grateful to Ioan but like a child, I pouted all the way to baggage claim and onto the airport express. The last time I visited was one of the few times I'd come without a family member. They'd normally stick me between my parents or a brother to keep me from getting distracted or worse, lost. I might have become friends with airport security a time or two.

I swore I wouldn't text Ioan. But just as I was annoyed, there was another force, a strange, exciting curiosity that had my fingers texting him as I exited the baggage claim and walked to the station building. *Landed. Headed to Paddington.*

I'd never met Ioan but his name gave me a picture of dark hair and pale eyes. He immediately sent an audio clip with step by step walking instructions to the ticket office. His helpfulness was eerie. And comforting. I'd lost my mind.

With a headphone in my ear, the other dangling at my hip, I listened once more to how he pronounced his name. He'd said *Yo-an*, something similar to Owen instead of the Americanized version Lacy had told me, closer to Ian. There was a warmth in the lilt of his voice. It wasn't familiar but it wasn't strange—somewhere in the middle. Much like me, I'd never had a solid place. I was too American to be English. And too English to be American.

The sandwich I'd eaten on the plane had long ago disappeared. My frustration with the man speaking into my ear grew with each passing second. Lacy must have told Ioan about my penchant for getting lost. That was the only reason he'd know. It was another mark against him —even if a part of me was curious.

The train attendant scanned my phone for the ticket and again, I was sitting. This time I had food in hand and my trip was limited to a few hours. What felt like a moment later, I woke with a start, only twenty miles from the obscure town of Lydcombe. Joy coursed through my veins. *Home.*

When I was a child, Grandad would take me to the black cliffs at the edge of his property, a steep trail leading down to the water. He'd squint his eyes and pretend he could see Wales. He'd pat my shoulder and tell me how Cornwall was once called West Wales. With a squeeze to that same shoulder, he'd let his hand fall back to his side, his other hand shielding his eyes. In a voice full of reverence, Grandad would say, "We're still connected, tied with the magic of our ancestors."

Like the dutiful grandchild I was, my belief in him and his theories was absolute fact. Nothing, not even my family's teasing, could convince me of the truth, but like most children, my faith shriveled with age. And now, as clumps of green and white rushed passed me, I wondered what version of my grandfather remained—if we were still connected like we once were.

My phone beeped with a text. Disappointment fell on my shoulders. It wasn't Lacy but rather Ioan. *William should be at Dartmoor station.*

Sighing, I laid my head against the seat. I'd been to my grandfather's house dozens of times. Ioan could call off his little babysitting gig. I didn't know William. Not that I knew who Ioan was either. I'd come to be with my grandfather, not Ioan. If I wanted to feel small, I would have stayed in California. The thought didn't sit well. I'd been all over the country capturing a story. Or as Lacy called it, chasing a story, and had never felt like I belonged, small or not.

A text came through. I closed my eyes for a moment, wishing it was Lacy. Peeking at my screen, I felt the now familiar frustration—Ioan. Again. *She's arriving in ten. Do not be late.*

Smirking, I texted back, *I'll let William know.*

The little bubble appeared. Ioan was writing back. The bubble disappeared. Then back again. The frustrated face of my oldest brother came to mind. If Ioan was anything like him, he'd abhor mistakes. Maybe my visit would be more entertaining than I thought.

I sent, *What is the penalty for tardiness?* I bit my lip to keep from laughing. An older woman with a gray bob a few seats opposite me smiled. She gave a nod, unwittingly encouraging me in my play. *Off with his head? His first born?*

Ioan texted back, *A black eye and eternal damnation.*

The train slowed but my interest was on my phone, no longer on the destination. Every interaction had been polite but short. He was a consummate professional. But until this moment, I had no idea what he actually did. He didn't live at the house which meant he wasn't an attending nurse for my grandfather. I texted back, *A black eye is a weak punishment. And eternal damnation ... too harsh?*

A split second later Ioan responded, *A black eye would mar his pretty face. The picture I'd take would be his eternal damnation.*

He didn't bother adding a smiley face or a goofy GIF. I half wondered if he was serious. The man was taking care of a eighty-five year old man—that would require a certain level of patience. And tenderness.

My phone beeped. This time it was Lacy—and for some reason, that was a disappointment. *The church was too dark. Had a musty smell. How's the travel?*

Before I could respond, Ioan sent, *You nervous yet?*

I chuckled. He'd thrown a gauntlet. I was the only daughter surrounded by heathen brothers. I would not back down. *The games have just begun.*

With me or William? His bubble appeared but he must have given up. Nothing else was sent.

The surrounding passengers were gathering their luggage. Slipping my phone in my pocket, I grabbed my luggage and filed out of the train car. The comfort of the sea wrapped around me, stilling my apprehension. I'd not realized I was nervous until the feeling left, chased away by the memories of Cornwall. I closed my eyes and breathed deeply.

"Sienna?" a crisp English accent asked.

I opened my eyes. A dark haired man who appeared to be a few years shy of thirty smiled at me. Charm rolled off his easy gaze and square shoulders. He would be a perfect specimen to photograph. "William?"

"That I am." His eyes twinkled and he grabbed my luggage. "The boot's a bit small."

He tossed a devilish grin over his shoulder and guided me to where he'd parked his expensive sports car—at least, I think it was. I was never into cars. It was silver and sleek. That was the beginning and end of my expertise. The way the light bounced from the smooth surface would make the photography tricky. He tossed my baggage into the poor excuse of a trunk—or *boot* as he'd called it.

My phone beeped in my pocket. William gallantly opened the passenger door. Slipping inside, I read the text from Ioan. *Are you spell-bound by Tall, Dark & Handsome?*

Yes. He oozes all that is charming. And just because, I added, *Did you really send a wolf to pick up a lamb?*

William slid behind the wheel. His phone lay on a wireless charger between us. It lit up with a text from Ioan. The first line read, *You were late.*

Giggling, I averted my gaze, my phone beeping in my hand.

"Tell me you're not leashed too?" William's voice was low, and I fought the rising laughter. William had no idea he was acting the part of predator. "For the record, I wasn't late."

"I wouldn't have noticed if you were."

"That I doubt." He adjusted the rear view mirror and shot me a dubious look. "If we were on a date, you'd know the very second I was late."

"Good thing we're not." I regretted the words the moment they left my mouth. The spark of determination was lit in his eye. He'd pegged me as a challenge. I should have gone the other way and fallen all over him but the die was cast.

"Is that a fact?" William arched an eyebrow.

"I'm only thinking of you." I motioned to his charging phone. "I have it on good authority that being late could result in a black eye or eternal damnation."

"You talked to him?" His gaze narrowed and his mouth hung open. In a flash, the doubtful look was gone.

Suspicion crept in. "Why is that a revelation?"

OF INK AND SEA

William shrugged, the playful flirt was back. "He's not the talkative type."

"He seems to have hit it off with my grandfather."

"That's because you're Liam's girl."

Warmth spread through me. *Liam's girl*. Someone claimed me. William chatted the entire drive to Lydcombe. Every few sentences he'd throw in a not-so-subtle *we should go* or *I'll show you*. William was a dime a dozen, a serial dater looking for a quick catch. Like my grandfather, I had dark facial features but our hair was a deep, earthy auburn—the bark on redwood trees after the rain. I'd spent my life having people turn to look at me and compliment my striking appearance. But like my grandfather had warned all those years ago—people caught butterflies because of their scarcity not because they loved them. I could hear his gravelly voice in my head, *Don't let someone flatter and cage you. Don't be a pretty prize.*

The older I got, the more I understood his warning. Lacy thought it was just another excuse for me to not stay in one place, including someone's heart. With William's blue eyes and dark hair, he was somebody's dream. Just not mine.

"I was given strict instructions to take you to the house." He pouted dramatically. "No time for a date today."

"Have no fear, I devoured a sandwich on the train."

His smile fell a little. "I thought you'd be more ... I don't know."

"Blonde? Tan?" Shifting in my seat, I focused on the gorse and heather, offering only my profile to William. The less I met his glance, the better.

"American." He slowed at the final curve toward the house. "Not that you're—"

"Very English." My phone beeped again. It might have been rude but I welcomed the distraction and checked. Sure enough Ioan had texted; he doubted I was a lamb. Grinning, I shifted my attention back to William. "I've been told that a lot."

"You're not at all what I expected." There was entirely too much pleasure in his statement.

"I've been told that a lot too." And not always as a compliment.

His tires crunched along the drive, bringing a slew of memories.

The weight on my shoulders lifted. The same electric current from my childhood hummed in my veins. William parked in front of the patchwork house. Built in the first century, its walls were older than my pedigree. From the street, my grandfather's home looked like three homes smashed together, not much different than the United Kingdom; England the largest structure with Wales and Cornwall on either side.

William grabbed my luggage from his car and whistled up the steps to the house. He assumed I'd followed but I'd felt the whisper of the sea. Obedient to tradition, I walked to the edge. The thin trail where I had supposedly followed my brothers down as a girl was overgrown and barely visible.

"So it's to be a sequel then?" A shadow fell across my view. *Ioan.* His presence gave an odd sensation, a thrilling comfort.

"Sequel? Don't we need an original first?"

"You don't remember?" He stood beside me, his accent strange. Not English or Cornish enough. Perhaps I wasn't the only one out of place. "Shall I grab a bit of rope?"

I refused to turn and face him, not ready to have my fictional version of who I imagined him to be rectified. "Who's to say I need help?"

"History." Keeping his gaze on the sea, Ioan leaned against an abandoned garden wall to my right. There was something familiar about him—or maybe it was the memory Lacy had put in my head. William called from the house but neither of us moved. Ioan whispered, "You don't seem to have fallen for the wolf."

"Maybe I'm the wolf." With folded arms, I turned to him, unsure of what I'd find. He kept his gaze forward, his jaw set. His shoulders were wider than my brothers' and he was maybe an inch or two shorter than William. His hair was dark and his eyes appeared light but there was something distinct about him. There was no surprise. I'd never seen him before, but he wasn't a stranger. His features were exactly how I pictured.

It didn't seem right though. I'd not had even a twinge of a memory with him in it. I let the odd sensation settle in my gut, brushing it off as inevitable. I'd not come for Ioan—but with all things Cornwall, I had hoped for something magical. It was silly and childish. Ioan was just a neighbor and I was just a lost soul.

Slowly, he turned his head, his pale eyes of green and blue meeting mine. His expression was unreadable in the afternoon light. "Promise me you'll not walk down alone."

That was unexpected. "You're not forbidding me to go?"

His eyes widened slightly. I waited for the subtle set-down, the reminder of my many mishaps. He rubbed his neck, his hands tanned. "I wasn't aware I was an ogre."

My face blushed. I felt every inch of its heat. There was a pull, a hum of electricity crackling between us. "Sorry ..."

"There's no need to apologize." He stepped forward, his words soft. He waited a beat. "Did William behave?"

"Yes—" I was suddenly dizzy. My heart raced. The sound of the ocean below seemed to sing to me, to invite me—*No.* I shot down that idea. "This ... can you hear that? I'm sorry. No, I'm not sorry. I don't know what I mean." The words were wrong. Everything was wrong. Fear crept in. Something had changed. But I didn't know what.

"If you feel the need, I'll grab a rope. All you have to do is ask." Ioan held out his hand, cupping my elbow. His touch cleared my head —the song cut off.

My heart leapt to my throat. *If you feel the need.* Like a hurricane, dozens of images flashed through my mind. The compulsion to jump in the heart of a violent protest, the curiosity of the homeless addicts —all of it—was a *need.* And now, the same pull wrapped around my waist, inviting me to the the waters below.

Like a caress, Ioan whispered, "Sometimes it's not enough to feel the warmth of a flame. Just don't go touching on your own."

❀ 5 ❀

S ienna
   Lydcombe, England: Present Day

❦

My camera felt heavy and awkward in my hands as I stood in my grandfather's bedroom. I'd come to document the man before me, but watching the shell of the greatest man I knew didn't feel right. Liam Rothesay's mind was inching toward the century mark, but his body looked as limber as when I'd been a child. He didn't speak to me when I entered the room, leaving William and Ioan downstairs in the kitchen. I didn't know their connection. They didn't appear to be close —although William had filled in for Ioan as my personal chauffeur. I was still a little shaken with the awkward conversation at the garden wall. Speaking with Ioan was oddly intimate. And overwhelming.

The late afternoon light fell into the room. When my grandmother was alive, she'd tease Grandad, asking if he'd fallen for the woman of the sea—an old myth of a Welsh woman and a Cornish man. Grandad believed the sea held the secrets of our past. The details of his myths were faded in my memories, like the sound of my grandfather's voice.

Circling him, I watched his earnest face, his eyes flicking about like someone watching a movie. I followed his gaze to the watery view outside the window. There was a boat or two but nothing out of the ordinary.

Kneeling before him, I lay the camera on the floor and clasped his hand between mine. "Grandad?"

His wrinkled brow furrowed but his gaze never wavered. On my knees, I doubted my reason for coming. My grandfather was in the chair, but his mind was out of reach. Sun spots and veins marred his hands and his long fingers were punctuated by arthritic knuckles. Out of habit, I checked the side of his left hand. As a lefty, his hand would be stained with ink from his hours of sketching. His hands were clean. And my heart was heavy.

My stomach growled and I made my way downstairs. William stood in the kitchen, twirling his car keys around his index finger. He flashed a beguiling smile as I walked in. "Ready for our fish and chips date?"

Other than the two of us, the kitchen was empty. I set my camera on the island counter. "Where's Ioan?"

"With his babies." William rolled his eyes as if to say, *where else would he be?* "Come on, let's go."

"What about my grandfather?" Grandad had lived the better part of his life in this house but it didn't seem right leaving him alone. Even if he still navigated the stairs—a worry struck me—should he be living on the upper floor? "Where's the housekeeper?"

Her name escaped me. I prayed she'd never know. The first day or so of returning, my head was a little fuzzy. If she found out, she'd hang me for sure. That is, if she still worked for Grandad. My parents had been vocal about Grandad's choice in housekeeper.

"Um ... good question." William just stood there, his face blank. "We could get take-away." There was a lilt at the end but not enough to be a question, just enough to hope. I wasn't biting. He glanced around. "Should I grab Ioan?"

"No." I waved away his question. There was something off about Ioan and I'd rather not be around him just yet. I would crack open his head and have a peek when I wasn't jet-lagged. William fidgeted again.

The poor guy had no idea how hopeless his flirting was, but I couldn't be completely heartless. "What are you doing?"

"Here?" He slipped his keys in his pocket, his shoulders resigned. "Or for a living? Marketing, if you must know."

I searched the fridge. If I was here to help, I might as well start with dinner. "Here. What do you do for Grandad?"

"Ha." William waited for the punch line. When I kept searching the fridge, he said, "Oh, you mean, why am I here? Right now?"

"Yeah, I know Ioan asked you to pick me up." Someone had gone grocery shopping recently. The veg was fresh and enough to make a salad—that would be easy. My cooking skills had not improved since I'd left home, not that my mother was the all-American housewife. Take out and leftovers had been my staple.

"He had another emergency." William circled the large island and jumped on the counter next to the fridge. "Happens a lot with horses."

"Grandad has horses?" My grandfather had never ridden. Nor had my grandmother.

"Uh, no." He chuckled. "They are Ioan's and you'll do well to remember just how much pride he takes in his babies."

Shutting the fridge, I stood opposite William. He swung his legs back and forth, looking like a mischievous boy. "Where are they? The horses, I mean."

"In the stables." William's smile dimmed. He, like so many other men I'd run across, felt lost when the topic wasn't on them.

"Grandad doesn't have stables." The lot was almost entirely surrounded by national land, part of the Heritage Coast. There were three homes along the thin line that butted up against a national preserve. The front gardens were pitiful, holding only enough space for a driveway before dropping down to the cliff and the bright yellow Cornish gorse. But then again, I'd never explored the other homes as a child. The sea had always been my temptation.

"Ioan has stables. His family has had horses since the beginning of time." William narrowed his gaze. "You don't know who he is, do you?"

"Not a clue." I folded my arms against the chill that crept across my neck. The wind picked up outside. I felt the pull of the sea once more, calling me. Like it had seven years ago, the whispers had become louder, more urgent. There had been a shift in the song I'd heard. I'd always blamed it on Grandad's Alzheimer's. He couldn't talk to me so the sea did it for him.

"Ioan Morgannwg." William waited for the shock. His eyes widened when I said nothing. He scratched his head and gave a nervous chuckle. "Doesn't ring a bell does it?"

"I have absolutely no idea what you're talking about." Something was off but I wouldn't confide that to William. My focus had always centered on Grandad and the sea. There wasn't much room for a neighbor.

"His mum was Lady Morgannwg." He winced at *Lady Morgannwg*, like it was an insult. "You know, *the* Lady Morgannwg."

The side door snapped open. The sound of boots falling to the floor echoed. Ioan's low voice carried. "William hasn't left yet?"

William straightened as Ioan came from around the side door. Impressed, I asked, "How did you know he was still here?"

Ioan eyed William, his expression unreadable like before. "William is not hard to find."

I felt a chill—there was more to how Ioan knew but I held my tongue.

"I was going to feed the poor girl." William slid down from the counter and clapped Ioan on the back. "Shall we get you something as well?"

"Doris will have your hide," Ioan warned and went straight to the sink, blood on his hands.

"Doris." I tossed a towel on the counter next to Ioan. "I couldn't remember her name."

"She loves me." William chirped. "Besides, she deserves a night off."

"What was the emergency?" Reaching over, I turned on the faucet, my arm brushing against Ioan's hand. A whisper tickled my ear. I whipped around but William wasn't near enough, he was still at the edge of the island. My heart hammered in my chest. I could have sworn someone whispered in my ear.

"Colic." Ioan didn't seem to notice my odd behavior. He scrubbed his hands and eyed my camera on the counter.

"I thought colic was something wrong with the stomach." Horses were as foreign to me as dogs. I'd never lived anywhere long enough to own an animal.

He turned off the faucet and gave his hands a hard fling. "It is. But I have to shove a plastic tube up their nose with mineral oil." He wiped his hands on the towel before folding it neatly on the counter. "It hurts like hell and bleeds like the dickens."

William grabbed his stomach and laughed a touch too loud. "I'm going to colic if we don't get food soon."

"You've two hands." Ioan checked the thermostat on the wall and then walked up the same stairs I'd just come from.

"It's hard to get a word in." William *tsk*ed loudly. "He just doesn't stop talking."

"Right." Exhaustion settled on my shoulders. I stifled a yawn but knew jet lag would win if I didn't start moving. "Do you know which room I'm staying in?"

William's lip curved to a devilish grin. "No, but I'd love to find out."

"That wasn't an invitation."

"Yet." He cocked his head to the side.

I'd be wasting my breath. "I thought you were going to get food?"

"Oh." He was caught. He'd wanted food to be a date but I needed to be alone. Being with William, even if I didn't know him well, was exhausting. "I'll be back." He paused a moment before leaving, his pride a little bruised.

My luggage was in the grand living room just off the kitchen. The ceiling was high and imposing, the aura Tudor-ish and ancient. My beat-up suitcase stood in the center, the handle still extended.

A breeze fanned the pages of an open book on the table next to my case. The windows on either side of the fireplace were open, the wind chilling. I slid each window closed, the sound echoing in the spacious room. Nothing had changed in years—possibly generations. The walls —except for a few of my grandfather's sketches—were still lined with chairs and paintings, each from a different era. The other living room on the opposite end of the house, dubbed the *Great Room* had two pianos, both from centuries before my grandfather's time. My suitcase was the most modern item and yet it was by far the most abused belonging.

I went to close the book but paused—my hand over the pages. In the center was a drawing of an old inkwell. The sketch wasn't one of Grandad's; his were charcoal or a broad ink. This was the work of someone else. A whisper caressed my neck. I jumped to a stand. No one. I was alone. The page fluttered from my movement. I gathered the book to my chest, the whisper coming once more.

The floor creaked. I spun around. Ioan stood in the doorway, his back bathed in the light from the kitchen. "Are you well?"

"I didn't hear you." The edge of the book cut into my arm. I relaxed, hoping he didn't notice.

"I gathered that." He stepped into the room and scanned the walls.

"What are you looking for?"

"For whatever you won't tell me." His voice was smooth, not a hint of emotion. And alluring.

"You scared me." It came out defensive, but I didn't care. Lacy trusted him and possibly Grandad, but I didn't. Not with something so sacred—odd how an eerie feeling, like a whisper, could feel intimate.

Taking another step, he searched my face. "I thought you were a wolf."

"Says the man who sneaks up on people." Silence filled the space between us. A warning rang in my head but I didn't know if was for the whisper or the man in front of me. "Where are you from?"

If he was surprised by my question, he didn't show it. "Everywhere."

"Are you always this exact?"

"Only when people are vague." He held out his hand.

I retreated, my calves against my suitcase. "I wasn't vague."

"I didn't scare you." He took another step forward, his hand still outstretched. "But I'm fairly certain I know what did."

"You do not. And I don't need your help." I pushed at his hand. I was standing just fine on my own. He could keep his hand to himself.

"The book, Sienna."

"Oh." Embarrassed, I handed it over. My name on his lips settled the air between us. "Sorry, I didn't know it was yours."

"So it seems." With a frown, he searched my face again. "Wales. I was born in Wales."

No wonder Grandad liked him. My grandfather loved all things Welsh—the language, the people. All of it.

"I didn't mean to intrude." It was my grandfather's house, and here I was, apologizing to a stranger. My arms felt empty, as if they missed the book. Or maybe Ioan's drawings reminded me of Grandad. "Who are you?"

Ioan arched an eyebrow. "Didn't William already tell you?"

"He said you were Ioan Morgannwg." The chill tickled my neck. He'd known about my conversation with William—I wondered what else he knew. He seemed to have no qualms telling William he was late or telling me to be careful at the edge of the property. "I'm not from here. I don't know what that means."

"Does it matter?" There was an edge in his voice. It made him appear more human to me. For the past few days, he'd been little more than a character in my head.

"My family says you can reach Grandad. Something no one else has been able to do in years. So yeah, I think it does matter." I hadn't meant to raise my voice but I had. Not a week before, I was in another room, arguing with a police officer about the validity of my questions. That man had thought me impertinent too.

"I'm not him."

"What?" Recoiling, I stumbled back from him. He'd read my mind. *No.* That was impossible. "What did you say?"

"What did you think I said?" He emphasized each word, like I would do with my nieces and nephews when they didn't understand something.

"Don't patronize me."

"Wouldn't dream of it." He arched his stupid eyebrow again.

"Answer the question." I growled and then sighed. Jet lag. That was the reason for me feeling unsettled. It had to be.

"I am Ioan Morgannwg. My family's land borders yours." His voice was soft again, alluring. He bent down and gently took my hand. I should leave—an electric hum crept up my arm from his touch. A peace settled into my gut. "What scared you?"

I kept my chin down, his chest covering my view. My pulse calmed, slow and steady. I was on the edge, trying to decide if Ioan was worth trusting. The electric hum became stronger. I would trust—just this once. "I thought I heard something. A whisper."

"What did it say?"

"I don't know." I rubbed the bridge of my nose with my free hand. "It wasn't words. I know it doesn't make sense but I *did* hear it."

"I am not the one doubting." His hand was still holding mine. A delightful thrill ran up my arm.

A door opened, echoing to the room from the kitchen. "Three plates of fish and chips," William called out to the house.

Ioan retreated, his hand falling away. He reached down and grabbed my suitcase. "I'll put this in the blue room."

Without another word, he left, taking the long way around to the upstairs room. William's hopeful face appeared in the doorway. "Ready?"

I nodded, fighting the urge to look over my shoulder at Ioan. A flicker of an image appeared in my mind, Ioan with his back against the hallway, his book in one hand and my suitcase handle in the other.

❧ 6 ❧

K enan
  Coch Bay, South Wales: 1606

❧

JOWAN PACED THE LENGTH OF THE SMALL BOARDING ROOM IN
Morgannwg Castle. The rest of Kenan's men had snuck back to the
army just outside the clearing. "How long?"

"A few hours at most." Kenan had hoped to be on his way to
Lydcome by now but his father had warned him. *Morgannwg will not
succumb easily.* Kenan's men were only twenty large. The rest of the
army were paid mercenaries employed by his father. The mercenaries
were bound by their pockets, not honor. His time fighting the Dutch
war had taught him the world was larger than his father's land, and
honor could not be purchased. But more than anything, Kenan had
learned the ugly side of man. He'd left as the younger son, filled with
innocence and eager for his father's approval. He'd returned bloody
and broken—and little regard for his father's whims.

"I don't trust them." Jowan stretched his neck and rolled his shoulders. "There's secrets in these walls."

"There's secrets in every wall." This was why Kenan had purchased his own land. He'd not be shackled to Lydcombe or his father. That was his brother's fate.

Jowan rubbed his face and neck. "Are we taking payment back to Lydcombe straightaway?"

Kenan smiled, taking in the chipped walls and ancient furnishings. "I know what you're asking."

"Then answer it." Jowan inspected the other bed, peeking below and around the crooked frame.

"If there's payment, we'll take it home."

Jowan's head snapped up. "Lydcombe isn't home."

"Ay." Kenan toyed with the handle of his sailor knife. The blade was sharp but short, fitting nicely in his palm. "Our men will sail home, my father's will take the long way round."

"Truly?" There was hope in Jowan's eyes.

"You'll hold your wife by the week's end." Kenan felt a twinge of jealousy. Jowan had married his childhood love, moving his growing family to *Ynys Wair,* an island Kenan had purchased from his spoils of naval warfare.

Kenan had kept the island's church and brought a priest, promising the man freedom from the king's church and a new roof. The grateful priest knew the reason. The island in the middle of the Bristol Channel was ideal for smuggling, and the church, the perfect hiding spot. Having Jowan's brother as the presiding priest helped. All three of the men in the Wair family looked like twins, the father included.

"D'you hear that?" Jowan whispered, a hand on his pistol. "Footsteps."

A soft knock and Jowan was at the door, pistol in hand. He opened the door, his back rigid. He tossed a look over his shoulder to Kenan, his eyes dark with suspicion. "It's for you, Ken—"

Palming his knife, Kenan gave a grateful nod. Jowan had cut himself off. Whoever was at the door didn't need to know Kenan's name. Jowan retreated, his hand falling to his side. Lady Morgannwg stepped forward, a young boy carrying a pitcher trailing behind. He set the pitcher on the table and left without a word.

Kenan bowed, his hand behind his back. "My lady."

"My granddaughter says you will not leave." Her shrill voice echoed in the small room. "How is it that Rothesay thinks so ill of my son that he holds us hostage?"

"Lady Morgannwg, let us speak plainly." Kenan ignored the subtle shake of Jowan's head. The man had wanted to quit the castle hours earlier. He'd thought bringing the rest of the army to storm the walls and take by force was the quicker way. Kenan would have agreed had he not witnessed the women. To breach the walls of a man's home was one thing, but to turn out his women was another. "Your son does not have the mind—"

"How dare you." Lady Morgannwg raised her hand and cried out.

Jowan spun her around, snatching her hand. Struggling, she spat at Jowan's feet.

"I'm not here to injure you, my lady." Kenan kept his voice low. "And what is said in this room shall not leave it."

"You expect me to trust you?" Her voice shook with rage.

"Your son borrowed money from Rothesay but never paid a shilling. Ah, you can hiss all you want, my lady, but your son looks the thief. When Rothesay sent men, they either never returned to Lydcombe or they came home empty-handed. Your own grand-daughter—"

"Tread carefully, soldier." Lady Morgannwg narrowed her gaze.

Kenan's father would expose the tender feelings, twisting and turning until he'd gained all he wanted. "Let her go, Jowan."

The soldier's eyes widened before obeying. Kenan sat on the stiff bed with a sigh. "I don't want to be here any more than you're wanting us here."

Lady Morgannwg rubbed her wrist but held her tongue. Her eyes followed Kenan's hands as they searched for the missive. He held it out, his finger underlining the payment options. "The lands will be forfeited to the nearest male relative who is of age, if Morgannwg is not fit. And if the earl is sound, there's to be a payment."

"If my son took his money, where is it? The land is desolate. We're a bleeding estate."

Kenan paused, searching the woman's face. Her granddaughter was practiced in the art of deceit—was Lady Morgannwg her teacher?

There'd been whispers of Rothesay's greed, but Kenan's father gave solemn measure to a man's word. Would Rothesay cheat a man of dull wit for land and title? "James Rothesay is his nearest male relative and will inherit everything."

"No, he will not." She jutted her chin, appearing closer to her son's age.

"Rothesay's left no stone unturned." Kenan tapped the parchment and read, *"House of Rothesay*. He wouldn't have those words—"

"This castle is all Rothesay will get," Lady Morgannwg snapped. "The rest is set aside."

"A dower?" Kenan knew the answer before he asked. If Rothesay took the castle, he'd only force the earl from his home, not the ladies. There was something missing. Kenan's father would not order his guards and son to capture an impoverished estate but Rothesay had seen enough value to pay mercenaries.

"We thought my son was ill." Lady Morgannwg winced. She was dancing around her son's dullness. Either that, or she was hiding a secret. "My husband made the necessary arrangements to ensure the family was provided for. His will gives everything but the castle as support to the dowager."

She pursed her lips. "Rothesay's men went away empty handed because there's nothing to give."

Jowan shot Kenan a doubtful look. They'd both witnessed Miss Morgannwg's attempt at seduction. Kenan said softly, "Rothesay will shut him in debtor's prison, my lady."

"He's protected by his title."

"Rothesay will strip him of those protections. You know this, or you wouldn't have tried to protect him when we first came." Kenan lowered his gaze. "I've known Rothesay my entire life, my lady. He is not one to cross."

"Do not cross a mother's love." She lifted her chin, defiance in her bones.

"I do not doubt your love." Kenan peered up at the woman, his guilt at the ready. Her desperation showed in the quiver of her lip and the clenching of her hands. "But even love has its limits."

"Return to Rothesay." She threw herself at Kenan's feet. "Please, tell him we've nothing."

Kenan didn't reach for her. He knew a caged animal when he saw one. She couldn't be trusted. And neither could her granddaughter. "I have my orders."

Lady Morgannwg's head snapped up, her gaze intense and dark. "You will regret this day."

"I already do," he whispered and stood, retreating from her touch.

"Part of you knows this is wrong."

"My dear lady, I know that you are worried for your child. I know your son is a simpleton. And I know Rothesay's ambition knows no bounds." He gave a subtle nod to Jowan. This conversation was over. "What I do not know is who is telling the truth. My orders are written and I will follow them. Wrong is for the court to decide."

Jowan offered his hand to the woman.

"No." She recoiled, her teeth bared like a rabid dog. "Wrong isn't decided by the courts." She waved at the weapons on the bed. "Right is taken by the sword. Your Rothesay is nothing but a brute. He'll kidnap or maim anyone to get what he wants. He can pay his armies and raise his wealth, but he'll never be right."

"What would you have me do?" Kenan asked quietly, ignoring the subtle shake from Jowan. The man didn't trust the woman, and Kenan didn't blame him. "Have you nothing to appease Rothesay?"

Lady Morgannwg's shoulders fell. "Rothesay knows we have nothing."

"Then why would he go to such great—"

"He knows of my granddaughter." The woman's voice hushed to a faint whisper. "Elyna was raised to be a nobleman's wife. Not another mistress to be cast aside."

Kenan felt the dread. This was what his father was after. Rothesay would take the castle and the daughter. Elyna Morgannwg would give him a son—all that Rothesay wanted would be his for the taking.

Lady Morgannwg begged, "I will not shackle her to Rothesay."

Kenan had watched his mother's heartache, his father's lust well known. His mother no longer resided at Lydcombe. She'd removed herself to London, taking the last of Rothesay's restraint with her. "I cannot return without payment, my lady."

"Rothesay will never have Elyna." The woman's eyes darkened.

"Mind your tongue, my lady." Kenan hated himself—and hated his father more. "Rothesay doesn't take kindly to threats."

A smile tugged at her lips, looking more like a snarl. "It's not a threat. It's the truth."

7

S ienna
Lydcombe, England: Present Day

WILLIAM POURED MALT VINEGAR OVER HIS FISH AND FRIES—OR *chips* as he'd called them. He'd offered ketchup but I was struggling to eat anything, my mind not on food. A fear had crept in, one that I hadn't thought of in years. The last time I visited Grandad, I was completely and utterly devastated. He hadn't recognized me—he'd called me by another name, not even my grandmother's name. I was supposed to be his favorite, a fact I clung to when my family pointed out how very black sheep I tended to be.

Aside from my grandfather, every sibling, cousin and blood relative of mine was ambitious, either in academia or business. Grandad, on the other hand, traveled the elected route of a second English son, the military. His older brother succumbed to complications of polio. He'd never had children nor had he married—handing over the Rothesay title and estate to a man who would have never afforded it otherwise. Grandad's inheritance gave my aunts and uncles the life of an English aristocrat while my grandfather was reluctant to speak of it. But at my birth, Grandad had come alive, our bond immediate and, until Alzheimer's, unbreakable.

William speared his fish with a fork, reminding me of Grandad's melancholy toward his privileged life. *My success was always brought about by death, in my career and in my family. Titles are a curse.*

"So?" William arched an eyebrow. From the look of it, he'd asked me a question.

"Sorry, I think I spaced a bit."

"A bit?" His smile was warm and his eyes had that twinkle quality. I hadn't really looked at him until that moment. His easy fascination with me put him at an arm's length, but now, I noticed how quickly he could charm a woman. His voice was pleasing, as were his manners. He'd made sure I was settled before tucking into his own food. His shoulders were defined despite his lanky frame. He must have shaved this morning but the faint beginning of a five o'clock shadow was appearing. The angle of his jaw and the cheek bones would make a beautiful portrait. And yet, he'd never have my heart.

Glancing at the stairs, I wondered out loud, "Does he ever say my grandmother's name?"

"He probably does." William pulled his food across the island and sat on the stool next to me. "And here I thought you were deliberately ignoring me." His wide smile said otherwise. "It can't be easy. My parents have a good row now and again, but even when they're at each other's throats, I can't imagine one being without the other. I think either one would be lost. Like their foundation just up and left."

"Do you remember her? My grandmother?" I tried another bite of fish. The coating was crisp and the fish tender and flavorful but my stomach stomped its foot in protest.

"A bit, yeah." He took a long pull of soda or maybe it was beer. I didn't recognize the brand. "She was quiet, like him."

"I don't remember her." The few memories I did have were just before she died. The funeral, on the other hand, was seared into my memory. To a child, the viewing was eerie. She looked a thousand years old and absolutely terrifying.

"I remember you," he said softly, stirring vinegar and mayonnaise into the corner of his takeout box.

"You probably remember Lacy." She was hard to miss. She might not have a drop of Rothesay blood in her, but she was baptized with the same easy charm and hungry drive.

He chuckled. "Everyone remembers Lacy."

Elbowing him, I teased, "Ah, did she break your little heart?"

"She left a string of broken hearts." He wiped his mouth after devouring the last of his meal. "She was older than me but I had to try."

"I have no doubt you tried." Lacy wouldn't have given him the time of day. Until a few years ago, Lacy had a type and kept herself on a strict diet of men. William would have fit the bill except he was too young and the worst offense—he lacked the well-heeled vocabulary she'd wanted. Brian was bald and divorced, two strikes against Lacy's idea of the perfect man. But his gentle nature won out. Again, I glanced at the stairs, wishing I could ask my grandfather about love.

"Yeah, well." William shrugged. He tossed the takeout box and sat on the kitchen counter by the sink, directly opposite the counter where I sat. The extra box for Ioan lay untouched. "She didn't even go for Ioan which is odd."

My stomach did a little flip. "Why is that odd?"

He tapped his fingers against his soda can and motioned to Ioan's takeout box. "I don't know. The whole Mr. Darcy thing. Ioan's always had the brooding thing going for him. Girls seem to flock to him."

William wasn't really asking about Ioan, he was asking what type a guy I liked. Funny, it didn't matter which country the male species hailed from, they appeared to think the same.

"I've never been a flocking kind of girl." It was the safest answer I could give. His smile stretched a little too wide—false hope. I stifled a groan. "I never stay anywhere long enough to flock."

William chuckled, determination in his eyes. My comment was supposed to deter, not encourage. He set the can aside. "Is that a fact? Well, how long will Lydcombe hold your interest?"

"I have no idea." This was the truth. Ironically, in the states I'd always have a couple projects lined up. I didn't want my health coverage to lapse, but in Cornwall, I was an English citizen. My parents offered to pay me a stipend for stepping in to help Grandad. I refused. Even Ioan mentioned a salary, but when I would visit as a teenager, Grandad and I made a pact, neither of us would rat each other out to our family. We gave each other glorious freedom. He could eat all the salty and fried food he wanted, and I could spend hours traipsing all over Cornwall without a brother or parent to comment on my lack of direction.

"So, what do you do?" William slid to his feet. Energy flowed from and around him. He couldn't sit still for anything. He tossed the can in the trash under the sink. I felt a little annoyed at how comfortable he was in my grandfather's kitchen. "Before taking care of Liam, I mean."

"I'm a photographer."

"Really?" He cocked his head to the side. He, like everyone else, struggled to picture me as one. His gaze flicked to the camera on the counter before pulling out his phone. A minute later, he turned it around. "This your work?"

His screen showed the vacant stare of an eight year old, her blonde braid slung forward on her shoulder, framing her face. Her older cousin had come to school with a gun and a vendetta. The girl snuck into the cupboard with her teacher's cell phone and called the police. While reporters poked and prodded her with questions, the girl became withdrawn. Her cousin hadn't shot anyone because of the girl's quick thinking—but what the reporters never asked was how she felt about him dying. Her cousin had pointed the gun at the principal and was shot, sinking to the concrete with a thud. The girl had saved the school but not her cousin.

"It's painful looking at someone like that." William scrolled up. "I mean, being that cute and that sad. Heartbreaking."

That's the reason I never sent the other picture. The girl had looked directly into the camera. I was thousands of miles away and still, I shivered at the void in her expression. At the tender age of eight, she was broken.

"Oh, now that's awesome." William flipped the phone back around, showing the action shot of a police horse clearing a makeshift barricade, the officer poised for combat. The police were ambushed by rioters—I never got the whole story, my next project had me on a plane an hour after the photo was taken. "How did you decide on photography?"

"I never know how to answer that." I twisted the fork between my fingers. My stomach was empty, but like a toddler it was still pouting. "I guess I just kind of fell into it."

"How do you fall into photography?" He scanned me, his eyes lingering on my food. "Did you start off in front of the camera?"

"Is that your way of asking if I was a model?" I had to hand it to him, William was more subtle than most. I was striking—like a neon flag. I'd turn a head but only for a second. Nobody takes neon anything seriously. Sadly, William's comment slid him farther down on the datable list. The side door opened and closed.

"I'm about as average as you get. Height. Build." I held up a hand when he opened his mouth. "Not asking for compliments. Just stating the obvious."

"She means if you're going to flirt at least be original." Doris gave a pointed look at William. "Just ask her out. Get the rejection over with."

I jumped from the stool and fell into Doris' embrace. Her name might have been forgotten in my foggy brain, but her love was always remembered. Doris was pushing seventy and was built like an ox. Her thick arms hugged me like an old, worn blanket. She stepped back and said, "Let me look at you, darling girl."

"How come I never get *darling boy*?"

Doris ignored William, her eyes misting. "Welcome home."

Home. The word pierced me. I blinked, surprised at the lump in my throat. Doris gave a slight nod, her hand squeezing mine.

"How is he?" I whispered.

Her eyes flicked to William and the fish and chips on the counter, my question forgotten. "Who brought that into my kitchen?"

William held up his hands. "She was starving."

"Are you hungry?" She softened, letting go of my hand. "How's the stomach?"

I shrugged. "Give me a day or two and I'll be fine."

Doris shooed William out of the way. "Make yourself useful and go get Ioan."

"See what I mean?" He jutted a thumb at Doris. "The girls flock to him."

"They'd flock to you too if you moved your hands more than your mouth." Realizing what she said, she frowned. "You know what I mean. Move it, boy."

"*Darling* boy."

"Darling-boy-who-wants-to-live-to-see-another-day, go get Ioan." She winked at me and set the kettle on.

William playfully stomped up the stairs.

Doris and Grandad met in the military. She became the house-keeper at my grandmother's insistence—Doris had played matchmaker when my grandfather was too oblivious to notice my grandmother's undying devotion. When Grandad inherited the estate, Doris soon followed.

She traded my food for a small stack of lemon and ginger biscuits. My stomach all but drooled. "I'd forgotten about these."

Doris beamed. "Well, they've always seemed to do the trick."

"I'm the only one who seems to get sick after coming home." *Home.* There it was again. Lydcombe was always home.

"Lydcombe just likes to put you in a little time out. Maybe it feels the same way when you leave, a little heartsick." The kettle whistled and Doris tossed in a teabag, squeezing lemon and honey in the cup. "There you go. You'll be right as rain."

"How is he?"

She hesitated, her eyes flicking to the stairs. "Some days I swear he's improving. And other days..."

Grief settled in the silence between us. I'd come to document Grandad. My career consisted of quick snaps of the camera. Only when I was far away from the subject did I stare at the photos. Only then did I wonder about their families and history. With Grandad, I already knew the family. I *was* the family. My reason for coming now seemed wrong.

"What helps?"

Doris grinned. "You mean other than my cooking?"

"That goes without saying." To prove my point, I shoved another biscuit in my mouth.

"Ioan."

My gaze shot to the stairs. He wasn't there. When I looked back at Doris, her brow was furrowed.

She pursed her lips. "So you feel it too?"

"Feel what?" I refused to be the first to admit anything. My parents thought I had a pretty face and an empty head. I didn't need anyone else to think that way.

She tucked her chin. "Nothing, love. Nothing."

The storm outside protested, rebuking me for not telling Doris the truth. Maybe my parents were right. "I feel something."

"You've always felt something here."

"This is different." Or maybe I was different. "As a child, we believe everything, from Santa Clause to the tooth fairy."

"Those are fairytales, love. Nothing but entertaining stories for lulling babes to sleep."

"So why do I feel something now?"

Doris paused, her eyes lit with mirth. "My darling girl, you're in Cornwall. These stories are real."

I rolled my eyes. She was just as guilty as my grandfather when it came to local myths.

"Doris?" Cradling my cup of tea, I let the warmth calm me. "What does Ioan do? I mean, why is he here?"

"He brings Liam's memories alive." Her conviction was set. She believed Ioan made a difference—which meant it was as good as scripture. She pulled out celery, onions and carrots. She must be making a soup.

I settled in against the back of the stool. Doris' cooking had a healing quality, like how most of my American friends spoke of chicken noodle soup.

"Lacy said my parents are suspicious." My tone was light. Doris didn't need any ammunition. Her frustration with my family was an ever burning fire. She liked exactly three Rothesays—one of them was buried in the cemetery and the others were currently in residence. "I don't remember Ioan. Lacy says he dragged me out of the water. I feel like that's something I should remember."

"You wouldn't remember." Doris paused in her chopping. "If you had something in your mind, nothing else was important. That, and you weren't exactly coherent."

"I wasn't drowning though." My parents would have told me—rather, they would have teased me endlessly about my inability to stay out of trouble. Mom had made a picture book when I graduated high school of all my broken bones. It was a running joke in my family. No one else had so much as a bloody nose.

Doris began chopping again. Her silence pricked my curiosity.

"I didn't drown, right?" A chill swept up my neck, caressing my cheek as it left.

"It was a long time ago." She scooped the celery and onions into the pan, the sizzling a comforting sound. "Ioan didn't give a lot of details."

"Weren't my brothers there?" Lacy had told me they'd received a tongue lashing from Ioan.

The stairs creaked, silencing the conversation. William appeared first, his eyes full of mischief. Ioan followed, his voice so low, I couldn't understand what he was saying. And then Grandad—a hand on Ioan's shoulders. His wrinkled gaze found mine and, for a moment, I saw my grandfather. My heart swelled and a spark of joy lifted his lips to a ghost of a smile.

The moment passed—his eyes clouded over—and he was once again the shadow of the man I loved.

8

Sienna
Lydcombe, England: Present Day

DORIS WAVED ME AWAY, NOT ALLOWING ME TO HELP WITH THE
dishes. The rejection hurt more than I cared to admit. If I wasn't in
the kitchen, I'd have to face my grandfather, the man who only spoke
to Ioan and Doris. My presence made him uncomfortable. That was
clear as day. To add insult to injury, Grandad ignored William as well—
making it harder to maneuver the man's blatant flirting.

"Go on, now." Doris shooed me once more.

"I think I'll just make some tea." I reached for the kettle but was
stopped by her hand.

"Darling girl, tea can't heal the heart." She pulled me around, her
gaze searching. "Liam doesn't do well with strangers—"

I sank at *strangers*.

"—ah, you're not the stranger." Doris squeezed my arms. "Listen to
me, child. Liam doesn't do well with William. He's the stranger."

I slid from her grasp. She could try to soften the blow but the truth would not hide. "Grandad doesn't remember me. I've known that for years."

"He does." She reached for the kettle, ignoring her earlier sentiment. "He just gets a bit muddled at times."

"By muddled, do you mean forgetting his granddaughter?" The words held an edge. I didn't smile to soften the tone. This was Doris. If anyone knew how much I loved Grandad, she did.

"No." Doris was entirely too chipper. "He knows who you were and who you are."

My heart fell to the floor. She was trying to ease the pain, but the more I stood in the kitchen dancing around that fact, the harder it was to bear. "How come I don't remember William or Ioan?"

Doris brightened at the change of subject. "Ah, William was probably too busy chasing the girls." She caught herself and added, "He'd be stealing a *cwtch* from a girl or two."

"And Ioan?" I didn't miss the way she swallowed hard or the pause in her tentative smile. "What aren't you telling me?"

The kettle whistled. I placed a hand on Doris' arm, stopping her from reaching for it. She gave a weak smile. "Ioan's a good man."

The eerie sensation was back. "But?"

She lowered her gaze. "His mum was a little strange. He kept to his estate."

"Why?" There was an enormous elephant in the room, but I couldn't put my finger on it. Jetlag was stealing my patience. "Again, what aren't—"

"Your parents didn't allow the Morgannwgs around the house." Doris kept her chin tucked.

"That's for Grandad to decide, isn't it?" There should have been more loyalty to my parents but for the life of me, I could never toss my grandfather over. Not for my parents. Not for anyone.

"Ay, love. And there was a big row about it." Doris smiled, her eyes lit once more. "Lady Morgannwg wasn't right in the mind, but that's no reason to treat someone so harshly." A faraway look crossed her face. Doris knew more about my grandfather's early life, and that of my aunts and uncles than anyone. "I hate to admit it, but I watched that poor boy take care of her and prayed many nights for her to let him go. I suppose she did in her own way."

I tried to imagine a feminine version of Ioan but couldn't. A part of me softened toward him, even if I didn't fully trust him. Fate had given him a worse hand than mine. Doris hadn't mentioned his father. I didn't dare ask about him. "His mother died, then?"

Doris nodded and poured me another cup of tea. "I thought Ioan would pack up, head to a city. Somewhere. Anywhere."

"Why didn't he?" I cradled the cup and smelled the fragrance of home.

Her gaze flicked to the stairways. "Your grandfather."

The calm fled in an instant, my pulse racing once more. "That's kind of out of nowhere. The family's banned and then he shows up one day?"

"He was only banned around you." Doris' voice was so soft and low it took a second to register. Avoiding my gaze, she sipped her tea.

"Which is why Grandad recognizes him and not me." A surge of jealousy overcame me. Like an old habit, my mind ran with the feeling. Ioan had taken charge of my travel plans because of his self-appointed position. No wonder my parents were suspicious. They'd not wanted Ioan near me, only to receive a phone call about him visiting Grandad. The details were a little fuzzy. I couldn't remember if he'd texted Lacy or my parents first. Either way, Ioan had inserted himself as the pivotal man in Grandad's life.

"Easy now." Doris gently stole my cup of tea, settling it on the counter. "I know a storm's coming and it's not Ioan's fault."

"I've said nothing."

She *tsk*ed. "You were never good at hiding your thoughts, love."

"Why does everyone give Ioan a pass?" There was less bite to my voice but I felt—rather than saw—him listening to me. He was upstairs walking my grandfather through his bedtime routine. There was no possible way Ioan could have heard me and yet he cocked his head to the side as if he'd heard every word. Again—impossible. I couldn't see him any more than he could hear me.

"Ioan never gets a pass." Doris wiped the counter and gathered her things.

"Lacy." I held up a finger. Then a second one. "And her fiancé, Brian."

"Fiancé?" Doris' face lit, her eyes merry and hopeful. With one little word, the conversation would be derailed. "Well, look at that. Lacy'll be a beautiful bride."

William trudged down the stairs. "Lacy's getting married?" Doubt crossed his features, his gaze flicking between Doris and me.

"Yes, people do that." Doris shook her head and hitched her purse to her shoulder. "They commit to one person."

"I can commit." He gave a nervous smile. Doris had hit her mark. It didn't help that it was in front of me. He hadn't a clue I'd already pegged him a serial dater.

"To more than one night? Not likely." She chuckled, her smile good-natured.

William had enough sense to not contradict her. Eyeing Doris, he nodded to me. "What's your schedule tomorrow?"

"Leave the poor woman alone." Doris sighed like an impatient mother.

"I don't know yet." That was the truth of it. Nothing in the house had changed since I'd last visited. Grandad had sketches throughout but I didn't want to snap a picture of his work. I'd wanted to capture him. Sir Liam Rothesay, the grandfather. I hadn't a clue how to do that when he no longer played the part. "I don't know what's on the docket for me."

"Relax, Sienna." Doris cupped her keys into the palm of her hand. "Do nothing for once. Can you handle that?"

"Are you wanting to do something?" William arched his eyebrows, trying to understand what Doris meant. "We could walk into town like old times."

"Old times?" Doris smiled wide, a twinkle in her eye. "Oh, child. It's a lost cause."

Movement caught my eye. Ioan descended the staircase without a sound. He entered the bright kitchen. In the darkened light, his eyes were a pale blue, startling against his dark features. His expression darkened at William, sending an eerie chill from across the room. I folded my arms against the feeling—his eyes flicking to mine. Without greeting Doris or William, he adjusted the thermometer on the wall to his right.

Doris' head pivoted. "Ah, Ioan, will you be staying tonight?"

William straightened, his expression hopeful. "I can stay."

The idea of entertaining William exhausted me. I didn't have the stomach for dancing along his subtle flirts. Stifling a groan, I felt the weight of the jetlag. "I'm here. No one needs to stay."

William stretched and sat on the stool nearest me. "You're exhausted. I can—"

"Go home." Ioan's voice was soft and low. Oddly enough, the sound of him enveloped me, easing the frustration of being around William. "I checked on the horses earlier and made the cot in Liam's room."

"You sleep in his room? There are other rooms." I was both suspicious and comforted by the idea. From the surprise on William's face, he'd not considered that part of the arrangement either. "I don't think Grandad wants me in his room."

Despite me holding his hand, my grandfather had barely recognized my presence earlier. I was nothing but a ghost to him—the thought sent me reeling. In California, the rejection didn't hurt as badly. How was I going to photograph him? Maybe coming to Lydcombe was a mistake.

I blinked and looked down at my own hands. They were long and lean like his. When I looked in the mirror, I saw a younger, feminine version of Sir Liam Rothesay. An ache opened in my chest. A tear fell on my hand. My face flushed, embarrassed. I wanted to run and hide. I did *not* want William to try and comfort me. If he stuck around long enough, he'd see more emotions than he'd ever want to. Feelings— those were my specialty.

"It's time to go, William." Ioan leaned against the kitchen counter, his arms folded.

"I do you a favor and rescue this little damsel from the train—and you're kicking me out?" William had already begun to stand. He wasn't going to stay in my grandfather's room. I wasn't *that* tempting or he wasn't that chivalrous. "Oh, are you okay, love?"

"Mind your tongue, boy." Doris waved William toward the door, sending me an apologetic smile. "She's exhausted and you've worn out your welcome."

William clasped a hand to his chest. "You've wounded me."

She *tsked* at him, waving him out the door. "Go on now. Don't make me fetch your mum."

Their conversation was muted by the closing of the door. Ioan locked the deadbolt behind them, the sound echoing in the quiet house. My face flushed again, the embarrassment all too real. Ioan might be close with my grandfather but he didn't need to see my tears. Or maybe I didn't need his pity. He was more like my family than he realized. He'd stay aloof and logical like my brothers, descending to provide the perfect amount of sterile help, only to disappear when emotions came. A nagging fact wanted to argue the point. The logical and aloof thing for Ioan was to leave Lydcombe, not stick around caring for an elderly neighbor.

Silently, Ioan circled back and went to the window over the kitchen sink. He leaned forward and peeked down the drive. The sound of two cars starting had Ioan's shoulders relaxing.

"I'm assuming you're not a fan of William?" I should have left well enough alone. But I felt vulnerable around Ioan and wanted to crack his head open a bit.

He turned, a smirk on his face. "He's a fan of you."

"And that bothers you?" It was hard to gauge if Ioan was Team Sienna or not. He'd arranged for me to be here but that could have been for Grandad's benefit, not mine.

"He bothers you."

"That didn't even remotely answer my question." The man was infuriatingly vague.

Ioan rubbed his face, frown lines showing his fatigue. "I think he's an arse of the first order. That answer your question?"

"Then why have him pick me up?"

"One horse colicked and one delivered a colt. I couldn't leave them." He peered over his fingertips, his hands falling from his face. "William's only in town on the weekends. I figured there was only so much damage he could do in that time."

"He's very sure of himself." The slow hum from the ocean began again, a low whisper. Fear crept in. I'd felt like this as a child but not this strong. And not this frequent.

Ioan arched an eyebrow, his gaze searching. A vacuum, a complete void of emotion was present. I couldn't siphon any feeling, good or bad from his eyes.

The whisper grew louder. I needed a distraction. "You could have sent Doris."

"William owes me. I'd rather not be in debt to Doris. At least, not more than I already am." He waited a beat. The silence grew awkward but he didn't move, nor did he speak.

"I should go to bed." Neither of us moved toward the staircase. "Are you really going to sleep in Grandad's room?"

Ioan's lips quirked to a crooked smile, transforming his face. The uptick of his cheeks brightened the room. The tension dissipated. His pale eyes looked more green in the kitchen—and full of mischief. "Liam would die of a heart attack if he saw a grown man in the middle of the night."

"Then why—"

He chuckled, bathing the room in warmth. "William's allergic to actual work. He only offers to score points with a lady. You being under the same roof would have been an added bonus."

"It'll fade." My fingers rubbed the hem of my sleeve. It was an old habit my mother considered a failure in character. "Give it a few days and he'll lose interest."

"You've seen a William or two in your day." It wasn't a question. The eerie feeling was back. Ioan had seen something in me—or perhaps I was just tired. "I'm relieved to know I didn't send a naïve lamb to the wolf."

There was a note of approval in his tone. I hated that I liked it. "You never know, I could fall head over heels in love." I held out my arms, then hugged myself with dramatic flair. "Marrying an English gentleman, wouldn't that be swell? I can almost hear my parents cheering from here."

"Oh, he's English. It's the gentleman part he's lacking." Ioan narrowed his gaze. "The cot isn't actually set up, but are you wanting to sleep in Liam's room tonight?"

"No," I said a little too quickly. "He doesn't recognize me. I'd scare him more than you."

He moved to the staircase, his arm extended—as if *he* were guiding me to my bedroom. I was the granddaughter, not him. It was petty. Stupid. But Grandad had bestowed me with the title of Favorite Grandchild. I was special to at least one person in the world. And now, I was no one. I was a ghost. A stranger.

Ioan's face softened. He stepped closer—his face inches from mine. "I'll be across the corridor. If you're scared or hear anything at all, open your door and I'll be there."

"Why?" The whispers rushed into the house like a curious breeze, begging for me to visit the trail.

Ioan cupped my elbow—silencing the sound. "That is a question I cannot answer."

"Cannot or will not?" With his touch, I felt braver, bolder. I inched closer. The faint smell of hay tickled my nose.

"Either way, I won't tell someone else's story." His voice was gentle, but his eyes held a warning. He broke our gaze and stepped back.

I gripped his arm, keeping the contact. "But you'll watch over your neighbor?"

His eyes flicked to my hand, his shoulders relaxing. "Ay. I'll watch over Liam."

"And arrange for me to come?" The courage grew. I wasn't sure if it was from the contact or the lack of inhibition, a side effect of jetlag. "Again, why?"

There was a strength in him that was more than alluring—more potent than intoxicating. I was Sienna Rothesay, the eternal runaway date.

Ioan leaned forward, his breath on my cheek. "This is where you belong."

Peace filled me, singing to the pulse in my head. The temptation to close my eyes and wrap my arms around him sent a jolt through me. I pulled back, my hand no longer touching his arm. His face became unreadable again, his posture rigid. My heart pounded in my chest—my breathing shallow. I'd lost my mind.

"I'll be across the hall," he whispered and silently walked up the stairs.

❧ 9 ❧

 enan
        Coch Bay, South Wales: 1606

THE SUN BATHED THE OUTER COURTYARD OF MORGANNWG CASTLE
with comforting rays. Kenan stepped back from the castle's steward.
He felt Jowan's watchful gaze, the soldier's frustration evident. Kenan
couldn't blame him. Jowan's greatest weakness was his loyalty to
Kenan. They were brothers bonded by war.

Mumbling, Jowan turned from Kenan and recounted the pitiful
flock of chickens. Feathers were missing and the eyes were dull. The
animals were horribly malnourished and neglected. They most likely
hadn't been out of their cages in days. Kenan's hens on the island were
twice the size, the eggs a mixture of blue, green, and brown.

"I doubt they're laying." Jowan kicked at the ground.

Morgannwg's steward cleared his throat. "They are the last of my
lord's flock."

Kenan had assumed as much. The hens would need better food if they were to be productive at all. Lady Morgannwg entered the courtyard, her granddaughter at her side.

Jowan grunted in frustration. "The woman's mad, Kenan."

The steward tucked his head, his gaze on his worn shoes. He'd more than likely been paid with meager rations of food instead of money.

"She's a mother." Kenan's own mother had protected him from his father's mercurial temper. She'd not left until Kenan could stand on his own two feet. They switched places, the son becoming the protector. "The earl is simple. I'd not cross a desperate woman."

"If I don't get home soon, you'll have to cross my woman." Jowan scowled and double checked the knots of the cages. The man wanted to be home with his wife. Both men had hoped Lady Morgannwg would send more than the paltry payment of chickens and cows. They needed collateral to hand over to Rothesay. "This isn't near enough."

Morgannwg's steward winced at Jowan's words. It wasn't a secret the castle was destitute. Rothesay had a reputation—and it wasn't kind. But warfare had taught Kenan he couldn't save everyone. Some sacrifices were out of his control.

Lady Morgannwg lifted her chin as she approached, the frayed hem of skirts sweeping the neglected stones of the courtyard. "The animals should buy some time."

Kenan waved his hand, indicating the chickens. "This doesn't cover the penalties. It doesn't even touch the original debt."

"We have nothing left to give." She narrowed her gaze, a challenge in her eye.

Keeping his voice low and soft, Kenan said, "Your son will accompany us to Lydcombe, my lady."

"Are you mad?" Lady Morgannwg spat the words. She'd been isolated too long, her dominating behavior born from protecting a simple son. Kenan's father would have struck the woman at the first impertinent act. "Rothesay will have my son in jail. Stripped of his title before he reaches Cornwall."

"And you, my lady?" Kenan gave a subtle shake of his head to Jowan who inched closer. He hated his father's castle in Lydcombe and all that the baron stood for but Kenan had given his word. "Shall you take his place and accompany us to Lydcombe?"

She reared back, nearly colliding with Miss Morgannwg. "How dare you?"

Kenan rounded his shoulders and held out his hands. "I've orders to keep."

Lady Morgannwg cried out, her voice piercing the air between them, a wild look in her eye. "You know as well as I do that I cannot leave the earl unattended."

The steward fidgeted next to him. The lady's words confessed the truth. Her son was not fit to be earl.

"I will go." Miss Morgannwg stepped forward, a gentle hand on her grandmother's arm. The morning light brightened her dark auburn hair, her black eyes bright—and enticing. Kenan pulled his gaze from her face. He would not cave to a pretty face like his father.

"No." Lady Morgannwg did not bother looking at her. "We will find another way."

"I do not want to use force." Kenan gave a nod to Jowan and with his right hand, flicked his wrist. Jowan held up a fist. With the draw-bridge down, the courtyard would be filled with Kenan's men in mere minutes.

"Then don't." Lady Morgannwg's voice was thick with panic.

"My lady..." Miss Morgannwg stepped forward again. "Let us speak privately."

"No," her grandmother snapped, but froze at the worried look on Miss Morgannwg's face. The younger woman's curious glances had noticed something amiss. Kenan's men would need to hurry before the older woman discovered the men outside the walls. Lady Morgannwg touched her grey hair and straightened her back, her lips pursed. "Yes—"

"My lady!" A pudgy servant rushed forward, his forehead sweaty and cheeks flushed. "There are men ..."

Lady Morgannwg held up her hand, her first finger extended. The drawbridge swung up with a loud snap, the security gate crashing down, a sickening thud echoed into the courtyard. A guard yelled, waiving his hand toward the gate. Between the loud conversation,

Kenan gathered that a hinge had broken, a blessing and a curse. The broken hinge locked the security gate down and the drawbridge up. The men outside the walls were experienced soldiers able to scale walls and penetrate the impossible. The castle would be captured. Their escape cut off by the locked security gate.

Lady Morgannwg gave a nod to a partially hidden servant in the tower. Kenan kept his face impassive. He'd underestimated the woman. Her quick thinking gave her a few hours at most. He'd seen the dark underbelly of this estate, the crumbling corners and starving servants. They didn't have the men or the weaponry to defend themselves.

Miss Morgannwg slipped between her grandmother and Kenan, her eyes both wary and watchful. "Shall we speak privately?" Not waiting for permission, she tugged on the arm of a reluctant Lady Morgannwg, pulling her inside the castle.

Kenan and Jowan followed. Miss Morgannwg tossed an unwelcome glare to Kenan. She'd either not wanted them to follow or she was making her distrust known. The small group entered the earl's chambers—or what should have been the earl's chambers. The blue dress Lady Morgannwg had worn last night was on the rack in the corner. The woman must have moved into the quarters when her husband passed. With the stiff posture of the granddaughter, Kenan wondered who resided in the mistress chamber, a room reserved for the wife of the earl. The bond between Lady Morgannwg and her granddaughter was evident, but was the earl given anything indicative of his rank in his own home?

"How dare you?" The widow narrowed her gaze. She circled the room with her arms folded. "I give you payment and soldiers try to storm the walls—"

Kenan kept his voice even and his expression neutral. "My lady, the debt was called. Your payment wouldn't cover—"

"Perhaps we can come to an arrangement?" Miss Morgannwg blinked slowly, feigning an innocence Kenan knew did not exist. "Send the payment with your men." She nodded sweetly to Jowan. "And leave a man until we can pay the rest in full."

Jowan scoffed and Kenan held up a hand to his friend, his focus on the beauty in front of him. "It would take just under a fortnight for the men to return. What in your circumstance could change so drastically in that time?"

The women exchanged a knowing glance. Jowan cleared his throat and took a step forward. Lady Morgannwg's eyes widened, fear taking hold. Jowan held out an arm, indicating Kenan. "Is there anything of value under this roof that you've withheld from him?"

"I was given a horse that would fetch a high price." Miss Morgannwg's lips twitched, her smile beguiling. There was more than a horse. The woman was hiding something.

Lady Morgannwg's jaw clenched but she held her tongue.

"And the reason this horse was not part of the payment?" Kenan tasted the deception in the air. It didn't matter what pretty words came from her striking face, she was maneuvering an escape from Kenan's father. "I had come to extract payment, but when I saw the desperation within these walls, I held my men outside the gate."

Miss Morgannwg's eyes flicked between her grandmother and Kenan. Realization appeared to have sparked something in her. Kenan had dressed the part of a simple soldier, but carried the authority of something more. Miss Morgannwg lifted her chin. "Your men?"

"I do not want to cause more harm than necessary, especially in the presence of ladies." He folded his arms across his chest, the nervous energy from Jowan spreading to Kenan. He'd let too much slip. Kenan would need to sweep the little tidbits of information away, or pivot and let the truth garner trust. "Do you have a benefactor that would pay the earl's debt?"

"Rothesay will not accept payment from our benefactor." Lady Morgannwg waved her hand in the air as if the gesture would erase the tension. "We have given all that we can."

Kenan stepped forward. "Rothesay demands payment in full. That is the contract. However that contract is paid, Rothesay will honor the payment."

Miss Morgannwg whispered, "Charles Muiris."

Her words chilled the room. Kenan retreated, *Charles Muiris* echoing in his mind. Jowan was at Kenan's side in an instant. The feud between Kenan's father and Muiris was bloody—and well-known. The men were once like brothers until they vied for the hand of the same woman. As the son of a duke, Charles won easily leaving James Rothesay with a broken heart and shattered pride. Like toddlers, each man ran to the king over every squabble, their lands sharing a border. The pieces fell into place in Kenan's mind. Rothesay did not want the castle or the payment. He wanted whatever prize Charles was after.

Kenan wiped his hand down his face. Miss Morgannwg knew enough of the feud to withhold her horse. He glanced at Jowan, the man who'd stood beside him through the bloodiest of nights. Kenan would need his loyalty now more than ever. "You are entering dangerous waters." He swallowed hard and prayed for courage. "Lady Morgannwg, you cannot be ignorant of how this came to be. Rothesay will not rest until he has bested Muiris."

"Muiris never mentioned Rothesay." Lady Morgannwg kept her head high but her hands curled at her side. There was deceit some-where in her words. She would not have kept the horse if she was completely innocent. "He gave Elyna the mare two years before. Rothesay came calling just last year. We live in Wales, away from London and politics."

He gestured to Miss Morgannwg. "How did Muiris come to know of you? And what of Rothesay, how did you happen upon him and his loan?" He held up a hand to silence her grandmother. He wanted to hear the words from Miss Morgannwg. The gift from Muiris put her as the link between both men. "I have known Rothesay all my life. I know what he would and would not say. I will spot the lie before you can finish hatching it."

Miss Morgannwg smiled prettily, her head tilted like a child. "That is a heavy accusation when—"

"I will not ask again." Kenan's patience had run its course. His men were instructed to circle the castle if the drawbridge was down. With the dire state of the walls, a weakness would be found and the castle would fall. "Tell me everything now or I cannot help you."

Jowan scowled at Kenan's side. The soldier was done with these women.

Miss Morgannwg's smile fell. She glanced between her pacing grandmother and Kenan. "Muiris was my husband's cousin." She hesi-tated—either from a memory or from hatching a lie, Kenan didn't know. "He and his wife were coming to visit but she fell ill. She did not recover."

"And your own mother?" He'd wanted to ask about the husband but with Jowan's careful eye, Kenan didn't dare.

Lady Morgannwg paused her pacing. "She died when Elyna was a small child."

"I do not mean to harm either of you, but I need to know the truth. If I do not ask, and if you do not tell me the truth, I cannot protect you from Rothesay. Or Muiris." Kenan ignored the doubtful look from Lady Morgannwg and asked, "The earl is a simpleton and yet helped conceive a child?"

Miss Morgannwg's eyes widened, a blush touching her cheeks and neck. She'd not expected the indelicate words. "I beg your pardon?"

Lady Morgannwg's shoulders sank, her pride falling to the stone floors. "An unmarried woman has little protection and little voice. A married woman must obey her husband ..." Her voice trailed off. She inhaled sharply and touched her grey hair. "But if the husband cannot speak for himself, there is great power for a woman. Marrying a simpleton is an advantage."

"If I'd been born a son, none of this would have happened. I could be his guardian," Miss Morgannwg whispered.

Her grandmother's face softened.

"Why did Muiris gift you the horse?" Shouts carried into the chambers. Kenan's men had found a weak point. "Was he unfaithful to his wife?"

Lady Morgannwg's eyes were drunk with fury. "How dare—"

"No," her granddaughter whispered softly. "He is my husband's cousin and no, he was not unfaithful." She ran a hand over her skirt. "But he did make his intentions known."

A flicker of surprise crossed Lady Morgannwg's features. She spun around, offering her back to Kenan. "He'd left the horse for Elyna as a gift for our hospitality." She turned her profile toward them. "That was the lie I was sold."

"It was not a lie," Miss Morgannwg said softly. "He was grateful and still had no son to inherit."

Kenan didn't know Muiris well nor did he know if his land was entailed, shackling inheritance to only male heirs. Kenan was the second son and would inherit nothing from Rothesay. Kenan's older brother was born with a crooked spine and twisted legs. He could not ride a horse nor could he wield a sword. Rothesay had yet to forgive his firstborn for being a cripple. But Muiris had no son, crippled or not. Nor did he have a spare like Kenan waiting in the wings.

And now, Morgannwg had no heir.

Jowan shook his head, whispering, "She is not the bird."

Kenan fought the smile. He'd rescued an abandoned falcon chick discarded from the nest. The spirited predator had nipped Kenan over and over again. The bird grew to a majestic gyrfalcon, a bird only the king could own. Over time, Kenan gained the falcon's trust and taught it to circle in the air until Kenan was alone, instead of landing on his arm. If Kenan were ever caught with the bird, the penalty was severe.

But he would rescue the falcon again—Kenan smiled. "I've no desire to claim this predator."

Miss Morgannwg narrowed her eyes, looking very much like the cunning falcon. "Speak plainly."

Kenan waved his hand in the air, indicating the area where the stables lay. "Did you welcome Muiris' attentions?"

She lifted her chin. "He left the horse and a letter. He knows of our desperation and believes himself to be our savior."

Lady Morgannwg relaxed at her granddaughter's confession. "He is not wrong. You need his protection and a male figure—"

Miss Morgannwg gave a subtle shake of her head.

"Do you wish for him to be your savior?" Kenan prayed she did. If Muiris could rush to their aid, Kenan would stall. Once he received payment, Kenan would march his small army home to Lydcombe. More than anything, he'd be free from his father's demands.

"It doesn't matter what I wish." Miss Morgannwg's voice was low and soft. "Better to be a second wife to an ancient man than a number-less mistress to a cruel one."

❧ 10 ❧

S ienna
Lydcombe, England: Present Day

THE MIDNIGHT WIND PUMMELED THE WALLS OF MY GRANDFATHER'S home, the house complaining at the assault. I entered the blue room, my heart thumping. During my birth, my mother had wailed against my father and grandfather, blaming them for not listening to her. She'd sworn up and down that I was coming early, but she was never silent about any of her aches. Not then, not now.

Seated in the café down the quaint street from my grandfather's house, a storm had rushed in, railing against the coast in a matter of minutes. My mother had leaped to a stand, her hand on her belly. She'd screeched like a stuck pig. My grandfather—according to my parents— had kept to the periphery with my mother, but at that moment, he jumped into action. His attention split between the storm and my mother. My father tried desperately to calm his wife while Grandad called the ambulance on the café's phone. When I screamed my first breath, grandfather clasped a hand to his chest, a tear falling down his cheek. He and my grandmother raced home to prepare a room for their newborn granddaughter.

Because I was born in the midst of a storm, Grandad believed I was linked to the sea. He'd caused a hurricane of activity and before I'd arrived at the house, the walls were painted blue and both a crib and rocking chair were assembled. The room shared a wall with my grandfather's. He was known to sneak in at night to hold me, singing an old lullaby, the love between a Welsh woman and a Cornish man.

The room was still small, holding a thin bed and the same rocking chair from my childhood. But the view—oh, the view was of my sea—the same view Grandad had stared at earlier in his own room. The only difference, he could open his window. Mine was nailed shut the night I was born.

The sound of the ocean nestled on my shoulders, accompanying me while I readied for bed. With my back against the headboard, I faced the darkened night. My grandfather was a Cornish man who fell in love with the sea, traveling the world and falling more in love with the waves each year. Only when his older brother passed away did duty call him home. No one else in the world understood the allure of freedom, of not having roots to hold us down. Every one of his children had snagged a degree and a spouse of equal stature. *Nobility begets nobility* was a favorite of my father's sayings. Grandad thought differently. Title and rank were more of a weighted noose that slowly tightened every year. A fact he mentioned when I'd visit.

I lifted my hand to the window, a palm to the glass—barely acknowledging that I'd somehow left the bed—and closed my eyes. The whisper grew stronger, becoming notes instead of words. A song. An old lullaby from another time. Sharp pain shot through my fingernails. I jumped back—the pain growing. Little bits of old white paint were caught underneath my fingernails. I'd tried to open the window. *No.* It wasn't me trying to open the window. I hadn't had the conscious thought to do so.

The room went cold. My hands shook and my teeth chattered like the nervous tapping of a harried telegram operator. I threw the edge of the comforter up on the bed and ducked under the frame. Grandad's weather-beaten chest was still there. I pulled on the cold, metal handle, shimmying backward, the wood scraping against the floor. Cracking open the lid, the hinges yawned. Too dark to see, I blindly felt for the old alpaca quilt my grandfather purchased half a century ago, my hand raking the inside of the chest.

Wrapping the soft Peruvian fabric around me, peace filled me. The deep blue color had long ago faded—the only reason I knew its original color was the slew of photo albums my grandmother had taken. I didn't have Grandad's gift of art but like my grandmother, I knew where light and beauty met. For a man forever searching for adventure, my grandfather had been wholly satisfied with his quiet wife. In the corners and in the shadows she could be found, camera in hand. I was eight when Grandad gave me one of her old cameras. It'd taken me years to realize the weight of his gift. My grandmother had been gone for awhile by that point but Grandad was determined to let her legacy live on.

Fiddling with the hem of the blanket, I felt a tear slide down my cheek. Grandad was the only one who could have appreciated my humanity award. I placed a hand on the wall we shared. He was both near and far. So many times I'd wanted to call and talk to him, share my stories—both those that sink the heart and those that lift the soul. But I hadn't talked to him in ages.

The sound of scraping vibrated from Grandad's room. I winced, realizing how loud I must have been when moving the chest. Gingerly, I tip-toed to my bed and gently, softly pushed the chest back under the bed. The sound from my grandfather's room began again—this time louder.

Wrapping the blanket higher on my shoulders—to keep the hem off the ground—I peered into the hallway, cursing when the hinge squawked. I'd done the same thing when I was a teenager bent on sneaking to the woods just beyond my grandfather's property line. Grandad would hear me every time. Instead of lecturing, he'd quietly descend downstairs and pull his boots on. About half a mile from the house, he'd begin whistling. We'd walk a few yards apart until my mind stopped racing and my curiosity was satiated. Without a word, I'd turn around and we'd walk side-by-side back to the house. Whenever he'd accompany me, I'd never feel the pull of the ocean—a fact I learned the last time I visited. The silence of not hearing him was more than I could bear.

Grandad was talking in his room, his voice carrying. The sound of furniture being moved echoed once more. I snuck along the corridor, keeping to the right side instead of the squeaky left. This house had more groans and complaints than any other home I'd lived in.

The doorknob leading to Grandad's room turned. In the hallway, I froze, one foot in the air and my hand on the wall. He didn't recognize me during the day. Seeing me in the dead of night would be terrifying. His door swung open. He hooked his arm around the doorframe, his hand patting the wall for the light switch. The hallway flickered to life. Grandad shuffled to the doorframe. My heart beat wildly. He glanced at his feet, noticing the black half-circle at the threshold. I snuck closer. The black was shiny but I couldn't tell if it was a sticker or a paper thin mat. Frowning, Grandad huffed—gone was the easy-tempered man from my childhood. He lowered his foot but then pulled it back, his eyes wide. He was scared of the half circle. I crept closer.

Grandad grunted and tried his other foot. Twice he lowered his foot to the black half circle, only to rip his foot back as if he'd been stung. He scoffed and slammed the door shut, the sound echoing in the nearly empty corridor. I leaned into the wall, my quilt pooling at my feet.

The soft hinge of the door at the end of the hallway sent my heart racing. Muted light spilled onto the worn wood floors, Ioan appearing at the threshold. His hair was spiked on one side, flat on the other. The sound of Grandad slamming the door must have woken him from a deep sleep. A palm to his eye, Ioan yawned and lumbered into the hallway, the wooden floors creaking in complaint.

"Go back to sleep," my whisper sounded more like a frog fighting a cold.

Ioan blinked, and then arched an eyebrow. "Have you slept?"

"Sure." With my back against the wall, I slid to the floor, tucking the quilt around me. The sound of furniture scraping across my grandfather's wooden floors set me on edge.

"Sun downers." Ioan scratched his eyebrow with his thumb. Sighing, he walked to where I sat and held out his hand. "That's what they're called. Sun downers. They're lively when the sun goes down."

"How long has he been like this?" I placed my hand in his. Touching wasn't common for me and yet the act felt natural. And oddly intimate.

"Being awake at night? Ah, that's been the last year." He helped me to a stand with one hand, the other grabbing the blanket from off the floor. "Rearranging the furniture, that's been in the last month or so."

Tentatively, I took the offered quilt. Other than my grandfather and me, Ioan was the only person I'd ever seen touch the blanket. Grandad had purchased it in Peru, a country he desperately wanted to remember. He'd complained that he was stationed there for too short a time. I loved that the original blue color was my favorite, the same shade as the sea outside his—and my—window. I'd wrapped it around myself thousands of times in my life. Every one of my siblings turned their nose and refused to touch it, saying it smelled too old and musty, despite its frequent washings.

Ioan offering the quilt felt odd. Not wrong, just out of place. Or maybe I was the one who didn't belong.

"He does this every night?"

Ioan helped tuck the quilt around my shoulders, his eyes still sleepy. "Every night."

"How do you get any sleep?" No wonder he texted my cousin.

He shrugged. "Honestly, sometimes I don't hear him."

"He just roams the house?" Visions of my grandfather running rampant in the night had my heart racing. This was much worse than I'd feared. Grandad should be in a nursing facility, not in this home. "What if he goes out into the street? Or drowns in the sea?"

In two long steps, Ioan was kneeling at Grandad's door, his finger tapping the black half-circle. "This keeps him in the room." He picked at the seam, revealing the silicon bottom. "I place it here every night after he finishes his bedtime routine. Don't worry, it doesn't damage the floor." There was an edge to his voice at *damage*. "His mind doesn't know it's not a real hole."

"I'm more worried about Grandad than the floor." In the middle of the night, I felt hope. Ioan was different, the epitome of an eccentric, but I'd never been more grateful for a stranger.

"Tell that to your parents."

"I'm sorry." My cheeks became hot. As did my ears. Thankfully, Ioan didn't glance my way. There was no doubt how the conversation went. Ioan probably gave them an update—and the accusations immediately followed. My parents believed there were always ulterior motives. Ioan must be there for a reason, to take something that wasn't his. They'd thought the same thing when my old mentor offered to fly me to the British Virgin Islands after the hurricane. *He must be after something,* my mom had insisted. I had lowered the speaker volume. My parents didn't know I was already knee deep in debris. I'd only told them I was going, omitting the vital information that I'd already arrived.

Ioan stood, his eyes more alert and his frame more limber. "As far as they're concerned I'm a Morgannwg. And Morgannwg's are good for nothing."

"Why?" I shouldn't have asked but the night had a way of softening secrets.

He shot me a lopsided grin. "Am I one of your subjects?"

"Subjects?"

Ioan motioned to my hand. "Photography. Am I one of your victims you'd like to portray?"

"Oh." I stared at my hand, as if seeing it for the first time. My photography hadn't been discussed in this home in ages, aside from William's failed attempt at flirting. "No, I was just curious."

"Isn't that where it starts?" He turned toward the stairs. He paused at the first step; apparently, I was expected to follow. "You're curious and start asking questions only your camera can answer."

"No, that's not at all how it works." I gripped the blanket. My voice was firm and a tad too defensive. Ioan didn't know me or how I worked. He took another step, his face unreadable. I followed—and silently cursed myself for following. "I'm either hired by a media company or sometimes I'm given a heads up. For the most part, I know who I can sell what pictures to."

"Are you saying it's all a business transaction to you?" The idiot took another step. He didn't bother to check if I was behind him.

"That's not what I said and you know it." It came out as a growl. He didn't flinch. Dropping the quilt, I hurried after him. "You asked if you were my newest subject. Like I'm a scientist and you're an experiment. It's not like that. It's not a business transaction either."

His gaze flicked to my hand on his forearm. I hadn't realized I'd touched him. "Then what is it?"

Anger flared in my chest. Who was this man? He was a neighbor, a virtual stranger, who'd decided that I needed to defend my career to him. A man who felt more at home in *my* grandfather's house. "You want to know what it's like?"

Softly, he whispered, "That is what I asked."

I stepped closer, fury building in my veins. "What you're asking is for an explanation that doesn't exist. I arrive—it could be a riot or a shooting or a debate—but I'm there with a camera in one hand and a press pass in the other. Most of us are looking for a *money* shot. One that will get a fat check to replace a broken camera or busted computer—"

"But you?" There was an urgency in his words. He inched closer, his eyes shadowed in the staircase well.

"Me?" I snapped. The man hadn't let me finish before demanding another answer. "It's a compulsion. It's a drive to find something. It could be a flower in the middle of a business highway, smack in the middle of protestors disrupting traffic. There's beauty in nature refusing to cave. It could be a child's tear-stained face, his eyes trained on the athlete winning gold. Humanity, in all its forms is worth capturing. It's not business. It's not science. It's ... it's ..." The words hung between us.

A fear crept in, followed by a thought. I sank to the stairs, my head in my hands. I'd been a photographer for years—and I didn't have a clue why I did what I did. Was I truly as rudderless as my family accused me of?

"Perfect." Ioan's voice caressed my ears. He sat beside me. "It's perfect."

"No, it's not," I spoke to the stairs. He'd not listened to a word I'd said. "You missed the point."

"I believe that's the idea." He sighed and stretched out his long legs on the steps below. "You do not have a point or an idea to prove."

My heart sank. I was too tired to argue. This was not at all how I thought visiting Grandad would be.

"Hear me out, darling girl." Ioan mimicked Doris voice. "There is beauty in freedom and there is power in beauty."

I shot him a look. He had to be joking.

He wasn't smiling. Nor was he frowning. He leaned against the wall opposite me. Bending his leg, he tapped his knee against mine. "Your parents calculate everyone and everything against their value system. Unless it can appreciate or be improved upon, there is little to no worth."

He'd clearly spent some quality time on the phone with my family. I doubted they ever spoke to Ioan in person—they rarely spoke to Grandad, let alone this supposedly inferior neighbor.

"You." Ioan paused. "You capture what is here. Not what you could make out of it or what it should be, but what it is at this very moment. That should be celebrated. Not derided."

I stared at him, studying his face for any signs of sarcasm. He sat there, relaxed and easy in the staircase of my childhood like he belonged there. He'd spoken to me as if he knew me. Anger and doubt wrestled inside me, each trying to decide who would take over. "You said there is beauty in freedom."

"Ay." He nodded, his eyes never leaving mine. "And power in beauty."

"Why?"

"You can learn and expand your mind. There is power in knowledge but we can easily get boxed into our way of thinking. Our right and wrong." He arched his eyebrow. "Your parents are very sure in their right and wrong."

"That has literally nothing to do with beauty. Or freedom."

"Does it?" He leaned in. "Beauty and freedom are two things your parents will never have. There is power in both."

"Both can be taken away. Beauty and freedom are both out of our control." I flinched at my tone. It was far too defensive. He kept speaking as if he knew me far better than the few minutes we spent in each other's company. He was waxing poetic in the dead of night.

"You've changed the definition of beauty. And freedom," he whispered softly.

Dozens of faces flashed through my mind. Some old, some young—but all of them had a story to tell. All of them were given a chance to be heard. My humanity awards were given because of the characters, not for grandeur or the subject's beauty. The idiot next to me was right. There was a power, an intangible force that took over, when I looked through the lens of my camera. Faces became stories, stories became human. My heart lifted and for a moment, I didn't feel lost.

❧ 11 ❧

S ienna
Lydcombe, England: Present Day

❦

IT HAD BEEN A WEEK OF SLEEPLESS NIGHTS. GRANDAD HAD A penchant for rearranging furniture. All of it.

Every. Night.

Cracking an eye open, I flinched, the sun far too bright. I'd forgotten to close the curtains and now paid the price, the waves carrying the sun's light out across the sea. My feet were twisted in the covers—I must have tossed and turned throughout the night. Kicking at the blanket, I realized I'd slept on top of the bed with only the old quilt wrapped around me. My grandfather moving around in his room was not a distant memory, but speaking to Ioan on the staircase last weekend was.

Ioan had grown quiet and stoic after pouring tea. He was turtle-like when he spoke, emerging for an intimate conversation, only to slink back inside himself when I wanted more information.

The smell of Cornish potato cakes wafted up the staircase and into the room. Saturday in Lydcombe. The sizzle and distinct smell of butter-fried flour sent my mouth watering and my mind racing with memories. Doris would have English bacon—completely different than the thin, fatty American bacon—and sausage, tomatoes and eggs. Every item would have a crispy layer of fried crunch.

My younger brother Matthew was my only sibling who relished the English breakfast with me. My older brothers were bonafide Americans who vacillated between strict vegan or pescatarian diets, both of which were exceptionally organic. Doris would cook for an army, only to see my family snub her food. Whatever was leftover, she'd package up and hand it over to me, always with a wink and a smile. With my belly full of fried cakes and eggs, I'd scamper off to the chicken coop while my parents would sit and drink Doris' tea, giving thinly veiled insults. My father and his siblings had always felt a little misplaced around Doris. She had unconditional loyalty for Grandad, an unpardonable sin. She refused to bend, nor would she blink when they begged her to change his diet.

My stomach growled, impatient at how slowly I dressed. I had no idea when I'd actually gone to sleep, but from the ache in my bones and the puffiness of my eyes, it had to've been exceptionally late. The groaning of the floor as I made my way down the staircase welcomed me. Every creak and grunt of the house was a warm embrace.

"Ah, did the cakes get you?" Doris beamed, scrubbing away at the frying pan.

Ioan was pouring our tea. He'd not bothered to look up. Doris nodded to the plates on the island just as Ioan set two cups down. Watching Ioan in my grandfather's kitchen made my stomach sour. I had never cooked with Doris. She would shoo me and my grandfather from the kitchen. Help wasn't welcomed, at least I thought.

"Where's Grandad?" My grandfather could tuck into his food like a champ, a knife in one hand and a fork in the other.

"He's already eaten." Doris shook the excess water from the pan and set it on the counter to dry. "He'll be restin' for a few hours before needing another meal."

I flicked my wrist and read my watch. "It's nine."

Ioan sat at the counter. He'd not looked at me yet. The man was a horrible mystery—one I didn't know if I wanted to solve. He cut into his tomato and cakes; neat little squares appeared where food once was. Lacy had done the same thing for her fiancé's youngest child. He smirked as if I'd spoken out loud.

Blushing, I turned my attention to my food and shoved a mini mountain of cakes and eggs into my mouth.

"Have you been to the island?" Ioan asked, a twinkle of mischief in his eye. He'd timed his question perfectly.

Doris wiped down the counters. One look at my chipmunk status, her grin stretched across her face. Nothing made her more happy than watching her cooking disappear. "Look at that. Reminds me of so many mornings."

I struggled to swallow the brick of cakes in my throat. Ioan reached over, settling my cup of tea closer to my hand. The man had an infuriatingly sweet smile on his face. I shot him a glare. He winked —the idiot *winked* at me.

Delicately, he speared some of his squares and waved his fork at me. "So, have you been to *Ynys Wair*? Or should I wait until after breakfast to ask?"

Glaring, I folded my arms. I was my grandfather's daughter, of course I'd been to the island. Ioan would've known that. "What do you think?"

"Your breakfast is getting cold." He stifled a chuckle and slipped his food into his mouth.

My mind raced to find something to ask while he chewed, "Have you ever been?" I sucked at this.

He nodded and swallowed his dainty bite. "I'm a Morgannwg. Of course I've been."

Doris stiffened at *Morgannwg*. She shot him a pitying look but kept her mouth shut. Ioan didn't seem to notice, his focus on my plate.

Stabbing the last of my cakes, I started in on the tomatoes. "What does that even mean?"

Doris froze, her back to us. She was in the middle of chopping vegetables for the next meal.

Ioan sat back in the stool, folding his hands neatly over his stomach. The morning sun from the windows behind us rose just a touch, casting an otherworldly glow about his head. My frustration—not that I understood where it came from—dissipated; replaced with an urge to capture the moment. His long black eyelashes appeared almost golden, his hair reddening with the rays. But his eyes, the alluring green and blue of the sea—in an instant, he was beautiful. He paused in his talking, the words lost to me. A flicker of something crossed his features, morphing to another face. Or another time.

I reached out, my hand touching his face. He froze, his eyes pale—heavy with grief. The slamming of a door broke the moment, stealing the breath from my lungs. We jumped apart, down from our stools and away from each other.

"That smells divine," chirped William, his voice too bright.

Ioan and I mumbled some sort of greeting. Doris stood there, her mouth open and eyes wide. She'd witnessed me touching him. My face was on fire, my ears burning with embarrassment. Ioan was no better. He fumbled around, grabbing our plates and cups. Doris said nothing, her head pivoting between us. I wanted to crawl in a hole and die.

"What's on the docket today?" William was either the least observant man I knew or horribly optimistic.

Ioan murmured something in Cornish. I didn't know enough to understand. Whatever he'd said shook Doris from her stupor. She snapped her towel at him. "Foul boy."

"Is that allowed?" William smirked, enjoying Ioan's setdown a little too much. "Never thought I'd see the day when Doris gets after Ioan."

"He's still my darling boy." Doris softened, her eyes full of maternal adoration. I felt a twinge of jealousy. Selfishly, I'd thought I was the only recipient of Doris' care. Ioan had made himself at home in her heart as well—Grandad being the first. She waved her hands at both Ioan and me. "Now, off with you."

"You said Grandad won't be up for hours." The untethered feeling came again. I didn't have a project or anything to focus on. My parents thought I'd come to help Grandad and I had done nothing of the sort. Doris and Ioan had everything under control. I'd also not really taken pictures which *had* been my plan. All I had done was stay up with Grandad while he went stir crazy at night.

"You should visit the island." Doris didn't look at me as she said it.

"Oh, you've never been?" William had taken the bait, but the sigh Doris gave meant the idea wasn't for him. He glanced at his watch. "When's the boat leave?"

"Ten." Ioan looked everywhere but me. And William.

"Perfect." William shoved his hands in his pockets and twisted to face me. "You have plenty of time."

"For what?" I followed his gaze as he took in my unbrushed hair and day-old clothes. I'd dressed in yesterday's outfit. What I'd give to disappear. "It was a rough night."

Ioan smirked but thankfully didn't reveal anything more.

"Oh." Doris tucked her chin, scrubbing extra hard at the already clean counter. "The man looked rather haggard this morning."

"He's getting worse," Ioan whispered to her. "More restless."

My heart sank. "What do we do?"

"Tell the nurse when she comes," Ioan said with a shrug. His apparent carelessness made my stomach twist. I stepped closer, my pulse pumping in anger. His gaze flicked to mine, his eyes full of sorrow. I froze, my own heart now firmly in my throat. He swallowed hard and whispered, "Go to the island. I'll handle the nurse."

"I came to help." It'd come out as a pout.

"And you are." He lied so easily it was tempting to believe him. He nodded to the waiting William. "Go."

"How is that helping?" I folded my arms but felt childish. "I didn't come for a vacation. I'm quite literally no help."

"A holiday never hurt anyone." William rocked back and forth on his heels. Nervous energy swirled around him. He was the very opposite of Ioan in that way, only similar in their dark facial features. William was lean and wiry while Ioan was wide and solid.

"Work never hurt anyone either," Doris murmured. She wrung out her rag and laid it on the rack above the sink. "Bring something back from the island. It could pull a memory from Liam's mind."

Ioan smiled fondly at her. Jealousy reared its head. They shared a bond that I thought was mine and mine alone. "Ay, memories are always good."

Bringing back a souvenir was not helping. I wasn't a child and didn't need some menial task to keep me occupied. The very idea stung.

"Grab some ginger chews." Doris waved William toward the door. "Sienna'll be ready for you when you get back."

"Ginger chews?" William wrinkled his nose. "Those are disgusting."

"Ay, but they help her motion sickness." Doris rolled her eyes as if everyone knew what ginger chews were. She shut the door behind him and turned to me, hands on her hips.

"I don't get motion sickness." Although I appreciated that she'd bought me time.

"You've been green for days." Doris arched an eyebrow. Apparently she hadn't lied for me. "It's a bit quick for you to jump in a ship after flying here."

Shrugging, I made my way to the staircase. "I only get sick flying here."

"Only here?" Ioan's low voice carried over, echoing in my mind. "Have you ever wondered why?"

There was a challenge in the question and for the first time I realized why he was a constant irritant in the short time I'd been here. Every word, every thought—every gesture—was a battle. A play at some twisted sort of chess game that I'd somehow stumbled into. I didn't know the rules, nor did I really know the players.

Marching up the steps, the frustration grew. I'd felt hoodwinked into coming to Lydcombe, and now I felt like nothing but a pawn. At the stop of the stairs, I faced Grandad's door. I'd come to help him, but secretly, I'd come to see if there was some way, by some miracle, I could feel a connection with him once more.

I closed my eyes and placed a palm to the wooden door. A whisper caressed my ear. My eyes shot open. My heart raced. I spun around—I was alone. There was nothing. I was the only thing that haunted his house.

Turning the handle, I walked into his room, the smell of the salty air tickling my nose. The window and curtains were open. Grandad was asleep in his bed, his mouth open and hair disheveled. With his face relaxed, he looked like the man I'd adored for all of my life. It was a cruel joke to be so close to him and yet completely out of reach.

"He does remember you," Ioan said softly behind me.

"Don't lie to me."

He walked to the window, shutting it without a sound. "I would never lie to you."

"A souvenir won't bring my grandfather back."

"Have you ever thought you might have it backward?" Ioan folded his arms, his gaze boring into mine. "That you're the one needing to be brought back, not him?"

"Can you just go?" I didn't want to do his little dance. Not when I needed to spend the next six or so hours with William.

His face softened. "Do you need me to go with you?"

Relief filled me—and I hated it. "You are the most aggravating person I know."

He smirked. "Maybe you need to spend more time with William. That'll cure you of your opinion."

❧ 12 ❧

enan
Coch Bay, South Wales: 1606

MISS MORGANNWG LIFTED HER CHIN, REVEALING THE STONY resolve in her eyes, the color nearly black. Emotions swirled, looking eerily similar to an angry ocean storm. Her dark features offset the deep auburn of her hair. Kenan knew she was a rare beauty, one that Rothesay would fight to obtain. The feud between Rothesay and Miss Morgannwg's admirer, Charles Muiris, would die down only to reemerge at the slightest provocation. Both men felt wronged by the other. Kenan doubted either was innocent. He'd witnessed his father's ambition too many times to trust the man's judgement. Standing before two desperate women in a destitute castle did not soften Kenan's suspicions. His men, and his father's mercenaries, would breach the walls soon, the castle neglected for decades. Kenan needed a plan before his father's men—soldiers bought to remain loyal to Rothesay—could try their hand.

"I've answered your questions." Miss Morgannwg swept phantom dust off her skirt, the hem beyond repair. Her delicate skin was smooth and fair, so unlike the Mediterranean women Kenan had met in his travels. She turned her dark eyes to him. "Now give me a reason to trust you. Answer me, are you a mere soldier?"

"I am many things and I have been many things." Kenan felt Jowan stiffen next to him. "A soldier. A sailor."

Miss Morgannwg frowned, tossing an exasperated look to her nervous grandmother who sighed and wrung her hands. "A careful man it seems."

She narrowed her gaze and pursed her lips, the deep red matching her hair. Her fingers trembled. Her thumb and forefinger stained with ink. She was learned enough to correspond—igniting Kenan's suspicion.

"You do not trust me any more than I trust you. The only truth I know you've said is your desire to be elsewhere." Her lips tugged to an innocent smile. "We share that same goal. I do not want you here either."

The chit was impertinent, Kenan would hand her that. "I am trying to assist you." He nearly added *child* at the end of his sentence. "Have you any idea the trouble you're in? You're smack in the middle of a turf war. You're surrounded by starving wolves, the only shred of meat for miles. You'll be split in two if you don't get help."

She lifted her chin. "You cannot offer help if you're one of the wolves."

"They will tear you to pieces, woman." Kenan pointed to where the walls outside the earl's chambers stood. "There will be no castle. There will be no estate. If one man cannot have you, the other will make sure no one will."

"And yet you are here on behalf of Rothesay." Miss Morgannwg stepped closer, her voice biting. "Your words are tainted."

"I've no choice." Kenan wanted to be on his island or on his ship—anywhere that didn't house a nippy woman bent on making him the villain. Exhaustion sank into his bones, his resolve weakening. "I am bound to my—"

"Kenan," Jowan warned, a hand on Kenan's shoulder.

Lady Morgannwg's mouth fell open, her eyes narrowing. It would be just a moment before her mind pieced together who Kenan was—or rather who his father was. The little trust Kenan had been able to lay down would be gone.

"You've been bought by Rothesay." Miss Morgannwg hadn't noticed her grandmother's silence. "You cannot help us."

"I doubt Muiris can either." Kenan stepped from Jowan's touch. "But I've been bought by no one." He shot an apologetic look to Jowan before kneeling in front of Miss Morgannwg. "I am the second son of Lord Rothesay. I can promise you he is determined to be paid. This was my last errand, described as a simple collection of debt." He kept his gaze on Miss Morgannwg, feeling the weight of her stare. She'd flinched at his admission but had not retreated. She was stronger—or more stubborn—than he'd given her credit for. Rothesay would love her fire—only enough to break her will and feel the rush of domination. "A combined force will breach the walls in mere minutes. We have little time to devise a plan. I know my father and what he is capable of —trust me, there *will* be payment in some form or another."

"I sent a missive to Muiris before you arrived." Miss Morgannwg gave a subtle shake to Lady Morgannwg. They were planning a strategy. Kenan stifled a groan. They needed to work together—at least for a moment. "Your men had a little skirmish a few towns back. A maid came to the castle to warn us."

Kenan shot Jowan a questioning look. The man shook his head, holding up his hands. Kenan pinched the bridge of his nose. It could have been a mercenary. "There are some men in our company that do not hold to honor or moral obligation. They are simple mercenaries who are paid by my father—and the very reason we need to act. And act now."

"I will not hear from Muiris for weeks. If at all." Miss Morgannwg rubbed her ink-stained fingers on her skirt. "In truth, I've never written him before and do not know if I'd sent the letter to the correct residence. He spoke of London and of Cornwall."

Cornwall. Kenan's father lived in Lydcombe on the northern edge of Cornwall, an estate facing the Bristol Sea—facing the same Welsh county where he now stood. Rothesay could easily intercept communication. Kenan's father held court in England while Kenan's island was the only land mass standing between the Welsh shores and the Cornish cliffs. It was blessedly peaceful being surrounded by mercurial waters and powerful tides—a perfect hideaway for stolen treasure.

Slowly, Kenan folded his arms. "My men were to return to my home after payment while my father's were to return to Lydcombe." He held up a hand when Miss Morgannwg made to interrupt him. "My home is an island in the middle of the channel—directly between Lydcome and this castle."

Jowan groaned and shook his head. They'd spent enough time helping each other win battles to know each other's mind. Jowan had figured out what Kenan was planning.

"Few sailors can pilot the waters, and even fewer can find the harbor." He tugged at the collar of his shirt, he wouldn't admit it, but the sudden warmth was from hope forming in Miss Morgannwg's eyes. She was nothing but a temptress, a siren to avoid. And yet there was pride in helping her. "We can send word to Muiris that you have been taken as collateral, a payment for your father's debt to Rothesay. It would buy us time for Muiris' interference and still keep the contract with Rothesay."

"Your father will have our heads." Jowan began pacing by the window.

Lady Morgannwg's mouth lay open, her eyes wide with shock. She'd not recovered from Kenan's revelation of his parentage. He couldn't blame her. His father was fair haired, his eyes beady and nose hooked —his features and character closer to the rodents scurrying along the castle walls. Kenan was tall, his shoulders broad from years of wielding a sword, and his eyes pale green. He was his mother's son, in kind and character.

Miss Morgannwg's brow furrowed at Jowan's pacing. "What will your father do?"

"He holds no rights to *Ynys Wair* and has never set foot on the island." Nor did the baron have access to a boat limber enough to navigate the narrow harbor. The inlet was a haven for smuggling, not warfare. Several coves were filled with tea, wool, and spirits made abroad. Every settler on the island knew and each had a part to play when a new ship passed by. Only Kenan's ships knew the inner harbor on the west, leaving the dangerous cliffs for foreigners. The cliffs faced the busy path between Cornwall and Wales. Powerful waves and angry tides shoved passing ships dangerously close to the rocky shores. Worried sailors would give the island a wide berth, never knowing the safe harbor hidden on the other side.

"If your father cannot reach the island, how will Muiris?" Lady Morgannwg sat on a chair, her back bent and her pride gone.

"He won't." Kenan winced at the growing chorus of shouts outside the walls. The time had come. "We will go to him."

"How do we know you can be trusted?" Miss Morgannwg's gaze bore into him. "What benefit will deceiving your father give you?"

Kenan tried to shrug but couldn't pretend he was without guilt. "I promised Rothesay I would extract payment."

"And what if Muiris does not write back? What if he decides against paying the debt?" Miss Morgannwg's voice became small—the façade slid from her frame, revealing vulnerable prey. She glanced at her hands, her lips pursed. "What happens then? They'll not breach the castle while I'm gone?"

"There is nothing of worth in this castle."

She winced. "There are people, Kenan."

"Rothesay knows Muiris is interested or he wouldn't have sent me. Rothesay doesn't want payment, he wants you—for the simple reason that Muiris desires you." Nothing made Rothesay more rabid than Muiris having a prize.

"And what if Muiris no longer wants me?" There was too much hope in her eyes.

"Then we pray Rothesay never finds out." Kenan's stomach twisted. He was about to play a dangerous game. Jowan was right. There was no difference in saving this woman than when Kenan rescued the winged creature. Kenan was beyond his reach, rescuing the royal falcon and now his father's impending mistress.

Lady Morgannwg stood from her chair. Her posture was meant for noble courts, not soldiers. With her chin lifted and shoulders back, she walked, each step lofty and determined. She held out her hand. "Promise me." She sniffed, the haughtiness gone. Her shoulders curved in defeat. Blinking back tears, she begged, "Promise me, your father will not have her."

"No." Jowan growled from behind Kenan. "He'll promise refuge on the island, nothing more."

A tear slid down her cheek. She clutched Kenan's hand. "Promise me."

Jowan was at Kenan's side, whispering, "Promise nothing. For all our sakes."

"I'll be fine." Miss Morgannwg laid a delicate hand on her grand-mother's. "He cannot promise what he cannot control."

"You are Rothesay's son." Lady Morgannwg swallowed hard, emotions welling in her eyes. "If Muiris does not come, you must protect her and—"

Kenan retreated. He would do no such thing. His father would never forgive Kenan, nor would Rothesay allow his son to live after such a betrayal. "He would rather slit my throat—"

"She will not leave without an assurance." The woman's voice shook, rising in panic.

Kenan shook his head. "I cannot promise to take her, Lady Morgannwg, but I can promise she will be safe in my care."

"Kenan." Jowan spat and murmured a stream of curses. He growled once more and went to the window.

"Swear it." Lady Morgannwg slid a ring off her finger. With a quick flick, the top hinged open, exposing a needle. She grabbed Kenan's hand and pricked his thumb. A bubble of blood appeared. "Swear that she will be safe in your care."

Miss Morgannwg shook her head, her hand wiping the blood from his thumb. "No."

Her grandmother pricked Miss Morgannwg's hand where Kenan's blood was smeared. She nodded to Kenan once more. "Swear that Elyna is in your charge. In your care."

"I swear it." Kenan ignored Jowan's curses and Miss Morgannwg's shocked expression. "Elyna Morgannwg will be safe in my care."

Lady Morgannwg sank to her knees, clasping Kenan's hand. "Thank you, my lord."

Jowan grabbed her arm and pulled her to a rough stand. "Say your good byes. The men are here."

The sound of swords clashing and wood breaking erupted in the courtyard. Kenan would need to act the captor, not the savior. Miss Morgannwg whispered a *thank you* in his ear. He turned to warn her of the trek ahead but her arms were wrapped around her grandmother. Kenan pivoted, no one was close enough to whisper. He wiped his thumb. The injured skin was dark, the color of ink instead of blood. Warmth crept up his hand, swimming slowly in his veins and settling in his chest. He felt a pull to Miss Morgannwg—and then a rush of fear. The men his father had sent—half of them never returned. He would need his wits about him. Instead of being a savior, he feared he'd become the prey.

❧ 13 ❧

S ienna
  Lydcombe, England: Present Day

MUFFLED VOICES GUIDED ME TOWARD THE KITCHEN, THE SOFT
morning light from the sea at my back. I glanced at the door capping
the hallway, wondering if Ioan was still here or if he'd returned to his
home and horses. A flicker of doubt came alive. Or maybe it was fear.
There was an element of danger with Ioan which didn't quite make
sense. My parents disliked him and his mother, but my cousin trusted
him. Lacy had not questioned his motive once. A feat, considering she
was a no-nonsense senior PR executive. Her job was to sniff out prob-
lems before they arose.

But she was in California. A lump formed in my throat. She was
getting married. Her happily ever after was coming in like a speeding
train while my life was still stagnant. My grandfather's room was
behind me, he'd not woken from his morning nap yet. I was supposed
to be here to document his life. The thought didn't sit well. It twisted
and turned in my stomach.

I closed my eyes, feeling the same pull I had as a child. Opening my eyes, I gave in and let myself be walked forward—past Grandad's room. The pull lessened at Ioan's door. With my palm on the door, an image appeared in my mind. Ioan had a hand on the muscled, dark brown neck of a horse. He turned his head as if he could hear me. His lips quirked upward, not quite a smile—just a whisper of delight. The horse nickered impatiently. Ioan gave a nod and the image evaporated.

I pulled my shaking hand back, cradling it against my chest. *Impossible.* I'd seen Ioan as if he were here, in front of me. I spun around. No one. I held up my hand. It trembled but appeared normal. *Normal?* There was nothing normal about this. There had to be an explanation. A reason for seeing Ioan in my head.

Cornwall had always been special—magical, even. But this, seeing a vision or daydream of someone else? No. That had never happened. Not once.

I knocked on the door, praying he wasn't there and somehow knowing he wasn't. A day dream, or whatever, I saw in my head had told me Ioan was with one of his horses. Opening the door, I held my breath. Ioan was staying in the room where my brothers used to stay. The bunkbeds were gone, replaced with a queen bed in the center. Muted gray walls were freshly painted. From the faint smell, it'd been in the last few months. Which meant Ioan had probably done the painting. I didn't know how I felt about that, if I was supposed to be grateful or irritated.

The sketch book I'd found in the living room downstairs was on the nightstand, a pouch full of pencils next to it. The window in his room had the worst light, at least for most of the day. Facing the west, Ioan's room would get the early afternoon light until the sun dipped behind the town's church tower. It didn't make sense for him to be in this room, not for sketches and not for Grandad. He should be in my room, a better fit in every way.

A thought wiggled in and I wondered if Ioan normally stayed in my room. He'd even called it the *blue room*. Between my grandfather's dementia and Doris' adoration, Ioan would have free rein of the house —something my parents could not be aware of. If they knew, they'd be on the next plane. I winced, wishing more than ever they would stay in

California. The expected guilt at not wanting to be near my parents didn't come. Cornwall had a way of feeding my independence—my rebellious streak, according to my parents. They believed I left my manners and my mind in California when we'd visit. There was love and freedom in these walls.

Glancing at my hand, a thrill traveled up my arm. I should be scared at my little vision. At least cautious, especially regarding Ioan. All I felt was a growing curiosity—with Ioan and with Lydcombe.

Muffled voices carried up the staircase, and with a groan, I remembered my impending boat trip with William. The hours of little sleep pulled at my hands and feet. Each step felt heavier than the last on my way down the stairs, my fate inching closer to my mood—irritable and dark.

Like a kid waiting for Christmas, William wore an eager smile as he sat in the kitchen, chatting away at Doris who finished putting dishes away. She gave an apologetic smile the moment I entered. Ioan was nowhere to be found. According to the strange image in my head, I knew where he was. That was a secret I'd keep tucked away.

Visiting the island was Doris' suggestion. Earlier Ioan had all but shoved William toward me. Just a week ago, Ioan warned me of William's womanizing tendencies—not that I hadn't picked up on William's not-so-subtle hints at a date or two. With Ioan's cat-and-mouse game of being tender one moment and stand off-ish the next, I wondered, who was the true wolf I should be scared of? Maybe Ioan was the true predator, the man who could do the most damage.

William's coat hung on the rack by the side door. Mine was tucked under my arm. It was the last piece of clothing my grandfather had bought me. He'd always kept a pair of my boots, jeans—all cold weather clothing here at the house. My parents thought it odd, but having something here in Lydcombe made me feel slightly less homeless. Like I had an anchor someplace in the world.

William cocked his head to the side, an impish smile on his face. He must have asked me a question again. He was like a teething puppy. If I wasn't careful my shoes would get chewed, or worse, the little guy would get antsy and urinate on my boots.

For the first time, I wished Ioan was here, not William. I felt a flicker of panic. My stomach didn't like that idea at all. It didn't matter. Both men would soon start to tease me like my family. Even Lacy's patience had thinned the last few years. Not that I would blame her. Only Grandad stubbornly saw me as adoringly imperfect.

On cue, William ran a hand through his dark wavy hair, chuckling. "Is there anyone home behind that pretty face?"

Doris shot him a scowl and wiped her hands on her apron. Shaking her head, she muttered something indiscernible. She turned the corner, more than likely gathering supplies from the cleaning closet.

"I've had maybe half a night of sleep in the last week. So, nope. No one's home." I pointed to my face, hoping my smile softened my words.

"Even with Ioan here?" His green eyes darkened a moment.

"What does Ioan have to do with anything?" I didn't bother meeting his gaze.

There was more to his question which made little sense. With William's sleek jeans and tailored shirts, he was every inch the English aristocrat. I didn't recognize the brands, but money and prestige was something I could see a mile away. The easy cadence with how William filled a room, he was a man who was raised with expectations, from the world and for himself. Ioan worked with his hands, callouses on his palm from shoveling manure and caring for horses. Fear crept in. I'd touched Ioan's hand only once—my eyes flicked to the kitchen where I'd sat with him a few hours earlier. Part of me was scared of Ioan. The other part had a growing hunger to know him.

Rubbing my eyes, I forced myself to relax. There was one way I could sidestep William, giving him a chance to volunteer as my grandfather's night nurse. "Maybe you should take a turn in Grandad's room."

William grinned. "I'm not sure Liam would appreciate that."

"His furniture would."

Doris returned to the kitchen, broom in hand. "Oh, Sienna. Is it that bad?"

"No. It's fine." The last person I wanted to inconvenience was Doris. The woman had worked hard for my grandfather every day of his adult life. "If you stayed because of what I said, Ioan would kill me."

William brightened—far more than I wanted him to. He slid from the stool with surprising grace and held out his arm. "Shall we?"

"Take the rain coats." Doris nodded to the bench under the coatrack. "Or you'll be sniveling by the time you get back."

"I already have two in the car." William brushed his fingernails against his chest.

"Oh, you've learned how to be a gentleman, have you?" Doris laughed, her voice deep and comforting. "Bring her home in one piece or—"

"Ioan will kill me." He rolled his eyes and drew a line across his neck.

"Ioan?" Doris waved the name away. "He's the least of your worries. I'm the one who wields the knife in this home."

"That went dark rather quickly." William winked at me, charm rolling off him. "The sooner we leave, the sooner I can return you to your knife-wielding-protector."

"You think I'm teasing," Doris warned. The twinkle in her eye destroyed any threat.

William chatted and joked as we walked down the street to the harbor, my camera bag strapped across me like a seat belt. More than once I was tempted to ask why we hadn't driven. The walk was short, but William struck me as someone who'd use any excuse to show off his sports car. It wasn't until we neared the harbor that I realized parking was limited, if not impossible.

As the last passengers to purchase tickets, attendants ushered us onto the ship with nervous grunts. It'd been years since I'd sailed the channel. My grandfather believed these waters were the trickiest in the world, the current and winds always at odds with each other. This ship was motored and still only ran half the year. Most tourists believed there was treasure buried on the island, but wrongly assumed the old inhabitants were pirates. Grandad had told me they were actually smugglers, and our ancestors. Although, smuggler souvenirs didn't sell as well as gold-plated trinkets and treasure maps. The gift shop abandoned the truth long before my time. Grandad believed there was a treasure still on the island and not the hidden wool or liquor from the original owners. He believed there were myths and legends—stories that gave us hope. He believed wrongs could be righted by a second chance, a second life. He was a romantic in every sense of the word.

"I did bring the ginger chews." William scanned my face. "Doris really will kill me if I bring you back green and sickly."

"I'm fine." The low hum of a whispered song tickled my ear. "But if you don't mind, can we sit by the window?"

He cupped my elbow and guided me up the steps to the covered upper deck. There was just enough wind to keep the airflow without chilling my wimpy California body.

William sat next to me on the bench. It wasn't two seconds later, he began to fidget.

"Maybe you need a ginger chew."

He smiled sheepishly. "Sitting still has never been my forte."

"I'm shocked."

"You're a tough nut to crack." He nudged his knee against mine. "Tell me something no one else knows."

"I'm not tough. And I do crack," I said with a shrug.

He blinked before throwing his head back, laughing with abandon. His shoulders shook while mine sank. He was trying far too hard. "Oh, come on. Tell me something Ioan doesn't know."

"What Ioan doesn't know?" Oh, the poor boy. William thought my disinterest was because of Ioan. "I could write a book—no, I could write millions of books with what Ioan doesn't know." Holding out one finger, I said, "This is how many years old I was when I broke my first bone." I held out two fingers. "This is how many fingers I've broken— like I said, I'm not tough. I crack, literally."

The realization came slowly in his green eyes. The mid-morning sun ricocheted across the waters, illuminating his face. He would have been a perfect model for some sailor magazine. My fingers itched to pull out my camera. I wondered if he'd be encouraged by me taking his picture. The idea murdered any temptation for photography. He gazed out the window, unwittingly highlighting the angles of his jaws. "You are definitely ... not what I imagined."

"I'm not Lacy." I mirrored his pose, the water holding my attention. It always beckoned me. It always would. "The only Rothesay I resemble in any way is my grandfather."

"You do look like him," William offered gently.

I felt his gaze on me. "I've been told that a lot."

"Maybe that's why Ioan is so protective of you. He has a thing for Rothesays."

"He has a thing for Grandad," I said too quickly.

William shook his head and, with folded arms, turning his back to the water. "Ioan's a Morgannwg. They're known for being a touch mad, but they mean what they say."

At that, I met his gaze. "And just what has the almighty Ioan said?"

"That I better not repeat history." William shrugged while a chill swept across my neck. Ioan had said the same thing to me when I first arrived, referring to my tendency to slip from my grandfather's trail to the sea below. William *tsk*ed. "Ioan and Liam have that same belief, that history repeats itself until whatever wrong from in the past is rectified."

"What does that have to do with you and me?" Silently, I cursed. The last thing William needed was *you and me* coming from my mouth. I hurried to add, "And Ioan."

William ran a hand through his hair. "That's what I was hoping you can answer."

"And you believe it—or him? You believe in that idea?" My throat tightened. Whispers began circling me, like a breeze of voices.

He faced me—in a moment, so quick I nearly missed it—I saw a flicker of fear. He winked, the emotion gone. "I believe in a great many things. You being just one."

❧ 14 ❧

S ienna
    Ynys Wair Island, United Kingdom: Present Day

ᬽᬽᬽ

THE BRISTOL CHANNEL HADN'T CHANGED SINCE MY LAST VISIT AS A
freshly graduated college student. The sun quit its game of hide-n-seek
with the clouds and stepped fully into the late morning sky. No sooner
than its grand entrance, passengers spilled onto the lower deck below
us, their faces pivoting toward the warm summer rays. More than California ever could, England held court in the summer, the days early and
the nights short. And here on the Bristol Sea, surrounded by beautiful
blue waters, life felt absolutely perfect—if only my grandfather were
beside me instead of William.

An hour into our journey, our little ship was nearing the halfway
mark, where land was no longer visible behind or before us. At this
moment was when Grandad would wax poetic, his voice taking on a
husky quality. No matter how old I was, Grandad would repeat the old
myths he believed connected the island with his ancestors—and Wales.

The stories were faded in my mind, mixed with other happy memories of my time in England.

"Are you feeling alright?" William had become uncharacteristically still. I'd only known him a few days, but his inability to stop—talking or moving—was his most forthright trait.

"I'm fine." To prove my point, I smiled widely and batted my eyelashes dramatically. "Right as rain."

He straightened his stance, mischief in his eyes. "So you can flirt?"

I coughed. "Not even remotely."

"Just not with me." He held out his arm, motioning to the outer deck on the main level. "Should we join the crowd?"

"It's not you." It was a complete lie. Part of my hesitancy *was* him but the rest was me.

"Right." William flashed a dashing smile and waited for me to join him at the door of the covered upper deck. "I think that's my line. *It's not you, it's me.*"

Shrugging, I gave in. "You think I'm a catch—even a bit pretty in an odd, striking way—but in reality, you'll tire of me soon."

He spun his head around. "That's a rather dire outlook."

"It's the truth, no offense." Following him below to the wide main deck, I shrugged again. "Not only do I look a little different, you're used to getting girls easily and I present a challenge."

William narrowed his gaze, a nervous chuckle escaping. He rubbed his neck and glanced around. "Doris isn't the one with the knife. You've gutted me."

Circling him, I held out both my hands. "True or false, your longest relationship is a month."

He gave me a big thumbs down. "False."

"Liar."

It was his time to shrug. "Maybe I'm not the womanizer you painted me."

"What's your longest relationship?" Mimicking my mother, I narrowed my eyes and put a hand on my hip. This was entirely too much fun. I should have done this to every prospective suitor.

"Six months." William breathed on his fingernails before polishing them on his jacket. "And your longest?"

"Oh." This wasn't about me. "I never thought about it."

"A month? A week?" He whistled and shoved his hands in his pockets. "Wow. Who's the serial dater now?"

"I'm not the one chasing."

"Right." He gave a solemn nod. "That makes perfect sense. You're the victim in this situation."

I elbowed him. "Oh, come on. How many women have you dated this year?"

"Are you sure you want to go there?" He shook his head. "You realize how bad you're about to look?"

"I've dated zero men this year." Folding my arms, I leaned my back against the deck railing. Most men tried to control or possess. They weren't at all like Grandad. "Beat that."

He held up a hand. "What qualifies as *dated*? Because this conversation could take a quick turn."

"Going on dates with the same person." There was more to it. The sound of the sea was creeping into my head, making thoughts harder to form. "Repeatedly. Over a period of time."

William stepped closer, one hand lazily hanging over the rail, the other still in his pocket. "And ... how many men have you dated altogether."

"None." A cold breeze swept across my back, chilling me to the bone. It wasn't the weather. The chill had to do with something else, something intangible. I flexed my fingers in front of me.

"I can't tell if that's a good or bad thing." William cocked his head to the side, a mock frown on his face. "If you've never dated anyone that could mean you're ripe for the convent. Or ..." He tapped the side of his face, pretending to be deep in thought. "It could also mean you're an Olympic serial dater of the highest order. You're untamable against even the most ardent suitors."

Raising my eyebrows, I had to admit, I was impressed. "You should be in marketing."

He threw back his head and laughed, this time genuine. The warmth of his laughter had our fellow passengers smiling, despite not knowing the joke. In the spell of the moment, I was tempted. He was life and joy—what was I?

Lonely. The lump in my throat returned. As a child, I had buckets of joy and a thirst for life. When had I become a sad blob of nothing?

The passengers began murmuring, pointing to the island growing bigger by the minute. It looked so much smaller than I remembered. In my memories, the cliffs were gigantic and snow peaked, taking up the entire width of the horizon. Then again, everything was more dynamic when I was a kid—including Grandad. His words were gospel and his life immortal.

"Truce?" William stuck out his hand. He slid along the rail, creeping closer. "We pretend that we've just met and that our preconceived notions are utter rubbish."

"Tempting." This time I mirrored him and cocked my head to the side. "I did warn Ioan that I was the wolf and you were the lamb."

William grinned. "Duly noted."

I held out my hand but stepped back when he tried to shake. "In all honesty, I really don't know how long I'm here." My parents—and the few friends I did have—wanted me to settle down.

"So you've said."

"I came to help out with Grandad." It wasn't a complete lie. My parents thought that was the reason I'd come. The truth was much more selfish. I'd come to take pictures of him and all that made up the man I loved. The island. Lydcombe. If I wasn't careful, I'd start confessing these little tidbits. I should stop talking. He kept inching closer. "But Ioan and Doris seem to have everything under control. I'm finding it hard to justify staying."

William stopped, the silly grin no longer adorning his face. "Feeling useless?"

"Completely." Although I hadn't realized I was feeling that way until he'd mentioned it. "I love my grandfather but he doesn't recognize me. I'm a stranger. And yet Ioan and Doris who aren't family, are dearer to him than me."

"That's why I only come home on the weekends." He'd turned his head, his focus on the water instead of me. "My mum needs me, but she won't admit it. She was diagnosed with Parkinson's disease several years back. She goes out of her way to prove she needs no one. It's like a switch flipped in her brain. She became stubborn and ornery, every compliment or offer is some way to undermine her independence." He shook his head, a low sigh escaping. "Like I'm a miserable son who'd throw her away at first chance."

"What of your dad?"

"He just takes it." William rubbed his neck again. It must be his nervous tick. "I couldn't do it. Get barked at all day just for trying to help."

"Do you have any siblings? Anyone to help carry the load?" I felt like a fraud. Like I had any idea how a normal, functional family should act. If my parents struggled with a physical ailment, they would never admit it and they'd hire a fleet of the finest healthcare workers. I would not be trusted to help with anything. Even the diagnosis.

He gave a solemn nod. "Three. One in New York, one in New Zealand, and one in the ground."

"Oh, I'm sorry."

"I never knew him." William's face screwed up in frustration. "That sounded rather crass but it's hard to grieve someone you don't know."

"I'm still sorry." I'd never lost a sibling. I'd never lost a family member, except for my grandmother—and in a way, Grandad. Documenting loss with my camera was how I had experienced grief the most. "If I'm half as moody about my grandfather, I can't imagine how I'd be if I lost someone in my immediate family. Or if I knew I was losing myself."

He arched an eyebrow. "Losing yourself?"

"Your mom." I tucked my hands in the pockets of my jacket, feeling closer to my grandfather in that moment. "She knows her time is coming. Maybe not tomorrow but she knows the finish line is coming, or worse, she knows her ability to be in control of her body is coming to an end. I think that's more terrifying than death. I know Grandad was devastated by his diagnosis, wishing he had cancer instead." I grabbed William's arm, completely mortified at what I'd admitted. "Not that cancer is easier. It's just that he was scared he'd be a burden. That he would be a man child."

"I know my mum's scared. I understand that part." He smiled softly, his green eyes flicking from mine to my hand. "It's the anger part. The barking at me and my father. That part I don't understand."

"Does she lash out to all the siblings or just you?"

"Just me." He pointed to the harbor of *Ynys Wair.* "But I can't really complain when we're about to see the aftermath of extreme brotherly dysfunction."

"We're English. I thought dysfunction is in our DNA."

"No, we're human. There isn't a country or culture in the world that doesn't have a family scandal somewhere in their history." He winked, although this time it appeared more forced than genuine. Our conversation had struck a chord. To be honest, he wasn't nearly as exhausting as I'd thought.

A breeze tugged the loose strands of my hair, carrying whispers— notes of a song. I gripped the railing to keep the temptation at bay. The boat's motor sighed, shifting to a slower speed and sidling up to the thin pier waiting patiently for us. The waves lapped against the poles of the pier, teasing and calling to me. We walked up the pier, the water fading from blue to greenish and finally to the shallow brown, colored by the sand just beneath the surface.

"Missing California?" There was a sharpness to William's gaze.

"No." With a shake of my head, I added, "I've only had eyes for this sea."

"Ah." He held up his index finger. "So you're a one-sea woman now are you?"

I gave a dramatic sigh and clasped a hand to my chest. With a fake English accent, I said, "To be true."

"Is it because of your grandfather?" His voice was softer, more sincere.

"Maybe." We stopped at the edge of the pier. The rest of our fellow passengers were filing into the quaint little shops, choosing among the pirate gift shop, an old fashioned ice cream shop, and the information building. "Despite my American accent, I was born in Cornwall. Maybe it *is* Grandad. Maybe it's my birth." With the toe of my shoe, I nudged some of the pebbles on the gravel road. "This—Lydcombe or the island—all of this has always been home to me."

"Me too." In tandem we walked up the road toward the church and the museum. Despite his long legs, William matched his pace to mine.

"I've traveled all over the world but I keep coming back here. Like some outside force has bound me."

His words pierced me. No matter where I lived or where I visited for work, the U.K. was home. And it always would be. Even if I couldn't stay anywhere for long. It took a full moment before I trusted my voice to respond. "I know the feeling."

"Where've you gone?" He folded his hands behind his back, his tone easy—the flirting long since forgotten. "Traveled, I mean."

"Sadly, I've really only traveled *in* the states." I held out my arm, indicating the island. "This is about as exotic as I come."

"But your parents—"

I groaned, cutting him off. "I know. They travel a lot. I'm always working when they go on holiday."

"That's convenient." He winked.

"Exactly." A warmth spread in my chest. William was still very much a charmer but I held onto the feeling. I couldn't trust him with my heart. But it felt glorious to be heard—to be seen.

❦ 15 ❦

K enan
     Penyl, South Wales: 1606

CLUMPS OF ELM TREES DOTTED THE TOPS OF THE DARK WELSH
mountains. The mountains surrounded Kenan's view as the trail crept
inward for miles before meandering back toward the coastline. The
late afternoon sun peeked through the branches, lazily sinking in the
sky. Slowing his horse, Kenan signaled to Jowan—they would camp
here for the night. His fingers played with his ring now back on his
finger. His family crest—or rather his mother's family—was engraved
on the band. As the only male heir of her line, the insignia was his.
Kenan's older brother—the first son, from the first wife—would
inherit Rothesay's barony.

Miss Morgannwg eased her grip on the reins, her black horse
nodding its head in response. She'd said nothing since she'd left her
grandmother's embrace in Coch Bay. Kenan had spared only a few
minutes for Miss Morgannwg to bid farewell to the older woman. They

whispered promises to each other. Lady Morgannwg repeating, *I'll take care of him.*

Kenan felt a twinge of guilt. He'd not given Miss Morgannwg a moment with her father. The earl was a simpleton and more than likely didn't—or wouldn't—understand what was happening. Kenan wondered if the earl was aware he'd fathered Miss Morgannwg or if the man had enough sense to know his daughter was saving him from debtor's prison.

Kenan frowned. It didn't matter what the earl did or did not understand. Kenan had needed to assert authority the moment his men—and his father's men—breached the castle. Lord Rothesay, Kenan's father, no longer led his men. He preferred the safety of his own castle walls, forcing his son, Kenan, to do his bidding. Kenan knew the truth, Rothesay's health was fading—while the man's temper was forever at the ready.

With a quick glance to the dark, red-haired beauty riding at his side, Kenan wondered who fared better—the lady with a simple father or the knight with a tyrant parent. Either way, Kenan would soon be free, unlike the fair Elyna Morgannwg. He still didn't know her married name. Rothesay wouldn't care. He'd take her, widowed or not.

Her gaze met Kenan's, her expression stoic. His pulse quickened. He broke the connection and spurred his gelding forward. He could not afford to look upon another man's prize—whether that man be his father or Muiris.

Kenan knew the heartache of pride and lust. Rothesay claimed every one of his children, daughter or son—each birth a blow to Kenan's mother. She'd been a faithful wife. Even now, living estranged in London, she kept her vows.

Miss Morgannwg's horse snorted behind him, stealing Kenan's attention once more. He was aware of the woman's every move—every sound. He silently cursed. He should have listened to Jowan and not promised her safety with his blood. Kenan's mother was Welsh. He knew the power of a Celtic oath. Kenan was bound to Elyna Morgannwg, regrets and all.

He winced at the memory of her farewell. Kenan had tried to warn both Miss Morgannwg and her grandmother of how he'd need to act when the men broke through the castle walls. If Kenan didn't show authority over the estate, his father's men would takeover. Lord Rothesay was well-known for not only his own cruelty but the low morals of the men he employed. Kenan knew firsthand of his father's mercurial temperament—he'd spent his life grateful for his mother's tender care.

The men had filled the courtyard, swords and pistols at the ready. Kenan had barked out orders, leading the suddenly submissive Miss Morgannwg forward. She'd not spoken since.

Flanked by his men, Kenan marched from the castle walls within the hour. He needed to reach the hamlet outside of Swansea tomorrow but his father's men were suspiciously slow. Their company should cover twenty or so miles a day. They had kept their pack light and agile. But they'd only managed ten today.

The worry on Jowan's face confirmed Kenan's fears. Barking another round of orders, Jowan circled back, his horse slowing to a walk next to Kenan.

"It's not escaped your notice then?" Jowan's voice was low. "It shouldn't take two days to reach Swansea."

"Ay." Kenan needed to send for his ship or he'd have to wait another week for the post. "Is there an illness? Or have the men become lazy while waiting for us at the castle?"

Jowan narrowed his gaze, searching the men. He glanced over his shoulder at Miss Morgannwg. "I'd think they'd be motivated now that we have something to show for our voyage."

"Is it everyone?" Kenan knew the risks of mutiny—his education on the seas had taught what fear could do to a man.

"No, but we are outnumbered." Jowan gave a subtle shake of the head. "What benefit is there to stalling?" He slowed his horse and motioned to Miss Morgannwg.

Miss Morgannwg swallowed hard. She lifted her chin and straightened her back. If not for the widening of her eyes, she'd be the very picture of nobility.

"My lady, might we have a word?" Jowan asked loud enough for the immediate men to hear, his tone warm and deceptively inviting. The deference was for the benefit of the men. If he showed respect, they would follow suit.

She gave the slightest of nods. Jowan dismounted and led the way to an overgrown fir tree. Kenan and Miss Morgannwg followed close behind.

Jowan pretended to examine her saddle, whispering, "Did Rothesay send you a letter to you personally?"

"No." Miss Morgannwg shook her head, her hands flexing at her side. She seemed too nervous for a simple answer.

Kenan asked softly, "Have you sent any other correspondence?"

A flicker of panic crossed her features. She pursed her lips, as if deciding on what to say. "I have."

Kenan rubbed his neck. Their plan was unraveling fast.

"What did you say?" Jowan spat at the ground. "Do not play me false."

"I sent a care package to my old maid." She narrowed her eyes. "I will not give you her name. She will not be pulled into Rothesay's clutches."

Jowan shifted his weight and folded his arms. "Did Rothesay send any correspondence to anyone in the house?"

She lifted her chin. "He wrote to my father only."

"Which meant your grandmother read it?" Kenan softened the accusation with smile. *Did you read it* was what he'd wanted to ask. Miss Morgannwg had the ink-stained fingers, not her grandmother. "Did Lady Morgannwg respond?"

With her reins in her hand, Miss Morgannwg shook her head once more. "She wouldn't. Rothesay has a reputation. She didn't trust him. His letters went unanswered."

Kenan rubbed his neck. Miss Morgwannwg was clever. She'd not admitted to reading the correspondence, only that Rothesay's demands were ignored. A dangerous game the Morgannwg women were playing.

Jowan wiped his face with his hands. "This could turn on us in an instant, Kenan."

"Ay." That was the obvious part. Kenan didn't need to be reminded. He needed a solution, not another warning. "There has to be a reason they're moving this slowly."

"What do you mean?" Her words were laced with suspicion. "We've only left Coch Bay this morning. We'll clear Swansea before tomorrow morning, yes?" Her voice rose when she said *Swansea*. The city somehow made her nervous.

"We should be in Swansea by now." Jowan let the reins fall, allowing his horse to nibble on the low grass. "These are seasoned men. They know how to march and they know how to strategize."

"You expect too much of them." Miss Morgannwg sniffed. "They're brutes who mistreat women."

Kenan's mind raced back through the past few days. She'd mentioned the woman before. "The men, they mistreated someone from the village?"

She nodded curtly. "That's why I sent the missive to Muiris. One of your men attacked an innocent woman. She told me Lord Rothesay's army was coming."

"You were still ill prepared for us to come." Jowan narrowed his gaze. His suspicion matched hers.

"And how could we prepare?" she snapped. "We've no money. No friends. We are at the mercy of men. And men can never be trusted."

"Even Muiris?" Kenan asked quietly.

"Is he a man?" Miss Morgannwg arched an eyebrow.

"Why encourage a man you've no intention of marrying?" Jowan folded his arms and leaned against the tree. "Seems to me you're the sex to be wary of."

"You can say what you like." She held out her hand, indicating the surrounding soldiers. "You've men at your disposal. I cannot defend the very home I was born to. I'm only as good as the child I can bear. And what if I marry a brute, or worse, what if I'm to be nothing but a mistress? My children will be at the mercy of that man's temper— they'll not have the protection of a last name."

"For someone so against men, you've thought a lot about tying yourself to one." Jowan hissed at the ground. "Tell me the truth, woman." He stabbed his finger in the air, pointing to her. "Are you scheming? Have you betrayed Kenan's trust? He risked—"

She scowled, her eyes wild with rage, a blush creeping across her face. "I'm aware of what he's risk—"

"As am I." Kenan stepped forward, standing between Miss Morgannwg and Jowan, the tension crackling. Kenan kept his gaze on a tall blond making his way toward them. He was the self-appointed leader of Rothesay's men. Kenan didn't trust him, the feeling mutual. "The stories of my father are true. I knew what I was risking when I took the oath with your grandmother. But now, at this very moment, we are being watched."

Jowan tilted his head, eying Matthew, the blond leader who was approaching. "Speak quickly. Our time is short."

"There's a reason our men are slow to move and we need to know if it's illness or strategy," Kenan whispered quickly. "It's too late in the season for the men to cross Severn River by ferry."

Miss Morgannwg scoffed. "Severn River? They're sailing to Lydcombe?"

"They'd need a skilled pilot," Jowan answered. "We board—if we can make the post—just outside of Swansea. They'll have to risk the ferry and the tides or march up to Gloucester. That'll add two or more days."

"How long 'til they reach Lydcombe?" She leaned in, suspicion gone.

"It should take seven, maybe ten days to be at Rothesay's feet." Jowan spat at the ground. The man had little tolerance for Rothesay or men of his ilk.

"And to your island?" Miss Morgannwg hesitantly turned her eyes to Kenan, desperation in the tremor of her voice.

Kenan cursed the pull, the softening of his stance. He was bound to this nymph. He needed to get her to Muiris before she wormed her way into his mind—or worse, his heart. Mystic and witchcraft were powerful tools, if Kenan believed the stories from his mother. He'd delicately avoided women and eager parents, only to fall prey to one blood oath.

Jowan cleared his throat. He'd been a little too observant for Kenan's comfort. Jowan took up the reins of his horse. "If we board tomorrow, we'll be at *Ynys Wair* by nightfall." He turned from Kenan and met with Matthew, the blond leader of the mercenaries.

Kenan was grateful for Jowan's interference. It'd give him precious minutes to gauge the woman's mind. If she was scheming, he could lose his head. Rothesay was a stranger to mercy.

"By nightfall?" Miss Morgannwg asked. "And then what?"

"With the wind, it's likely Jowan is right. The Severn River ferry would not risk the wind for another few months. Rothesay's men would not arrive in Lydcombe until we've been at the island for at least a week." Kenan rubbed the stubble on his face. He'd packed light, leaving the comforts of his rank and birth at home. "Our plan could work, but not at this pace."

Her face fell. She glanced about, her shoulders sinking. "How do you fight alongside men you cannot trust?"

"It's the only life I've ever known, Miss Morgannwg." He watched the pity form in her eyes—it was dangerous ground, confessing anything. He would need to keep his distance. She was a pretender—he'd seen the evidence at the castle. "We need time on our side or our little plan to outwit my father will backfire."

"What will happen to you?" She stepped forward, the worn hem raking the ground. "Will he go to the castle?"

Kenan retreated. He would not be trapped by a woman, oath or not. "How many days before we arrived did you send word to Muiris? A week?"

"A week?" She shook her head. "The maid arrived three days before you. I gave her the letter and she left with the scribe."

It'd be at least a fortnight—at the earliest—before Muiris' reply would come. "And he knows of your father's heavy debt?"

"Muiris knows my father is simple. And he knows we are destitute."

Kenan wiped his brow, the weight of his decision on his mind. She'd not answered the question. "Muiris does not know of the debt."

"No." Her voice broke and her eyes were downcast.

"The island is removed." He sighed and against his better judgment, would offer reprieve. "It's isolated by tides and winds." He cursed himself as he stepped closer. She glanced up, her eyes wary and her stance unsure. He pressed on. "I keep a post at a church just outside Swansea, manned by Jowan's family."

"His family lives in Swansea?" Her eyes widened and she covered her mouth.

She'd not taken to Jowan. She didn't know the loyalty of a man like him. Jowan's parents kept tabs on all communication to and from the island. Kenan trusted the family more than his own. Kenan's father had never been to the island and assumed Kenan's holdings were the sad church and the surrounding farm. Rothesay would never set foot inside either building. He'd never see the fine furnishings and several servants, keeping Jowan's parents comfortable.

"You'll be safe." His throat tightened. He'd once promised his mother he'd protect her—he'd taken her by candlelight, sweeping her away to London. It'd cost him his inheritance and a promise of servitude. The agreement with his father would soon be lifted—this was the last errand. "I promise, Miss Morgannwg."

"Elyna. If we're to flee together, you might as well call me Elyna," she whispered. "I suppose I should be thanking you."

Kenan tucked his head. She shouldn't have given him permission to be informal. "Do not thank me yet."

She lifted her head. A strand of dark, red hair fell forward. "And why is that?"

"You've entrusted your life to a smuggler."

❧ 16 ❧

S ienna
Ynys Wair Island, United Kingdom: Present Day

WILLIAM SAID LITTLE ON OUR WALK TOWARD THE ISLAND'S CHURCH and museum. I kept glancing at him, but he appeared to be deep in thought. Whoever this version of William was, I preferred him hands down over Cornwall William. That man was a flirt and exhausting. This new, quiet gentleman was easier to be around. He folded his hands behind his back. If we'd arrived earlier I would be tempted to take a touristy photo of the sunrise.

In companionable silence, we gently climbed the road, nodding to other pedestrians coming down.

Turning behind the peaked wall of granite lining the road, I felt my temperature rise. With the granite blocking the chilly wind, my body relaxed in the warmth of the sun. If we'd come in the late spring, pink poppies and purple soapwort would dot the field to our left. The church's graveyard should still have the whimsy flowers attached to stubborn vines. I'd forgotten the name but not the spirit. The plant could survive wild winds and clay soil, bringing forth a dainty flower, white in the center and lavender at the end.

The crowd of tourists grew as we neared the church and museum. William held out an arm, guiding me toward the courtyard in front of both buildings. "What strikes your fancy?"

"I'm not sure." My grandfather had always taken me straight to the museum, buying small bags of dried lavender on every trip. For as many times as he'd taken me, I should have the tour memorized. But for the life of me, I could never focus. My mind was always wandering, lulled by the scents and hushed conversations of the patrons. "Where do you want to go?"

William gave a halfhearted shrug. "If I were a good boy, I would visit my ancestor's gravestones." He winked, revealing the same Cheshire grin he wore back in Cornwall. "But I've never been accused of being a good boy."

Rolling my eyes, I elbowed him. "The church it is."

"I'm still surprised Ioan didn't take you." His tone was light but one thing I'd learned on this trip, William wasn't as shallow as I'd once thought. "This is kind of his thing."

"How?"

He shot me searching look. "This is *Ynys Wair*."

"Aren't your ancestors here as well?"

William stopped, a hand on my arm. "You really have no idea what all this means, do you?"

A whisper whipped around my hair, sending a chill up my neck. My stomach twisted. "Should I?"

"Sienna ..." He scratched his temple, an internal debate written on his face. "Ioan owns this whole island. He lives in that decrepit little barn—he even dares call it a house—but chooses to live there instead of here."

I swallowed the correction. Ioan lived at Grandad's house, not at the barn. William's error made me wonder what else he didn't know about Ioan. "It's not like there's a house here."

"There's a bloody castle on the other side of the island." He placed a palm to his forehead as if the idea pained him. "The man's just like his mum. Not right in the head."

"I thought the island was part of the historical society." I could have sworn that was covered in the museum. Not that I would bank on my memory at the moment.

"They lease the land from him. It's renewed every year." He shoved his hands in his pocket. "He wouldn't pay a nasty council tax. He wouldn't pay anything. He could live like a king here."

"A king of what?" I couldn't help but laugh. "There's lavender and chocolate. Oh, and a pirate shop at the pier."

William smiled but there was sorrow in his eyes. "You're right. There's not much here."

"Except your ancestor's gravestones."

He nodded, the mirth still not back. "The entire village exists for tourism."

"It's tempting, isn't it?" Folding my arms against the cooling breeze, I tried again, feeling a bit of guilt for taking the humor from him. "To look at all of this and wish for it, but you're William. Not Ioan. He would probably thrive here, secluded away from most of the world. How would you survive? The ship doesn't come regularly after October. What would you do for those six months of nothing?"

"I could pretend to be Hades and trap fair maidens in my lair for half the year. I could ply them with chocolates and an unending supply of lavender perfume." William met my gaze. The sadness melted away. Cornwall William was back which was still infinitely better than Sad William. "There's even a spiritual retreat in late April. I could be the savior for all women."

"Liar." Shaking my head, I started up the walk toward the graveyard tucked behind the church. "You'd be bored and a king."

"Probably." He followed suit, his hands behind his back once again. "But I'm bored already. Why not be bored somewhere else?"

"You don't strike me as someone who's bored."

"Oh." He cocked his head to the side, a sneaky grin firmly in place. "And what type of a man do I strike you as?"

"Mischievous for sure."

He tipped his back and laughed. "I do like to have a bit of fun. You can't fault me for that."

"Does it bother you?" I lowered my voice as we entered the old church. When I'd visited London several years ago, the ancient churches had the same smell, musty and solemn. Here, the windows and doors were kept open from sunrise to sunset, allowing the wind to sanitize the air.

"Bother me? Do I look like a man easily bothered?" His lips quirked.

William seemed to have given up on collecting me as a new trinket. I felt like a rather amusing puppy at his side. Before our little journey, I'd pegged Ioan as a tough man to know instead of William. Perhaps being enigmatic was a mark of a true Cornwall man.

"Your reputation." We walked on the outer edge, away from the ancient benches. A gray-haired pastor was eagerly talking to an elderly couple. By their accents, they were from Wales, not Cornwall. The island was smack in the middle between the two lands but claimed by none.

"My reputation?" William's smirk grew. "You mean the ribbing I get from the likes of Doris?"

"You either *are* a serial dater or you pretend to be." We filed through the back door, the archway round. And inviting. "It has to hurt or at least be a frustration that no one really knows you."

He gave a one shoulder shrug. "Does anyone really know Ioan?"

"Tell me about it." When William stopped, I waved away the comment. "I get whiplash from his moods."

William opened his mouth but must have thought better of it and snapped it shut. He pointed toward the far end of the graveyard where plain headstones lay instead of carved monuments. Following, I relished the quiet that always descended here. The few times my grandfather would accompany me to the small cemetery, he would watch me. The white noise, like a fan or the humming of a computer, would cease. Not even the whispers from the sea could reach me here. I'd made the mistake of telling Grandad of the whispers. The memory pricked at my heart.

Leaving William's side, I walked to a tall, thin stone monument in the center. A regal falcon was carved into the island's native blue-gray granite. Its wings were outstretched, tips of the feathers broken and jagged. The talons morphed into the four-foot spire anchoring the small statue.

Here—at the base of this very monument—I confessed the whispers. I'd placed a hand on the talons and told Grandad everything. He should have told me I was crazy. Blinking back tears, he kneeled before me and took my hands in his. He stared at our clasped hands, the tears falling.

His behavior scared me more than the whispers ever did. Or the songs I sometimes heard. Only once did he bring up the whispers— when he begged me to stay with him in Lydcombe several years ago. He'd told me about his Alzheimer's diagnosis. I'd promised to not tell my parents. To this day, I don't know if they found out on their own or if he finally admitted it. We were united—always. Guilt clutched my heart, squeezing with all its might. I touched the granite, the stone cool. "I should have stayed," I quietly told the wind in my ear.

"They're still here," William spoke behind me. "There was an aviary built for the falcons back in the early seventeenth century. Even after the master ..."

He kept talking but I couldn't hear the words. The notes of an old song danced in my head. A lump formed in my throat, and I wished my grandfather were here instead of William. I'd told my family I was coming to help Grandad—but here on the island I knew I'd been called home for something more. Something that had nothing to do with me. I wasn't here to reach Grandad or to help him improve. I was here to help him return, to die.

Fear didn't come. Nor did the guilt. The warmth of peace filled me, and the ground beneath my feet felt more sure. The last several years, I'd felt untethered, a flag waving wildly in the wind—but now, I felt the steady drive of a purpose. I wondered if Ioan had instinctively known or had felt the need. Or if it was all some happy coincidence that he pushed to get me to Lydcombe.

"... but being illegal never bothered them. Falcons. Smuggling." William's voice pulled me from my thoughts. He didn't appear to notice. He pointed to where he believed a castle stood. "I can't remember the name of the guy, but I know it was James Rothesay's second son. He was the black sheep of the family. Abandoned his duty and became a pirate."

"Kenan." Of course, I knew the name. When William looked at me I shrugged. "My parents paid an obscene amount of money to have our family tree put in a book."

"They never come here. Why care about genealogy?"

"They love their pedigree." We walked to the outer edge of the cemetery. About ten feet from the white fence, the ground dipped down into a low valley, a cluster of small, ancient homes lay in the belly of the island. "They're not fans of actually living in England or paying English taxes, but they take great pride in their ancestry."

"Where's your mother from?" His fingers tapped on the railing. The light from the afternoon sun gave warmth to his profile. The angle of his jaw and tilt of his forehead—he should have been a model.

"London." She was proud of her upper aristocrat heritage, even if she no longer had the accent. A bird flew low in the valley below us. "Why were falcons illegal? In ancient times. Why was that a crime?"

"Depending on which time in history, only the king and his family could have them." He leaned on the railing, his eyes squinting, searching the homes below. "This is England. There was class system for everything. Birds, Clothing. Accents."

I watched him. "Who were your ancestors?"

William fidgeted, uncomfortable with my question. "I'm from Lydcombe which means I'm related to half the town in one way or the other." He poked my arm. "Not everyone escapes to America."

"I was born in Lydcombe."

He nodded his head slowly. "That's right. I forgot about that little tidbit."

Turning from our view of the village, I added, "Which means we're probably related."

He pumped a fist in the air triumphantly. "See, I told you. Family scandal is our thing."

"My family doesn't do scandal." I was the wild card—the lone rogue —and I was hardly barbaric. Holding up my hand like a kid in class, I said, "Guess who's the reckless one in the family. Oh, that's me."

William's brow furrowed. "That's disappointing."

"Not sure how I feel about that. Should I be flattered that you don't think I'm wild?"

He offered his elbow. "I've been told I'm an excellent teacher."

"That, I have little doubt." Stepping closer, I looped my arm through his. A shadow of a bird flapping its wings was on the ground ahead of us. Above, a bird circled. I left William and followed the bird, hopping the graveyard fence.

"Sienna, what are you doing?" William called after me.

A rush of sounds and music filled my head. Pulling out my camera, I walked down the steep descent in and around the native gorse. The bird dipped down, its feathers the gray and blue of the island's granite. The animal circled above me and cried out. My heart raced at the sound. Grief. The animal was grieving. It swooped down. I ducked— my right ankle bent against a rock. A crack and pop—and I was down.

❧ 17 ❧

S ienna
    Ynys Wair Island, United Kingdom: Present Day

THE FALCON CRIED OUT, ITS SHRILL VOICE ECHOING IN MY MIND.
My ankle turned and then I was down, my elbow slapping against the
rocks and spiky moor grass. My camera was next to me. A quick look
and it appeared undamaged. The edges of the soft grass fibers faded
from green to white and then purple. My ankle throbbed, the pain
creeping up my calf. I focused on breathing and lay back against the
island. The falcon circled lower, its cries softer.

Slowly, my hand raked the grass for the camera. The lighting was
wrong. And the falcon moving made for a horrible picture but the pull
toward the creature directed my hands and eyes. Peering through the
lens, I almost heard the falcon speak. My finger shook, accidentally
taking a dozen pictures.

I heard William call after me from where he stood at the churchyard. I slid the camera back in the bag, strapping it across my chest.
The bird tilted its head toward William. It held out its talons and

landed next to my foot. I froze—the ankle forgotten. The feathers were less gray, containing more white than when it was flying above me. It pivoted its head, as if trying to get a better look at me.

Scooting up on my elbow, I leaned forward. The bird squawked at me, reprimanding me for moving. I giggled. It squawked again and walked forward, its long talons crisscrossing over each other as it stepped. The once regal animal now appeared goofy, its tail feathers waddling.

"Sienna?" William sounded closer.

The falcon flapped its wings, reminding me of Doris shooing me and my grandfather from the kitchen. The poor creature clearly didn't like William any more than Ioan did. *Ioan didn't like falcons?* He'd never mentioned it to me. I shouldn't know that fact.

A flicker of an image appeared in my mind. Ioan was bent over at his horse's side, a hoof in his left hand, a tool in his right. He paused. The falcon shrieked above me, blurring the image. Ioan dropped the hoof and straightened. I could feel the tension in his shoulders, the worry in his stance. He turned his head and whispered, *Are you alright?*

"Sienna?" William rushed to my side, shattering the vision. "What happened? Doris is going to kill me."

The falcon flapped its wings and took off in a huff. It began circling above us once more, screeching at William. The creature wanted him gone—and me to pay attention. To what, I didn't know.

"Where does it hurt?" William's question whipped me from my thoughts. "Did you bump your head?"

"My ankle," I murmured. The falcon and seeing Ioan in my head had distracted me. The whispers swirled, but like most people, William didn't seem to hear them. The pain down my leg was very much alive. Rubbing my temples, I focused on breathing. The voices became louder.

I'm coming, Ioan whispered.

My head snapped up. Ioan wasn't here. I grabbed William's arm. "Did you hear that?"

"How can you not? The bloody thing won't shut up." He shook his head and pointed a finger at the falcon. The falcon swooped dangerously close over William's head. "It's possessed."

An ache opened in my chest. I'd not wanted to come to the island —spending the day with William had seemed like an insurmountable, exhaustive task but once we'd left, he'd been affable. Charming, in a brotherly way instead of flirtatious. But he'd not heard Ioan's voice. Nor had he heard the other whispers. I felt suddenly alone. Isolated.

The only person in the world that knew of my whispers didn't recognize me any more.

The falcon cried again. William shook a fist at it. "Shut up."

"It's my fault." Leaning into William, I struggled to a stand. My ankle began throbbing and for some reason, so did my right elbow. "I came into his territory."

"There's no way you're going to be able to walk back up to the church."

I followed William's gaze, my heart sinking. He was right. The incline was tough enough but the rocks and shrubbery would be tricky with two solid ankles.

"Let's have a look." William kneeled at my feet, my right foot propped against my left. Gingerly, he lifted the cuff of my pant. "Oh, Sienna. It's already swelling. How in the world—"

"I told you I crack."

He stood slowly, sighing. "I don't even know how to tell if it's broken or not."

"Not much of a Boy Scout, are you?"

He arched an eyebrow. "My job is to make things pretty so people will buy them." He pointed to my feet. "There's nothing pretty about what's going on."

"You're a master of compliments."

"It's beautiful. Want me to take a picture for you?" William smirked, the tension easing from his shoulders.

"Hilarious." I rolled my eyes.

"Seriously, though. We need to get you up that hill before Doris and Ioan find out."

I swallowed hard. "He already knows."

His gaze flicked to mine. He scoffed. "Right."

I wasn't lying—but that didn't make the turning of my stomach stop. Fear shadowed my thoughts, creeping behind me as I tried hobbling up the incline. William was silent with only a few grunts here and there, helping me up and over the gorse and grass. A lump formed in my throat. Not from my throbbing ankle screaming with every step. No, the emotion was spurred from the realization of how lonely—how utterly alone—I was. Because there was a truth I hadn't acknowledged with even my grandfather. This wasn't the first time a vision had accompanied a whisper. To be fair, I'd forgotten, the moments long past. They were before Grandad lost his grip on his mind and before I could ever be called an adult. The memories were fragmented, but I'd see a man, his accent thick and his words odd. Sometimes I'd see a boy, and sometimes, I knew the boy saw me.

A pair of security guards descended, scrambling along the rocky terrain. I gripped William's arm. "Are you sure Ioan owns the island?"

"Yes, why?" His voice was almost as wary as his eyes. He'd not yet forgotten my comment about Ioan knowing what happened.

"He's going to kill me."

William chuckled, his voice light and warm. "Because you tripped and fell?"

"Since when does a security guard mean a good thing?" Not a week before, I tangoed with a police officer. Security guards were just as difficult to maneuver. My current batch of rent-a-cop was running toward us with more gusto than I wanted.

He smiled, his eyes dancing with amusement. "Please tell me you have a story behind that question."

"No comment." I winced as he brushed his leg against my ankle.

"Ay, woman. I swear if you've broken your ankle, you're writing my eulogy." He shifted his arms underneath me. He must be tiring.

"I promise I'll tell them the truth."

"Which is?" He sobered for a moment. "You and I both know you didn't fall *that* easily."

"The truth is I chased after a falcon." I motioned to my ankle. It was much easier to talk about the sprain instead of me seeing Ioan or admitting I'd felt a pull to a flying creature. "And *then* I tripped and fell."

He narrowed his eyes but didn't have time to question. The guards were upon us. He flashed his disarming smile and held out a hand. "Thank you for saving us."

The younger of the two guards rolled his eyes while the older, gray-haired man shook William's hand eagerly, saying, "Oh, this hill can be quite the devil."

"Seriously," William and I both said in unison.

The guards chuckled, elbowing each other. The older one playfully poked his companion. If they thought my ankle was a flirtatious ruse, me pretending me to be a *damsel in distress,* they were in for a major disappointment. "Best take the other side of the lady."

The younger guard gave a nod, sliding up next to me. "The name's Davey."

"Sienna." William waved his hand with a flourish. "Or you can call her, Lady Trips A Lot. And me—"

"Not Prince Charming," I deadpanned, earning a good-natured chuckle from the elder guard.

William clutched his chest. "After rescuing you from the falcon, this is how you treat me?"

"That's a sight to see, isn't it?" Davey whistled. "Today's the first time I've seen one. Harry, what about you?"

The older man—Harry it seemed was his name—glanced up, his face wistful. "Not in years, Davey. Not in years."

"I do bring out the best in people and islands." William gathered applause from his new friends.

He carried the conversation as we made our way up the hill. The pace was excruciatingly slow, but the hollow look in William's eye haunted me. Something had happened between the moment I fell and when the guards came. William had become the flirtatious idiot once more. Except this time, I could see the difference—the dampened smile, the hesitation in his gestures, the dimming in his eyes.

In what felt like hours, we were back in the church and the guards settled me onto the pew in the back. Harry squeezed my shoulder. "We'll make a quick call to have the physician look you over."

I grabbed his hand. The last thing I needed was a proper scolding for leaving the churchyard. The guards were kind but I was raised in a bureaucratic America. There would be forms and follow-up phone calls with emergency contacts. The less my family knew, the better. "Thank you but I think I'm good. I just need to get back home."

Davey and Harry exchanged a glance. William held up his hands. "I'm staying out of any decisions here."

"I promise I'll be fine." Pointing at William, I added, "The sooner I get back in one piece, the better."

William pivoted from me to Harry. "What's the quickest way to get Miss Gimp over here to the ship?"

"The island's physician can take a quick look and she can be on the employee return boat." He leaned over the pew, his face earnest and kind. "One of our perks is going to and from Cornwall on one of the employee ships. They're small but fast. Only a dozen employees use them on a regular basis."

"I'm fine." With a hand on the old man's arm, I tried to look as confident as possible. "I promise." I waved to my throbbing ankle propped on top of my other. "This is—I absolutely promise you— nothing new. I can't stay away from mishap even if I tried."

"Have you ever tried?" William mumbled behind me.

"The least we can do is get you on the employee ship." Davey's eyes were eager—reminding me of the Cornwall William. "It'll get you home in half the time." He checked his watch. "It'll be arriving at the dock in an hour and ready to return by four."

William shrugged. "It's not like we can explore the rest of the island anyway."

He had a point. I hadn't really wanted to come but now there had been a moment—with my back against the grass and the falcon crying out to me, I'd felt a different type of settling. Something I'd not felt in a really long time—something completely different than what I felt at Grandad's house.

"I know." I shifted—and silently cursed. My stupid ankle threatened mutiny. "One little fall and I hijacked our tour."

"You make it sound like we can't ever come back." William's lips quirked to a lopsided smile. "I do come home every weekend."

"Yeah, I suppose you do." I forced a smile. Coming to the island had solidified one thing—and that was my purpose. I knew I'd come to help my grandfather pass on. That would soon turn to an all-consuming task. Grandad had talked about my grandmother's last few months. He was at her bedside every hour. I ran a finger along the grain of the pew, feeling every inch of a farewell. Not just with Grandad but with the island. I'd just arrived and knew I wouldn't return for a long time. If at all.

I swallowed hard. The truth at the core of Grandad's death, the horrible fear that followed me like a rabid shadow, was what would happen when he passed. The last remaining link, the only true connection I had with my family, would be gone. There would never be a reason to return to Lydcombe. Or the island. The magic my grandfather believed in—would be gone.

❦ 18 ❦

K enan
  Penyl, South Wales: 1606

❦

THE NIGHT SKY BLANKETED THE COMPANY OF MERCENARIES AND former soldiers in silence. Kenan said little during the dinner, accepting the meager ration from Jowan. Kenan's oldest friend had been nervous since his confrontation with Matthew, the blond leader of Rothesay's mercenaries. Jowan didn't take to strangers in general, but his paranoia was heightened with the leader's questions. Both Jowan and Kenan had lived through mutiny attempts. A bond forged in battle could not be shaken. And now, as Jowan insisted on cooking their own food and eating separate from the rest of the men, Kenan didn't argue.

Elyna must have felt the tension and held her tongue as well. She had kept to herself for most of the journey. Her gaze drifted to Kenan every few minutes. When Matthew offered wine, she declined—even when he offered a second jug with a wink, confessing that the second round was the *good stuff*.

Kenan wouldn't have deprived her even with his suspicions. Jowan wouldn't defend her, he'd hated the woman and her grandmother at first sight. He'd be enraged if Kenan admitted to feeling a pull toward her. Even more so if Jowan knew how many times Kenan's mind wandered to thoughts of her. And if she did the same.

He should have paid more attention to his mother's stories instead of dismissing her words as superstition. If the stirrings Kenan felt were from the oath, he could not trust them. Nor could he trust Elyna's affection—if she held any for him.

Jowan had not yet forgiven Kenan for telling Elyna of their smug-glings—his feeling obvious by the abrupt words and stinging glares aimed at Kenan. The island and their illegal dealings were secrets only few people had the privilege of keeping—most of them living on the island. Rothesay would have Kenan's head. Or demand a cut of the profits for his silence.

"It's time we retire." Jowan voice was low, for Kenan's ears only. "We will tie our horses to the tent."

Elyna's eyes widened. She swallowed hard and glanced at the surrounding men, each in small groups of four to five a piece. The wine had softened the edge between Kenan's company and the mercenaries, adding the tension to her shoulders.

And Kenan's.

"Where will I sleep?" Elyna stood, her chin lifted.

Jowan pointed to both tents next to them. "There."

She narrowed her eyes at his gruff tone. "I've never been kidnapped by an army before, excuse my naiveté."

"Kidnapped?" Jowan growled. He stamped out the fire with more force than needed. "You weren't bloody kidnapped at all."

"Enough. Both of you." Kenan held out his arms. Nodding to Elyna, he said, "We'll put your belongings in the tent, but you will stay with us."

"What?" Jowan and Elyna said in unison.

Kenan stepped closer. "Something is amiss and I can't explain what or why." With a flick of his wrist, he indicated Matthew laughing in the midst of his men. "She will be in the tent with us until we are separated from the mercenaries."

Elyna's hands trembled at her side. Jowan shot her a glare. To her credit, she narrowed her gaze, not backing down.

"The sooner we get to Swansea, the sooner we can breathe a sigh of relief." Kenan threw the last of his meager stew on the dying fire, ending the conversation. He softened when he heard both Jowan and Elyna sigh. They were alike in their differences. Neither appeared to trust easily and yet were loyal to those closest to them.

When the company of men had settled down, Kenan snuck to Elyna's tent and collected her. Her feet made no sound as she followed him—twice he glanced behind to make sure she was following. Her ability to move silently made him question just how innocent, just how helpless, she truly was.

Kenan opened the tent flap, the moon's soft light casting shadows inside. Jowan sat against the opposite wall where the fabric lay against the trunk of a tree. Even in the dark tent, his expression gave little doubt into his reason for sitting up.

"I will take the first post." Jowan crossed his ankles.

Kenan murmured, "You're not even attempting to sleep?"

Elyna sat on the opposite end, folding her arms over her chest. "I can take the next post."

"You'll rest." Jowan leaned forward and sneered. "We do not need the help of a lady, especially one who wishes us ill."

"I do not wish you ill. I can help—"

Kenan whispered, "The men will hear you."

Turning her head, Elyna hissed. "I can hear farther than any man here."

"Your lies are endless." Jowan scowled. His mood would not change until he was back on the island and reunited with his patient wife.

Lifting her chin, Elyna smirked. "I heard your men approaching—both in the morning and with the greater numbers."

The memory came alive in Kenan's mind. Elyna had tried—and failed—to pull her grandmother inside long before the partially hidden servant had given the warning.

"Convenient that it's already passed." Jowan shook his head. "The memory I have is of you trying to seduce Kenan in the corridor."

"I did nothing—"

"Which speaks to Kenan's strength, not yours." Jowan's shoulders relaxed. He folded his hands on his lap. He was winning the battle and didn't bother to hide it.

"It matters not what happened before." Kenan tossed his blanket to Elyna. She would need the comfort more than him. He was used to sleeping on the ground, leaning into his saddle. His fingers played with his mother's ring on his small finger, his mind drifting to her. "We must tolerate each other for the moment."

"Some of us are less tolerable than others," Elyna whispered.

"Miss Morgannwg—"

Cutting off Kenan, she held a finger to her lips and tilted her head, listening for something. Or someone. For several minutes they stayed silent and still. Finally, she shook her head and said softly, "Can you hear that?"

Jowan scoffed. "I changed my mind. Kenan, you take the first shift." He scooted over to his saddle and stretched out. Instead of leaning against his saddle, he folded his blanket and covered his eyes with his forearm.

After a few minutes, Elyna whispered, "You should sleep as well."

"I'm not tired," Kenan lied. He'd marched most of the last month and was sailing before then. This was supposed to the beginning of his holiday. Soon it would be too dangerous to sail the Bristol Sea's mercurial waters to his island. He'd not told Elyna that time was not on their side. He'd kept that secret close. They had roughly a month before passage was no longer safe.

"Thank you." She wasn't looking at him, her gaze on the worn hem of her dress.

"Do not thank me yet."

"I wasn't talking about this." She made a circle with her finger, indicating the tent. A strand of her hair fell from her loose plait. She lowered her voice, inviting an aura of intimate confession. "I meant for the oath."

For the oath. The words echoed in Kenan's mind. He swallowed against the fear. He knew the oath would haunt him but he could not confess that to her. Not with her back hunched and her voice small.

"It meant a lot to my grandmother to hear it." She wrapped the blanket around her shoulders. "I know I'll not see her again. But those words will comfort her."

"We don't know—"

She waved away his words. "I don't know what lies ahead but I do know I'll not return."

"Then why did you agree to go?"

Pursing her lips, she inhaled a shaky breath. "For the same reason you took the oath."

Kenan coughed into his fist. "You've the advantage over me. I'm still struggling to know why I did it." He jutted his chin toward Jowan. "I'm sure I'm not the only one who wants to know."

She smiled, softening the night. "It was the right thing to do."

"I don't know about that." Kenan's focus was still on Jowan's stretched out frame. "It doesn't feel like the right thing to do at the moment."

"Because it's hard?" With a delicate hand she propped her chin, her elbow digging into her thigh. "Nothing right has ever been easy."

He felt the disappointment in her words. She'd never understand what it meant to watch over a company, to worry about them—worry for them. "These men are my responsibility. Taking your oath has put them in jeopardy."

"If you'd not taken the oath, my grandmother would have offered herself." She made a face, her lip curling into a scowl. "We both know Rothesay didn't want her."

"She would not leave her son."

"Never underestimate a mother, Kenan." Elyna's words filled the tent, the warning echoing in the otherwise still air. "She would have found a way to disrupt Rothesay's plans."

"An oath doesn't save you from my father. And it doesn't pay the debt."

She arched an eyebrow, a mischievous grin in place. Silently she crept forward and placed a hand on his. A current—a humming—ran up his arm, a whisper in his ear. He shrank back, breaking the contact. She cocked her head to the side and did it again. This time she gripped his hand. The whisper turned to words, a flicker appeared in his mind.

He appeared in his mind, as if he was looking through a mirror. *No.* He swallowed the panic. He was in her head, seeing through her eyes.

"Get back." He stood with a jump.

❧ 19 ❧

S ienna
   Ynys Wair Island, United Kingdom: Present Day

ை

DAVEY AND HARRY HELPED ME TO THE COURTYARD WHERE A PALE-
green car with *Royal Historical Society* was printed on the side. Car was a
generous term. It looked more like a big bubble. I'd spent my driving
years in California, the land of trucks and SUVs. Flying back and forth
from England had warned me of one American trait—bigger is better.
For the most part, I didn't subscribe to the belief but with my ankle
throbbing, the last thing I wanted to do was squeeze into the tiny two-
door automobile.

"*Fuldamoble*? An *N-two*? This is a dream. It has to be. I haven't seen
one of these in years." William circled the car, his tongue wagging. He
tapped the hood and nodded—his dreams had apparently come true.
He got down on his knees and peered at the undercarriage. "No rust?
This has to be what, a fifty-two? No, fifty-four?"

"At least take it on a first date before you get into her bits." Davey chuckled, his grin spreading from ear to ear. "Go ahead and look. There's not a speck of rust on her."

"You're kidding." William's head popped up. "That's incredible. How often do you have to tinker with it?"

"Tell you what. Take me to the harbor, and you and Davey can have your little date with the pretty princess." Pointing to the car, I added, "That is, if we can all fit inside."

"Oh, come on, now. Don't be cruel to my girl." William flashed a winning smile, his eyes crinkling in delight. "I'm pretty sure we should take two trips." He rubbed his hands together. "Or maybe three."

Harry shielded his eyes from the glare of the sun, his hands sprinkled with sun spots like Grandad. "I think I'll leave the joy ride to the young folks today." He waited for William to take his place next to me at the car. Harry dipped his head in farewell before rushing across the courtyard to a distraught mother with a screaming child.

Davey opened the passenger door on the left side. "William if you can squeeze in the back, we'll take a little drive after she's settled."

William shook his head, his eyes dimming. "No, I'm a gentleman. I'll stay with Sienna."

"I'm actually pretty talented at being by myself." Stifling a groan, I slid into the seat, the camera bag cradled in my lap. At five foot, four inches, my height was as average as the day was long. Never—until this moment—did I ever want to be shorter. "I think it's fair game. If you can survive the car ride, you should be rewarded with a drive."

William shrugged and followed Davey to the driver's side. By some miracle, William folded himself into the sliver of a backseat. We pulled away as the church's clock chimed three, an hour left until the employee ship was scheduled to arrive. Slow and steady, Davey navigated the populated courtyard, careful to give everyone a wide berth, especially the distracted children busy pointing at birds or flowers. Several other families joined in with the pointing. Leaning into the window, I peered upwards, eyeing the falcon once more. He was circling over our car.

"Somebody has a fan." William's breath was short from his cramped position in the back.

Guilt wriggled in. "Seriously, William, you should go for a long ride.

Go pop a wheelie or spin little donuts—whatever it is that makes you happy."

Davey rolled down his window and shot me a patronizing grin. "Pop a wheelie?"

"This car can't pop anything." William chuckled, making me feel infinitely better. "Except maybe the clutch."

"It's smooth as glass," Davey tossed over his shoulder. "We'll go slow around the curve to the castle for Sienna's sake but when we come back around, we'll speed up. You'll be able to hug the curves."

"Don't encourage him." Placing a hand on Davey's arm, I gave my best fake frown. "He's known for hugging curves."

"It's one of my many qualities." William sighed dramatically. "If only you'd cave to my charms."

Davey's eyebrows raised, realization on his face. He thought William and I were together until that point. His expression turned hopeful. He sat up straighter. "Don't worry, William. You've rescued her. Women can't resist a knight in shining armor."

"I'm not a damsel in distress."

"You're right. You're no longer in distress because of me." William leaned forward, his hand on my shoulder. "You're welcome."

I swatted his hand away. "Technically, it was Davey and Harry that rescued me."

Davey's mouth fell open, his eyes confused. "But ... William was the one to get to you first."

"What were you doing anyway?" William's voice shifted from mischief to genuine curiosity. "Other than pissing off a falcon."

Davey rolled up his window as my mind raced for an excuse. There wasn't a rational reason for me leaving the church's graveyard. Davey turned inland down a gravel road, leaving the tourist road behind.

"What's that?" I pointed to an empty guard stand, a level down blocking the road. I didn't truly care but I wasn't going to admit the falcon drew me in like a forgotten memory. With any luck, the guard stand would shift the conversation to something safer.

"It's really nothing. It was abandoned when the family left for good decades go." Davey put the car in park and unlocked the little stand with keys from his pocket. A moment later we drove past the lever. "Just a second and we'll be clear."

He got out of the car. I breathed a sigh of relief. William shifted behind me.

"You never answered my question." His head was next to mine. "Why were you chasing a falcon? If that's what you were really doing."

"William!" I shouted, pretending to be surprised. "You're worse than my brothers."

Davey was back in the car, saving me from answering—I felt William's gaze on me. He wasn't going to let it drop. I'd have to answer him eventually. In truth, I didn't know why. I'd been drawn to the sea, drawn to ink sketches—and that same drive pulled me toward the falcon. If my family had been with me instead of William, they'd be teasing me relentlessly of my thoughtlessness. And how I'd ruined their little tour. That is, if they cared at all about the island. They were more interested in museums and artifacts than a neglected strip of land in the middle of the Bristol Sea.

Driving inward on a road splitting the north valley from the south, I was grateful I would soon be alone. Bushy sycamore and beech trees rushed past us as Davey sped along the mountain road. Each valley took a much more gradual decline here than over by the church. The road was wide enough for an American freeway but lacked any center line.

This would have never worked in California, even in the outlying rural cities I'd visited on my journalist adventures. This island never had to worry about traffic with the small population of employees. The granite cliffs and low valleys obscured my view, making the island seem expansive. "How wide is the island?"

"Just under three kilometers." Davey slowed the car for an upcoming bend.

"She's American, Davey."

Sighing, I rolled my eyes. "I know what kilometers mean."

"What's the conversion, Einstein?" William crouched forward. "Three ... two ..."

"A mile, no. I think it's a mile and a half."

Davey winced. "That's a good guess."

"One point eight miles, thank you very much." William sat back.

I caught his smug expression in the reflection. "A mile and a half is close enough."

"You two sound like an old married couple," Davey said with a shake of his head.

"We're not dating," I blurted.

Davey raised his eyebrows. He clearly didn't believe me.

"See." William held far too much joy—and mischief—in his voice. "Even Davey thinks we should date."

Just as we rounded the curve, I heard a voice. *He's the only one.* I swallowed hard. Those words weren't mine. I didn't dare ask if anyone else heard them. A chill swept across my neck. The only thing that had changed was the view. The granite wall was now miles of ocean, the color matching Ioan's pale blue-green shade.

The road turned, creeping along the coastline, revealing the crumbling tops of a stone castle. This was the home that William thought Ioan should live in. "Are you still jealous, William?"

Davey nodded. "Just wait a bit."

A moment later, the small hill hiding the rest of the castle gave way. The crumbling stone wall was not part of the castle but of either an abandoned tower or barn. Just behind the roofless structure stood a simple castle made out of the darker, bluer stone. With its four stories, the home stood like a beacon at the edge of the island.

"Yeah." William's voice was a mixture of envy and resentment. "I'm still jealous."

"How did you know it was here?" It came out before I could stop myself. The tone of William's statement meant there was history between him and the island. Or between him and Ioan.

"Everyone knows it's here." William waved his hand in the air.

"I've been coming here since I was child." Grabbing the headrest, I turned but only saw his profile, his gaze on the castle. "Until today, I'd never, not once, heard of it."

William said nothing.

Davey cleared his throat. He apparently didn't like silence. He glanced over his shoulder at William before saying, "It's not common knowledge. I mean, I knew about it, but my parents worked here. They actually met here—"

"Another love story." William sat back against the seat, sighing. "Give a little romance and everyone looks the other way. Ioan courts the historical society and everyone calls him a hero. He's not paid a dime in taxes. He owns two thousand acres of British soil. Who's the pirate now?"

Davey and I exchanged a look of surprise. He gave a tiny shrug. We silently agreed to change the subject. He nodded at the castle. "You want to know a real secret?"

"Absolutely." I sucked at this. There was entirely too much enthusiasm in my answer for it to be genuine.

William grunted in response.

"That cliff just to the right of the castle. That's where the employee ship will go." Davey tapped on the steering wheel. "The harbor is tucked behind. In ancient times, the ships could stay hidden while unloading their cargo."

"The smugglers." Pride swelled in my chest. Grandad was right. His stories weren't fiction.

Davey grinned. "You are correct."

"She's a Rothesay, Davey." William shifted again. "Her family has memorized their lineage."

Davey's brow furrowed. Rothesay would mean nothing to him unless he lived in Lydcombe or came from money. He slowed the car as we dipped below to a small parking lot. A building the size of a two-door garage stood in front of the castle, completely obstructing the view. Three cars identical to the one we drove were parked under an ivy covered carport.

A whisper pulled my attention toward the harbor, two ships bobbing at the other end, one an ancient ship on stilts. Both were anchored to a thin walkway, leaving the main harbor vacant. I felt a pull, the same feeling I had at Grandad's house, wrap around my wrist, tempting me to go down—to touch the water. With great strength, I forced myself to focus on the castle instead of the water, the cold stones reminding me of Ioan. So close to the water and Grandad—and yet impenetrable.

❧ 20 ❧

S ienna
Ynys Wair Island, United Kingdom: Present Day

❧

EMBLAZONED ON THE BUILDING'S FACADE WAS *ROYAL HISTORICAL Society.* William was right, the employees were paid by *RHS.* Ioan was getting quite the bargain, no taxes and no maintenance cost. Davey parked as close to the entrance to the building as possible, his door hitting the lip of the cement. Shuffled between both of them, I limped inside the foyer. A large sectional was on the far left, a television mounted on the opposite wall. An *Employees Only* sign hung over the kitchenette to the right. Smack in the center was an empty receptionist desk. We were the only three people in the entire building. In a matter of minutes, I would be utterly—deliciously—alone.

Pointing to the sectional, I said, "I will be happy as a clam if I can lie down while you two play NASCAR."

William rolled his eyes. "Wrong country."

"Same language." With a hand over the camera bag, I hopped to the couch.

"I beg to differ." William put both hands on his hips and scanned the building.

"You don't beg."

"Are you sure you two aren't dating?" Davey chuckled and checked his watch. "We have about an hour before this place will be swarming with employees."

William bowed deeply like a butler, his hand circling with a flourish. "My lady."

"Oh, please." I waved them off. "Go have your fun."

He snapped to a stand. "Are you going to be alright?"

"Only if you leave me alone." Closing my eyes, I lay down.

They waited a few minutes before going, the door closing with a quiet hush. The tires crunched along the gravel parking lot. If I kept my eyes closed, I could hopefully catch up on the sleep I'd missed last night. Deep breath in, followed by a deep breath out. The sound of waves crashing against the rocks echoed in my ear—my heart began racing, humming in my veins. There was a quarter mile between the ocean and where I lay, not including the building's wall muffling the sound. There was no conceivable reason why I could hear the waves.

A memory burst through my thoughts. My grandfather stood inside the church, my hand in his. He bent down to my level and cupped his mouth, whispering, "Can you hear it? Do the waves call to you?"

I shook my little head. I couldn't be more than six years old, my parents arguing over who was at fault for my younger brother's sudden disappearance.

Grandad's smile faltered. "You can't hear the song they sing?"

"Do you want me to?" I'd have jumped off a cliff to see his smile back—even at six, I was his biggest fan.

"No, no." He stood slowly, his shoulders hunched.

"It's too hard to hear." I couldn't hear singing yet, not at that age. Only dreams and images came to me. "But I can see him."

"You see someone? A man?" Grandad's eyes doubled in size. I squeezed his hand, worried something was wrong. He blinked and returned to this kneeling position. "What does he look like?"

"Nothing." The voice didn't have a face. "He's blurry. And he likes the water." Like a seasoned grandparent, he didn't push for more information. I waited for the teasing but it never came. He never—to my knowledge—told my parents. It was one of many secrets that bound us together.

The waves against the rock down below settled into a rhythm. I'd given up trying to understand how I could hear the ocean. Squeezing my eyes tighter, I counted silently in my head. *Ten. Nine.* The face of my brother burst into my mind. We were traveling to the airport and he was bragging about all the addresses he was dividing and then factoring in his head, only to do it all over again. The memory pulled me down the rabbit hole of other moments. I was back in fourth grade, staring at my feet as my family laughed and shamed me about my inability to memorize multiplication facts. My breathing turned shallow, my pulse throbbing in my neck. My cheeks flushed warm. I was standing like a fool in front of my family while my youngest brother recited every factor perfectly. He was two years my junior.

Brains aren't everything.

I catapulted to a sitting position, my heart racing. No one.

With a finger to my throat, fear pounded in my panicked pulse. I hung my head in my hands but refused to count or do anything that involved numbers. Lying back against the couch, I noticed several concentric circles on the ceiling from roof leaks. The musty color showed they were old, but with the sterile environment they stood out. Tilting my head, I smiled and pulled out my camera.

They weren't all the same shade nor were they perfect circles—in their own right, they were pretty. Or maybe I was just bent on finding the elegance in the flaws. The creaks in my grandfather's house were music and the neglected trail was a harmony. Maybe that was what Ioan was talking about on my grandfather's staircase.

A few clicks and the image was captured. There was—there *is*—something breathtaking, something precious about capturing what *is* rather than what could be. Or what had been. The humanity award was given to me when all I'd done was capture the exact moment a child lost her cousin, or an athlete won a medal—or an officer protected his enemy.

The busy hum of people greeting each other wafted into the building. The employees had arrived. My solitude was gone. Any moment,

William would be back. Exhaustion settled around my shoulders with a heaviness that shouldn't be there. William was fine. The problem was me.

The commotion grew louder and I braced myself. With a quiet swish, the door opened. I gripped the armrest and pasted a smile for whoever was entering.

"And I thought my horses were high strung." Ioan's voice stole my attention. His pale eyes pierced me, stealing my thoughts. Just hours before, Ioan was in my mind. And now he was here. A fragment of an image one moment, reality the next. Ioan cracked a smile and offered his hand. "Where's Knight In Shining Armor?"

Without thinking, I slipped my hand in his. The callouses from hours of farm work rubbed against mine. An electric hum shot up my arm. There should be fear at this eerie connection—but the dizziness from the sea and the whispers dimmed. Ioan was both the cause of distress and the remedy. Grandad was the only link between. I'd heard of twins having an otherworldly bond. I'd photographed a woman who believed she was linked to an old ancestor. She could hear her thoughts. She was also a humanities professor that was not exactly beloved by her peers. She wore her outlier reputation like a badge. *Agents for change never fit in,* she'd say with mischievous smile.

With my hand in Ioan's, there had to be a true explanation. We were no more related than William and I. Our families were from Cornwall. It would take only a few centuries back to find every resident of Cornwall tying each of us to a common predecessor.

Ioan pulled me to a stand. Instead of helping me to the door, he bent down and turned up the hem of my jeans. I winced, realizing I'd not shaved my legs. Ioan chuckled. My humiliation was complete.

"Can you put any weight on it?"

Shifting, I winced. The stupid thing screamed at me like a tyrant.

Gently, he palpated the skin. "I'm not sure if it's broken. Only an X-ray can determine that. It'd be easier if it was."

"Easier, how?"

He peered up at me, his dark lashes framing the pale greenish-blue color. Outside in the sun, his eyes would turn more blue. I'd thought colors only changed in hazel eyes but apparently there was plenty I knew nothing about—including the confusing man at my feet. He tugged the hem of my jeans down. "Tendons take forever to heal. A break is fairly easy."

"I've never visited my grandfather without going to the doctor down the street."

Ioan smiled, his eyes sparkling. "It's tradition then."

"One I'd like to break."

He chuckled softly. "You're too busy breaking everything else."

"Hilarious," I deadpanned. "Can I get a schedule?"

He arched an eyebrow. "For what?"

"For your moods." I should have said nothing. There was a part of me that wanted to document his many moods with the camera strapped to my chest. It would be a dizzying social experiment that any humanities professor would love. "One minute you're gentle, even encouraging. The next, you're nothing. As in, no emotion."

"Is that all that's bothering you?" He slid his arm around my waist and shouldered more of my weight. His face was inches from mine, his skin holding a smattering of light freckles. There was a hint of hay, or maybe it was the scent of horses, but something comforting about him held my tongue. His gaze flicked to my lips. "My moods are the only thing that bothers you about me?"

No. I swallowed hard. There was no explanation for what I'd seen— or thought I saw. And heard. I couldn't confess my crazy just yet. But he'd come to the island. "Why are you here?"

His eyes widened. "Are you serious? Look at your ankle."

"How did you know?" No one had called Doris or him. "William has been with me every step of the way. Well, until he went on his little joy ride. I know he didn't call you. That timing wouldn't have worked."

His arm stiffened. "You tell me."

"I'm asking you." The building filled with employees chatting away, the commotion growing. I cursed under my breath.

He leaned in, whispering, "Let's get you to the house so we can talk."

My breath hitched. *So we can talk* held a promise of something more. It was silly but I was starved for answers, for something solid to hold onto. Warmth filled my chest.

Ioan took my camera and we hobbled around the building to a cement walkway leading to the side of the castle wall. The building was smaller than I'd thought. In my mind, castles were enormous mansions. The granite cliff appeared to have swallowed half the structure. Ioan shuffled my weight and entered a code on the handle. He nudged the wooden door open with his foot. The door swung open revealing a kitchen—a near identical kitchen that was in my grandfather's house. The dark cabinet held the same wooden grain. The granite countertops were different—opting for the same gray-blue of the cliffs. The position of the island and the stools, the exact number of cabinet doors and locations of the sink—all of it was exactly like Grandad's. The chill caressing my neck was back. The promise for answers was false. This was just another layer of questions and mystery.

Ioan gave a nervous chuckle and rummaged through the same drawer where my grandfather would keep his medicines. "Do you want to sit in the kitchen or the living room?"

"Please tell me you see what I'm seeing."

He filled a cup and came to my side, two pills in an offered hand. "Yeah, it's a little freaky."

"Why?" One little word wasn't enough. There were so many *why*'s I didn't know where to begin. He had been comfortable with my grandfather's kitchen because it mirrored his. "Why does this kitchen look *exactly* like Grandad's? How did you and my grandfather become so close? Why did you come—really, why did you come to the island?"

Ioan stared at the pills in his hand, this thumb rolling them around in his palm. "That's a lot of questions."

"Mind answering one?"

❧ 21 ☙

K enan
  Penyl, South Wales: 1606

KENAN TOSSED AND TURNED, UNABLE TO SLEEP—HIS MIND RACING
since Elyna's touch. Seeing through her eyes was madness. Or witchcraft. He was grateful when Jowan took his post. Not that Kenan
would sleep, but he could relax, sort out his fears without needing to
jump at every sound. He wondered if she spoke the truth, that she
could hear more than a man. Jowan's suspicion had felt misplaced until
Elyna had touched Kenan's arm. Perhaps the soldier's instincts were as
sharp was ever.

He and Jowan had tied Elyna's horse between theirs. They would
know if she snuck away. Or if she were stolen. The slow march to
Swansea still bothered Kenan. He didn't know the reason behind the
laziness of his company. Or what motivations Matthew held. Kenan
felt as if a noose were slipping around his neck. No matter what he did,
the rope would tighten. Kenan missed his island and the safety it

promised. Between the granite cliffs and low valleys, he was surrounded by loyal friends and protective waves.

Elyna whispered, "Kenan?"

He stiffened.

"Let him sleep, woman," Jowan warned.

Kenan silently groaned. He would need to sit up before they began arguing. If Jowan would soften, Elyna might relax—and let a secret slip. She was hiding something. Kenan was certain of it.

"He's not sleeping." She shuffled at the end of the tent. "And neither are the men."

"Get out of my head, woman. You're nothing but a witch—"

"Jowan." Kenan sat up, her warning echoing in his mind. He didn't trust the woman but he knew a power coursed through her veins. That he was certain of.

"If you don't believe me, go and see for yourself," Elyna hissed.

"Have you laid a trap for me now?" Jowan's voice was low. "Do not think I won't haunt you from the grave, woman."

"Jowan." Kenan rubbed his head, his friend's name coming out as a sigh. He sounded more like a tired parent than a trusted confidante. "We need each other. We'll sort the rest of this ..." He twirled a finger in the air, indicating the three of them. "We'll find the answers once we reach the island."

Jowan stood, his frame bent forward with the low ceiling of their tent. "Right or wrong, we're all awake. We can break camp and begin the day early."

"We won't win any friends." Kenan began gathering the few belongings in the tent. "Our men are few in number."

"No." Jowan paused at the entrance. "But it'll reveal who is foe and who is friend."

He left, his footsteps light and hesitant.

Elyna crawled to Kenan, placing a hand on his forearm. He fought the temptation to shrink from her touch. Her hair fell forward, caressing his skin. Elyna's face was inches from him. Her mouth parted and she spoke but Kenan couldn't hear the words above the racing of his pulse. She cocked her head to the side and pulled her hand back. "Can you hear it?"

"Hear what?"

She sat back, her brow furrowing. "You do not trust me."

"Do not cry foul when you're guilty of the same." He sighed. "I shouldn't have said that."

"I trust you more than Jowan."

Kenan smiled. The unsettling feeling in his chest calmed. She sparked both his nerves and peace within him. "That doesn't mean much."

She gave an answering grin. Her skin looked soft. And tempting. "We are bound, Kenan. It is like you've said. Until we get to your island, we need each other."

"I trust Jowan with my life." His voice was soft but the words were firm. "He's been at my side when no one else would. I'll not abandoned him—"

"For a woman." Elyna's smile faltered. "I did try to seduce you at my father's house, but not for the reason you think."

"And the reasons?"

"I knew you were a Rothesay man and would do his bidding." She averted his gaze and folded the blanket Kenan had given her. The beginning of early morning light cast an eerie glow in the tent. "The woman who'd warned us of your army had told me Rothesay loved the art of war." She placed a hand on top of the folded blanket. "Including women and children. Nothing is sacred to that man. The woman thought Rothesay wanted to win by dominating. I thought if I appeared submissive, you would report to Rothesay and he would lose interest."

Kenan had watched her mind take in the men. She'd scrutinized the small band the moment she'd stepped foot in the dining hall. Strategy, not lust, was in her eyes. "Your eyes betrayed you. You were not consumed with passion."

Her head snapped up, her eyes wide with worry. "I am sorry. I meant no offense."

"The shot to my pride was not fatal." He gathered Jowan's blanket and saddle next to him. "I do appreciate the candor." Trust was built with honesty, not flattery. Her confession soothed his suspicions.

With his saddle under his arm, Kenan slipped from the tent. The morning was not yet lit, the sun hours from peeking above the horizon. He saddled his horse. The animal flicked its ears and kept his neck taut. Something was wrong but Jowan was nowhere to be seen. The camp was silent—alarmingly so. Even the birds had not begun to stretch and chirp. He felt a chill and the presence of another. He spun around, only to see Elyna's worried expression.

He placed a finger to her lips and pointed to her horse. She nodded and began saddling. Kenan hurried to saddle Jowan's horse—leaving the tent upright. Several tents surrounded them but not the slightest sound—not even of men sleeping—echoed in their camp.

Elyna whispered, "They have him."

Kenan shook his head. Jowan would not have been taken, not unless there was a reason. He was a soldier with a keen mind and an agile body—Jowan would not be caught. Kenan whispered, "Stay here."

She said nothing, reins in her hand. Kenan felt torn. He'd promised to keep her safe but Jowan was as much of his charge as the woman before him. With a scowl, he left her and crept toward Matthew's tent. *Jowan can't be caught.* He repeated in his head. Kenan felt the disapproval from Elyna in his mind. He couldn't explain it but his head was somehow tethered to hers. Soon, Elyna would be someone else's problem. She would be Muiris' woman. The idea didn't sit well. But Jowan was his family. And his sole concern at the moment.

He kneeled at the entrance of Matthew's tent. Silence. He flicked open the flap—empty. Jowan would have come to this tent first as well. The early light was still too dim to see the outline of boot prints in the soil. Jowan and Kenan wore the same size in the same boot. It was deliberate—only the two of them knew this fact and had more than once led one soldier to the other after battle.

A muffled cry from behind him set his nerves on edge. *Elyna.* He stood frozen, not knowing who to search for—Jowan or Elyna. He'd left her alone despite the stillness, the impending aura of danger. And Jowan, he was missing.

His skin prickled—the distinct feeling of being watched came over him. He swallowed the rising fear and forced his mind to retrace the steps over the last few days. Slowly, he stood and flipped open the nearest tent. Three men were curled against their saddles, each face peaceful and calm. Kenan recognized the youngest one, closest to the entrance. The young man was Kenan's newest recruit, his family already living on the island. With his boot, Kenan ever so slightly—just in case his watching audience saw him—shoved the man's leg. The young man didn't stir. Kenan gently kicked at his foot. Nothing. Not a moan. Not a sound. *He's dead.* Kenan stood, too scared to enter the tent and check if the man was breathing.

A cry pierced the air—Elyna.

Kenan spun around. Murmured voices came from the same direction of the cry. He ran toward his tent. A circle of men stood in front of his horse. Matthew broke through the circle, his arms crossed. Nerves rolled off the man's frame. Matthew's ambition was barely contained. He looked very much like Kenan's father, unable to cage the greed. He stepped to the side, revealing Jowan's bent frame in the center. Jowan's accusation to Elyna echoed in Kenan's ears, *Have you laid a trap for me?*

Kenan stoked his courage and came closer, his back straight and his shoulders rigid. As Matthew neared, Kenan saw blood on Jowan's temple.

"And here comes the son." Matthew spat on the ground, his left hand cradling his right. He was injured, more than likely by Jowan. "Does your father truly think we are stupid? Does he think we'd not know when we're cheated?"

Kenan folded his arms. "My father thinks all men are beneath him. His son included."

"You cannot fool us." Matthew nodded to his men, a signal of some sort.

Kenan rubbed his neck, feigning boredom. In one night, he'd lost his men, except for Jowan. Kenan had mothers and fathers who would mourn their sons. He scanned the periphery for Elyna. "I would not accuse you of being a fool."

Two men burst through the circle, Elyna between them. Her mouth was bound by a scarf, her eyes filled with fury. Kenan felt relief. Anger was of better use than fear.

"Your father cannot pay an army with a woman." Matthew grabbed

Elyna's arm and tossed her to the ground before Kenan. "How will she pay our wages?"

"Or the wages of my army." Kenan held out his arm, thankful his hand wasn't shaky. He'd promised his men rest—this was to be their last errand for Rothesay. "But perhaps you've solved that problem. If there are fewer men, there are few people to share the spoils."

Matthew waved his hand, including his surrounding men. "A poor harlot cannot feed us."

"Or our families," another man from somewhere in the circle murmured.

"If my father played you a fool, he's done the same to me." No one would answer his gaze. He'd already lost the fight. "The blood of innocent men is on your hands, Matthew."

"No, Kenan." Matthew's voice broke, his eyes wild. He stepped closer. "That is on your hands."

"The men you poisoned. They had families." Kenan watched for the recognition. No one argued his guess. The mercenaries who'd been paid had slaughtered the men Kenan had cared for, led and guided the last several years. In an instant, their lives were snuffed. All for greed.

"Your father promised double payment." Matthew pointed at Jowan. "And we will have what belongs to us."

"Taking Jowan as trade will not win you my father's favor." Kenan, more than anyone, knew how little Rothesay cared for others' lives. His father cared for only one person, himself. Rothesay would bury Matthew for the insurrection. "His pride matters more than men or gold."

"But you are not your father." A gleam entered Matthew's eye, four of his men surrounding him. "You care for Jowan. You're like brothers, are you not?"

"You would trade my place with Jowan?" It was too easy. Kenan was walking into a trap. Elyna's gaze snapped to his. She was just as much his charge as Jowan was. "And what of the lady?"

"She comes with us." Matthew snapped his fingers. Two men were back at each of her arms. "But we will have your word that you be our prisoner."

"You accost my friend and now my father's mistress." He scoffed. "And now you want me to pledge my submission?"

Matthew stepped forward and with a loud crack, smacked Kenan across the face. Elyna cried out. Kenan lunged for Matthew—arms encircled him, holding him fast. Fists and feet pummeled his head— and then stomach. He struggled to breathe. He landed on the ground, the world growing dark.

❦ 22 ❦

S ienna
    Ynys Wair Island, United Kingdom: Present Day

SHOVING IOAN'S HAND ASIDE, AND WITH THE LITTLE PRIDE I STILL had, I limped to the barstool in his kitchen. Ignoring the goosebumps littering my skin was impossible. There were far too many questions bouncing around in my head. The similar layout of Ioan and Grandad's kitchens were just one of dozens.

Ioan put the kettle on, his motions mirroring Doris. His calm demeanor irked me. I'd thought she'd welcomed him into Grandad's kitchen because of how often he came—that he'd won her over because of his close proximity. But Ioan had made himself at home because in a way, he already was.

Silently, I snuck my camera out of the bag. I felt like a child spying on my brothers, but I felt infinitely more powerful taking a picture without Ioan's knowledge, as if my simple act gave me more control.

The soft light coming from the kitchen window warmed his skin, highlighting his broad back. There was a strength in Ioan—something

I'd only attributed to my grandfather. My father and brothers were heavy on the *pretty* and light on the *strong*.

Ioan turned around and folded his arms. If he'd been my brother, the stance would have been arrogant, an impending victory. My brothers had a way with words and facts. They could wield an argument better than a pugilist. But Ioan's dark circles under his eyes told a different story. His shoulders were forward, not quite hunched but not a hint of confidence. He leaned his back against the counter, both arms stretched out. We had battled my grandfather's Alzheimer's every night this week. But here, with only the center island separating us, he felt a thousand miles away.

I slid the camera back in the bag. Ioan didn't seem to care about having his picture taken. Or maybe he'd known what I was doing.

"Ask away." He rubbed his face. "What do you want to know?"

"You might want to sit." I tipped my head at the barstool next to me. "This is going to take awhile."

"My mother." Ioan frowned. He seemed annoyed by my frustration, making little sense to me. "She was close to Liam."

"Your mother—"

"She lived here." He gave a half hearted wave, indicating the house. "Katherine Morgannwg lived here off and on. And her parents lived here before then."

"What does that have to do—"

"I met Liam here." He lowered his eyes. "He used to come and visit. Your grandmother got seasick and rarely came. But he always did."

Whispers wrapped around my body, chilling me. Grandad had never told me about the visits. Or about the castle. Grandad and I told each other everything. He wouldn't hide something this big from me. Ioan had to be lying. My grandfather wouldn't—couldn't do that to me. "That doesn't explain why both kitchens are exactly the same. My grandfather's kitchen hasn't changed in at least thirty years. Maybe some granite, but the layout? No, that hasn't changed in probably centuries."

"Four centuries." Ioan shrugged. "But who's counting?"

"For the love of all that is holy, please quit playing games and tell me what is going on." My hands gripped the edge of the stool. I prayed my face was smooth. My pulse raced and I couldn't tell if it was from fear or anger. I hated that Ioan had another link to my grandfather. Another tie to Grandad's life that I would never have.

"Where do you want me to start, Sienna?"

"The beginning would be nice." I didn't bother hiding my irritation. I was well beyond that point. Until a few weeks ago, Ioan was a stranger—a forgotten memory of my childhood. He'd gone from unknown to center stage. His kitchen was just one example of the strange, the weird position Ioan played in my grandfather's life.

"The castle was built in the early sixteen hundreds."

"I'm not asking about the history or about centuries. Or anything that has to do with numbers."

His gaze flicked to mine. The faintest whisper of a smile appeared on his lips. He knew of my antagonist relationship with math. Or course he would know. The man knew every detail about my grandfather. Who knows what the two of them talked about—clearly they had more shared secrets than Grandad and I did.

"Why are you smiling?"

"I'm not." Ioan frowned dramatically, looking more like William. "Liam's house was renovated the same century this castle was built."

"After four centuries they would keep the same layout?"

"Both homes were remodeled again when Liam inherited his barony." The kettle whistled and just like Doris, he made a lemon and ginger tea for me.

"You don't want any tea?"

He shook his head. "I'm not the one who gets seasick."

"Airsick." It came out defensive. Ioan's knowledge of me felt like a betrayal from my grandfather. Grandad and I kept secrets only for each other. We were each other's safe person. We could love each other and never, *never* betray our trust. "I only get sick when I fly home. I mean here." Growling, I shook my head. "I meant Cornwall."

"You only get sick coming home? Interesting, that." His lips quirked upward again. "Have you ever wondered why? Lydcombe calls to you. The sea calls to you."

"That's low on my laundry list of mysteries." My hands cradled the hot mug. "Why did you come? Tell me the truth. There's no logical reason for you to know about my ankle."

"Logic has its place." He rolled his eyes. "Just not here."

"And by here—"

"What's your first memory of Lydcombe?" Ioan circled the island, his movements silent—his eyes on me. "Think back. As far as you can go. What's your first memory?"

Snapping my fingers, I said, "Oh, you know I've got it. My first memory is when I asked you a question and you answered it. When was that again?"

"Fine." He smirked and sat next to me on the stool. "You win."

"It's about time."

"Before I say anything ..." He eyed the door behind us. "Promise me this stays between us."

"You don't want William to know?" That made two of us.

He swallowed hard and leaned over the island's counter. "I don't want anyone to know."

"Why—" I cut myself off, the reason more than clear. I didn't want William to think I was crazy but having a crazy mother wasn't a battle I'd ever fought. "Because everyone will think you're like your mom?"

"Sort of."

"Was she—I mean, did she have the vision things?" I sucked at this. There was a reason my camera did the talking. My cousin Lacy was much better at navigating the minefields of delicate conversation.

"Vision things?" Ioan arched his eyebrows. "You feel the connection or visions, as you call them, and your first priority was to ask about the kitchen?"

"Why are you acting like any part of this conversation is normal?" The warmth from the mug spread. My cheeks and neck were hot. "Nothing about this is normal. Or logical." Irritation soured, turning to frustration. "I'm not a child. I'm not stupid. Why can't you just talk to me like—"

"I'm sorry."

"For which part?" I barked.

"I was hoping that you'd have answers. Not questions." He folded his hands and placed them in his lap. "Liam always seemed to have answers. I guess I assumed you would too. I can't solve this without him."

"Solve what?" It came out as a sigh. The same sound my mother made when I had another injury. Or another question about how the world worked.

Keeping his profile to me, he continued, "The tragedies. Our family and their curses."

I sat back, waiting for him to laugh or crack a smile. This conversation had taken a dramatic turn. Rothesay's didn't do drama. They didn't even own a television or watch soap operas. *Books develop the brain, t.v. rots original thought.* Under no condition would my family tolerate the idea of a curse.

Ioan began again, his words hesitant. "My mother was ...unstable. That part I know. But she was close with Liam. They were good friends. Toward the end, he was the only one that could talk to her."

"Is that why you're helping Grandad?" That would make sense. A curse didn't.

He didn't look up. "Liam was kind to her, but no, that's not the only reason."

Silence filled the space between us. The frustration grew. This was ridiculous. "Are you always this forthcoming? I think drilling a hole in my head would be less painful."

"You have a way with words."

"And you don't."

He tapped his index finger against the counter. "Liam knew things. He knew about this house. About the inkwell. About the sea. And how the drawings worked. They'd talk about it together."

No. He had to be lying.

Grandad had never talked about any curse. "*They* meaning your mom and my grandfather?" His words echoed in my head. *Curse. Inkwell. Sea.* I didn't know which threads to start unraveling. I only knew Ioan was wrong.

"Yeah—"

"And drawings?" The only sketches I'd seen at the house were Ioan's. Grandad loved colors. He believed the world was richer than black and white. And infinitely more vibrant than the gray of charcoal pencils. But more importantly, Grandad thought *I* was vibrant, full of life and color instead of too bright and too much.

"Yeah ..." Ioan sighed and slid off the stool. "I'd say follow me, but I think I'll just bring it."

"I'll pretend I have a clue what you're talking about."

He smiled sheepishly. "I'm in the dark as much as you are."

"I doubt that," I murmured while he quietly left the kitchen.

He'd been hesitant with any information, even seemingly insignificant tidbits. Having the same kitchen layout wasn't earth shattering. A bit creepy and odd but hundreds of homes in California had the same basic layout. The idea didn't sit right. Cookie-cutter homes in California were to keep costs down and production up. Seventeenth century England didn't care about either. There was no reason for these two homes, one in Wales and one in Cornwall, to be remotely similar. Lydcombe was an ancient barony inherited over several centuries while the island was only four centuries old.

"Here." Ioan held an old inkwell in the palm of his hand. His breathing was shallow.

"Are you scared of it?"

"No." His voice said otherwise.

"How old is it?"

He arched an eyebrow and straightened his stance. "You know what this is?"

"Yeah, an inkwell. An ancient one by the looks of it."

"How do you know that?" He placed the small cylinder on the counter. "It's the smallest one I've ever seen."

"Grandad has one." Leaning over the counter, I flipped the top of the lid over. The tiny hinge squawked a pitiful yelp. The cylinder wasn't more than an inch or two high and roughly the same in diameter. "Why so little?"

"Liam thought it was portable." He grabbed it and turned it over, showing a calligraphy-carved *M* on the bottom. "Both he and my mom thought it stood for Morgannwg."

The ache of my ankle started again. I'd sat too long on the stool with my legs dangling. The inkwell became infinitely less interesting. "I don't know the name."

"You wouldn't."

"Gee, thanks—"

"Easy, girl." He chuckled, reminding me of Grandad.

A lump formed in my throat. My grandfather was resistant to my temper and tongue. He was absolutely impervious to my antics. No one had ever loved me so completely. And no one ever would.

Ioan set the inkwell back down. "Your family wouldn't know the name because the last Morgannwg was a girl. The earl's direct line ended with her."

"Those pesky girls ruining everything." My smile didn't lighten the words as much as I'd hoped.

"Her father was considered mad," he said softly.

"I'm sorry."

"His room was considered haunted after he died." His voice cracked. He wasn't talking about history. This was too personal to be about ancestors. "He'd gone gold mining after the birth of his only child."

"He died in a mining accident?"

"No, mercury poisoning." He rubbed his temple. "Mercury surrounds the gold and then evaporates, leaving the gold."

"Gets married and dies."

"No." He swallowed hard and shook his head. "He wore the ring made from the mining. Mercury poisoning takes time. Eats away at the brain."

"Oh." The air tensed between us. He wasn't talking about some ancestors. "Did your mom have mercury poisoning?"

He nodded once. "But it wouldn't have mattered. She'd have lost her mind anyway."

"I thought mercury was ..." I had no way to put this nicely. "I thought everyone knew that mercury was bad."

"Mercury was still used in teeth fillings. Dentists thought it was safe as long as it stayed encapsulated." He took the untouched tea from the mug and laid it in the sink. He'd not bothered to ask if I was done. "By the time we found the source, it was too little, too late."

"They couldn't just take it out?" We'd gone from curses to inkwells and now to mercury. For the first time, I began to wonder if Ioan was like his mother. William had accused him. Maybe that's why Ioan and Grandad were so close, their grip on reality was slipping.

"Mercury collects in the kidneys." He rinsed the mug and turned to face me. "Mom's family used *Mercurochrome*." He rubbed his neck, and before I could ask what *Mercurochrome* was, he continued, "It's an antiseptic."

"And it has mercury in it?"

"Yeah, you could say that." He took the inkwell and slipped it into his pocket. "No one cares that she had mercury poison."

"Why are you putting it away?"

A knock on the door interrupted me. "How's the gimp?" William's booming voice echoed into the castle.

A fear crept in. Ioan knew William was about to walk through the door. The idea made zero sense but I knew it. I'd seen Ioan in my head and I could have sworn in some weird, crazy way, I had heard his voice as well. Was Ioan connected to all of us this way? Could he peek inside Grandad's head—or William's?

"You missed out on a *Fuldamobil*." William stopped himself and turned to me. "Actually, forget that was the first thing I said. Pretend I asked about your ankle first."

"Your sympathy is overwhelming," Ioan deadpanned. "Doris will be so relieved."

William grimaced dramatically. "You'll give my eulogy then?"

"Do you really want Ioan to summarize your life?" I shrugged when they both looked at me. They'd forgotten about my presence. "You two fight like scorned lovers."

William beamed like I'd given him the greatest gift. Groaning, I watched as he sidled next to Ioan and threw an arm around Ioan's shoulders.

"Tell me, dearest. What can I do to have your love once more?" William backed away, letting his hand drag across Ioan's shoulders. With a hand to his forehead, William gasped and sank to his knees. "Please forgive me, fair Ioan."

❦ 23 ❦

S ienna
   Ynys Wair Island, United Kingdom: Present Day

YNYS WAIR WAS A TINY SLIP OF AN ISLAND IN THE MIDDLE OF THE Bristol Sea. But only here would I be given a front row seat to the world's dumbest argument. William was still pretending to be head-over-heels in love with Ioan while Ioan was stifling his growing fury. William sighed in complete and utter contentment from the havoc he wreaked on Ioan and slid onto the stool next to me.

Oblivious to the rising tension, William tapped the granite countertop and glanced around Ioan's kitchen. He arched an eyebrow. "Hey, this looks a lot like Liam's."

Ioan folded his arms and worked his jaw. William's ability to irritate Ioan seemed to be exponentially volatile at the castle.

"It's probably time to leave," I said—although having zero idea of the employee ship's schedule.

Ioan glanced up. "They won't leave before the doctor gets here."

"I don't need a doctor." I'd broken enough bones in my life to know the difference between a sprain and a break.

"It's not for you." Ioan back was ramrod straight, his arms taut across his chest as if he was barely containing himself. He'd never been easy going, but this newer version was even more of a mystery than the man who cared for my grandfather. "There's always a doctor and a volunteer fire service on call." He sniffed at William. I wasn't sure why —William hadn't said anything against the island not having emergency services. "The shifts are two days on and two days off."

"I thought he said the doctor lived on the island." I kept my voice light and cheerful, but the surprised look on Ioan's face made me doubt my comment.

"Come off it, Ioan. *He* is Davey from security." William chuckled. "Sienna has more than one rescuer it seems."

A vein ticked on Ioan's neck. Ignoring William, his gaze flicked to me. "Only one doctor lives on the island, the other comes on the ferry."

"Who pays their wages?" William tapped a finger on the counter, his face a wash of feigned innocence.

"Oh, don't start." I groaned and rubbed my temples, my ankle throbbing with a vengeance. "I don't know what's going on between you two, but either start pounding into each other or stop talking."

William shot me a sympathetic smile. "It was just a question."

"Right." I slid from the stool. "My parents are champions at wrapping a lot into a simple question."

"Have you ever thought of therapy?" William grinned and offered his arm. "Sounds like there's a lot wrapped in your comment."

"For some reason, I doubt you've ever gone." Pointing to both of them, I said, "But you two should go for couple's counseling."

William scoffed dramatically, a hand on his forehead. "How dare you!"

I winced, his voice too loud. My head and neck were screaming. Ioan was at my side, whispering, "Let's get that foot up."

William dropped his act, his face sobering. "How bad does it hurt?"

"It's just my stupid ankle. And now my head. It's fine. I'm fine." *I just want to go home,* I almost added.

Ioan placed a reassuring hand on my back, his eyes giving a knowing glint. I'd not said the words but somehow he knew. I stared at him, wishing I could read his mind the way he appeared to see mine.

With a man on each side, I hobbled to the living room—the same layout as Grandad's. The sofas surrounding the grand fireplace were in the same *u* shape as my grandfather's, although the room was bigger. Come to think of it, the kitchen was slightly larger as well—the entire castle was bigger, slightly grander than Lydcombe Manor. Ioan helped me to the sofa and placed a cushion behind my bank, his touch both gentle and firm. The fury was still there, the current just below the surface. William appeared to still be oblivious, chatting away about how hard it must be living so far from a castle, sarcasm in every word.

Ioan straightened and sat on the opposite chair, glaring at William who'd sat next to my feet on the same sofa. "When you're done complaining about where I do and don't live, you could always move into your house on the island."

William froze—swallowed hard—and gave a false half-smile. "Your definition of a house and mine are worlds apart."

"Wait, you own a home here?" For as much as William crowed about how unfair it was for Ioan to own a castle and not reside in the stone walls, he'd forgotten to tell me that detail. "This, I have to hear."

"It's not a home." William lay back against the sofa, failing to appear relaxed. His jaw and shoulders were tight. "A house has a roof."

"No roof means no tax." Ioan leaned against the mantle, his thumb scratching his jaw. The island had to be the source of contention between them. The sparring was much more tame in Cornwall.

"Says the man who pays nothing," William murmured.

"Is that a fact?" Ioan arched an eyebrow. "I've two council taxes to my name that say otherwise."

"I thought council tax is paid by where you live." My parents had become U.S. citizens before I was born, granting me dual citizenship. If I stayed in Cornwall for too long, I would have to pay taxes—and I knew next to nothing about them.

"It is," William and Ioan said at the same time.

"You can't live in two places at once."

William smirked. "Yeah, Ioan, how does that work? Sienna would love to know why you're—"

"I'm not the one pretending," Ioan barked.

A knock on the door snuffed out the argument.

"Don't worry, I'll get it." William jumped to a stand. "We can't let the nobleman dirty his hands."

Ioan scowled, his pale eyes filling with heaviness. A flicker of an image appeared in my mind, Grandad comforting Ioan in this very room.

"Is there a time limit for how long I'm left in the dark?" With a shrug, I sat up. "I get that I'm not from around here but it's exhausting trying to figure out what you two are arguing about."

Ioan glanced above me and winced. Following his gaze, I froze. On the wall above me was a framed canvas painting—the girl was young, her hair a dark, deep red—the color of rain-soaked Redwood tree bark from Northern California. Her eyes were nearly black, her skin pale and smooth. She couldn't have been more than seventeen, maybe eighteen. The raincoat was the same color as the one Grandad had given me.

A chill ran down my spine. The girl was me. "What in the—"

"I can explain." Ioan held up his hands in surrender. He at least had the decency to appear sheepish. "It's not what it looks like."

"By all means, tell me what it looks like."

He sat where William had just left. I scooted away. This was beyond freaky. He hesitated, his gaze moving around the room, touching everything but me. "I painted it—"

"Yeah, I gathered that."

"I didn't mean to draw you or paint you." He rubbed his eyes and laid back his head. "The woman. I was trying to get the woman out of my head. But the more I drew, the more color I put on the canvas, the more she came out like you."

"That's from years ago. Explain that."

His hands slid from off his face, revealing a sheepish expression. "Yeah, about that ..."

"Do I want to know?"

"It was Liam's idea."

I threw a cushion at him. "Liar."

He caught the cushion and grimaced. "He said it would help get the woman out of my head and offered a picture as a guide."

"You're telling me that my grandfather gave you a picture, a virtual stranger—" I cut myself off. Ioan was a stranger to me, but not to Grandad. A lump formed in my throat. Grandad had this whole family, people he cared for, spent time with—that I knew nothing about. I didn't know Ioan or his mother. I didn't know he owned a castle that replicated my grandfather's home.

Ioan shot to a stand. "Yes."

"Yes to what?" The idiot wasn't getting out of this. He'd painted a picture of me—the *me* from years earlier. The *me*—I looked at the canvas once more, the shirt peeking out from under the raincoat. It was the last time I'd worn it. I wasn't a teenager, I was twenty years old. I wore it the last time I came—it was when Grandad didn't recognize me. "You're lying."

"Liam did give me a picture." Ioan hesitated. "But the painting changed after your last visit. After I got a better look ..." His voice trailed off and he looked to the door where William left.

"A better look?" I hadn't met Ioan at that point in my life. "Don't lie to me."

"I see you, Sienna."

I gripped the armrest of the sofa. This wasn't happening. Ioan might have known Grandad, but he was a stranger to me. And yet, Ioan had watched me. He'd *painted* me. I felt naked. Vulnerable.

"Hey, everyone ready?" William burst into the living room.

The details fell into place. I pointed to William. "You knew he was coming." Ioan had said *yes* to William's question of our readiness before William was in the room.

Ioan held out his hand and smiled too bright to be sincere. "Shall we?"

I folded my arms. "No."

William raised both eyes and leaned his shoulder into the wall. "Who needs couples counseling now?"

"Hilarious," I deadpanned. "You here all week or do I need to come back to see the rest of the show?"

William's mouth formed an *o*, his eyes wide. "I think I'll go wait in the car."

"I don't think so." Using the couch's arm rest, I rose to a stand. "What's the deal with the island? Why are you bent out of shape that Ioan doesn't live here?" I pointed to Ioan—his chin tucked. "And you, why are you on edge with William?"

He lifted his gaze, a question in his eyes. I wasn't going to bring up the painting with William in the room—but that didn't mean the topic was dead. We were far from done discussing that elephant.

"It's a long story." William jabbed a thumb over his shoulder. "And the ship is quite literally waiting to set sail."

"There's no sail," Ioan mumbled. "It can't *literally* sail."

"And the question is still not answered." I hopped toward William. "What is it with you Cornwall boys? No one can answer a question. No one can explain anything to me."

William nodded his head toward Ioan. "He's not Cornish."

"You know what I mean."

"Call it sibling rivalry." William grinned. "Lydcombe is too small of a town for two boys like us."

Ioan nodded. "Yeah, something like that."

"Liar." I limped across the room, refusing both their offers of help. It wasn't really my business why they argued, but I was a stranger in my grandfather's house and the lone wolf of my own family. I was tired of being an outsider. Coming home to Lydcombe used to be a respite, not a reminder of all I lacked. The lump in my throat grew bigger.

"Come on, now." William was at my side, a hand on my forearm. "Don't be stubborn."

"Oh, *I'm* the one who's stubborn?" My stupid ankle throbbed but I kept limping toward the side door—the same door I'd entered an hour earlier. The same door that I'd walk through in my grandfather's house. "I'm not the one holding onto a childhood grudge."

"If only it were just our childhood," William whispered, his hand under my elbow. "Ours goes back generations."

"Oh." My family clung to their ancestry like the last breath of a

OF INK AND SEA

drowning swimmer. Hobbling from William's touch, I pivoted back to Ioan. "If you're both from Cornwall, how do you two have a grudge?"

"I wasn't born in Lydcombe." Ioan's low voice carried to where I stood. "I was born in Wales."

"Straight across the sea." William smiled wide, his eyes glinting with mischief. "He was *literally* born across the sea."

The lump in my throat disappeared, my mouth dry and my nerves on alert. "Where in Wales?"

"Coch Bay." Ioan pursed his lips, a sad frown forming.

"Why do you look like you're about to apologize?" I glanced between the two of them. William appeared confused while Ioan's shoulders slumped. "Why is it a big deal that you're from Coch Bay?"

William's brow furrowed. "He's Lord Morgannwg. Why are you surprised by this? He's the Earl of Morgannwg."

"He's the Earl of Morgannwg?" I clung to the wall and waited. William had announced Ioan's title as if I should be in awe while Ioan was cowering like a dog caught with his head in the trash. "What exactly am I missing?"

"It's how he gets away with all of this." William threw both arms in the air, indicating the castle.

"What does the island have to do with being an earl?" Most of my life was spent in America, a country that outlawed nobility in all its forms. Earls and castles weren't something I studied. That was my family's department.

"That's an Ioan question." William winked. "The emergency crew is here and so is our ship."

"We should leave," Ioan said gently.

William playfully elbowed me. "We can always come back."

"I'll grab her camera." Ioan nodded to the door. "Will you make sure they don't leave us behind?"

"Sounds like a plan." William saluted us both and left.

"Why is it a big deal?" I asked Ioan's retreating form.

"It's hard for William to swallow." He returned with my camera in one hand and a book in the other. "Me being a Welshman and owning English land and title."

"I thought that argument was buried a few centuries ago."

"William was the perfect kid with perfect parents and a perfect lineage." Ioan held out a sketch book. "I was the kid who had nothing going for him. Like Liam, my family inherited only after a string of mishaps."

"What's with the book?"

"It's a place to start." He swallowed hard. "At least, for me it was."

❦ 24 ❦

K enan
     Penyl, South Wales: 1606

THE AFTERNOON SUN TORE THROUGH THE BRANCHES OF THE ELM trees. Kenan blinked against the onslaught, the light piercing his eyes. His head throbbed. He took a shuttered breath, his side hurting with every move. The early morning assault from the mercenaries had left its mark. He leaned against the stump of a tree, the men's voices too low to understand. He needed to steady himself before escaping.

"The less you move, the less you'll hurt," Elyna whispered to his right.

He stifled a groan. The woman was nothing but misery. Elyna's hands were loosely tied and she sat cross-legged next to him. Her dark red hair fell over her shoulder, framing her face. Her smooth, pale skin against dark features—she was beautiful. And dangerous.

Kenan blinked, his head still dizzy. His wrists throbbed from being tied. He glanced at Elyna's wrists. She was secured by a simple slipknot, and from the angle of the rope, she'd tied herself. The blasted woman was a pretender. "You've made new friends."

"Are you always this trusting?" Elyna smirked. "They had me tie you as well."

Kenan held up his wrists. He'd made his living as a smuggler but had never seen this knot. His life—or death—could be determined by the type of rope or knot. "And why would they want you to tie it?"

"They tested it." She lifted her chin, a slow grin appearing. "They tested mine as well."

"Matthew would recognize a slipknot." The leader of the mercenaries was cunning. And careful. Elyna was lying. "How long have you known him?"

Her eyes widened. "You think I'm in league with them?"

"What are you hiding?" Kenan didn't bother hiding the growl. She winced at the sound. "Your face. Last night. When we said Swansea."

She lowered her gaze. "There are things in Swansea that should stay there. That's the beginning and end of it."

"Jowan is like a brother to me." Kenan spoke slowly, his dizzying mind forcing him take small breaths between words. "Blood oath or not, I'll avenge his—"

"He's not dead." She huffed and scooted closer, her lavender scent stilling his spinning mind.

"What are you doing, woman?"

"Hold still." She pulled the end of her rope, releasing her right hand. With both hands she tugged at the ends of Kenan's rope in opposite directions, freeing his wrists. "There. Now you're free."

He stared at the rope in his lap, his bruised head not able to understand what was happening.

"Run away." She waved her hand. "Go save your comrade in arms."

"You know I can't."

"I free you from the oath." Elyna didn't look at him as she spoke. "Go on your merry way."

"You can't free me." He promised to keep her safe. A moment ago he'd been tempted to leave her, believing she was in league with Matthew. But now, she'd untied him. Kenan didn't know what to think.

His mind hadn't been clear since h'd stepped foot on Morgannwg land. "I've not fulfilled my part."

"I'm safe." She smiled weakly. The slight tremor in her breath. She *was* hiding something. "They'll not harm me."

"They'll slit your throat for a farthing. It's what they do." Mercenaries held no honor, their swords loyal to the highest bidder. Elyna was valuable only because a nobleman desired her. And Rothesay's devotion was as fickle as his health. The moment Rothesay tired of Elyna, she would be tossed aside.

"They won't cut my throat. They'll burn me." She dipped her chin. "Or bind my feet and toss me to the sea."

The wind carried her words, swirling around Kenan. "What did you do?"

"It's not what I did, Kenan." She rubbed her hands together. "It's what I am."

"And what are you?"

"I'm a Morgannwg." Her hair fell forward, shielding half her face. "Your friend calls me a witch. My family is different."

"Jowan didn't mean what he—"

"You weren't awake when he told them of my hearing things. And how I've trapped you with witchcraft." She straightened, and tucked her hair behind her ear. A finger to her lip, she cocked her head to the side. "They're coming."

"Where's Jowan?" Kenan whispered and retied his wrists with a loose knot.

"He was tied to a tree." Elyna's lips curled to a mischievous smile. "By me."

"Is that when he called you a witch?"

The smile faded. "No."

"Help him to his feet." Matthew's voice bellowed, several men trailing behind. He snapped his fingers. A man on either side roughly pulled Kenan to his feet. Matthew shoved a parchment to Kenan's chest. The man's eyes were wild. Matthew's plan was not going as smoothly as he'd hoped. "Sign the letter."

"My father won't pay a ransom." Kenan kept his wrists together, pretending to be tied. He swallowed the rising bile. The sudden movement sent his stomach reeling.

"We've got his whore and his son." Matthew chuckled, his lips forming a sneer. He'd been wronged before. Kenan had seen his kind before. Matthew would trust no one.

"I'll help him," Elyna said softly. She glanced at Matthew coyly, feigning an innocence she didn't possess. "I've an inkwell in my pocket."

"And just why do you have an inkwell?" Matthew sneered. "Why would a lady have need of a quill?"

"I helped my father address his tenants." Her lie came quickly. Their tenants couldn't have paid a penny in months. Morgannwg's estate and his land were destitute. She held up her hands. "If you'll untie me, I can help him sign."

Matthew snapped his fingers at his men. "Do it."

The nearest man helped untie her, his face confused. He'd noticed the slipknot. She could have untied herself. Elyna shot Kenan a nervous look. She produced a small canister in her palm. Interloping Celtic ringlets were carved on the outside. Kenan's mother wrote him from the same canister, keeping her ink separate from his father.

Matthew held out a quill. Elyna curtseyed, playing the submissive woman. Matthew turned his back to her and began whispering to his men.

Kenan shook his head—and winced, his head dizzy. The woman was a nymph, nothing more than a temptation to regret. She laid the paper flat against the ground. She hid the nib of the quill behind the inkwell and cut the inside of her arm. The edge of the quill filled with blood. Before Kenan could say a word, she grabbed his hand and cut the inside of his hand. She wrote *free* against his palm.

"What are you doing?" Kenan whispered.

She ignored his question and dipped the quill in the inkwell. "Here."

"What did you do?" Kenan waited for the pull to slip away, to be free of his blood oath.

"You know what I've done." She didn't look him in the eye but leaned closer. Her hair caressed Kenan's face. Her lavender scent tempted Kenan. "Sign your name. You'll be able to sneak away without being tied to me. Go save your friend."

"You said Jowan was alive."

"He's tied to a tree. Alive, for now." She wrapped her hand around his, forming each letter. "Don't worry about me, Kenan. What you said was true. I am not as innocent as I appear."

"I cannot leave you behind."

"You're a good man, Kenan. But you don't have a choice." Elyna smiled, her eyes crinkling. She turned with the parchment in hand. "Sir?"

Matthew grabbed the paper and offered it to the same man who'd untied her. "You leave now."

"Sir?" Elyna batted her eyelashes. "Might I accompany him?"

"No." Matthew grabbed her forearm and shoved her aside. "You'll do as your told."

"Rothesay has not set eyes on me yet." She scrambled to her feet, her pride at the ready. "You'll have a better chance at a ransom once he's seen—"

"He would simply steal you from my men." Matthew folded his arms and spat on the floor at her feet. "Rothesay is cunning. Be careful who you trust." He kneeled and retied her wrists.

She lifted her chin. "But, sir—"

Matthew smacked her across the face. "You'll stay. And speak when spoken to."

Leaving a man to stand over them, Matthew barked orders to his men, his hands waving wildly.

"Are you alright?" Kenan inched closer to her.

"If you tell me to mind my tongue, I'll stab you with the quill." Her face was calm. "I know how to handle men like Matthew."

The image of Elyna at her father's castle appeared in his head. He'd thought her a conniving woman but now wondered if she was playing her part of surviving prey. "How many men shadowed your father's door?"

"You were not the first. Nor will you be the last." Elyna fiddled with the knot.

"If you sneak away, they'll know you returned home," Kenan

warned. These men were mercenaries. What they lacked with strategy, they made up in force. With Matthew showing signs of ill temper, Kenan should stay at her side.

"I'm not going home." Elyna sat back with a sigh. "He tied a blasted brilliant knot."

Kenan slipped his hands from his ties and helped make quick work of Elyna's. He clasped her hands in his. "Look at me."

She shook her head. "I won't promise you."

"I made an oath."

Elyna smiled, hesitantly meeting his gaze. "You've made two."

"No." Kenan squeezed her hands. "I didn't say a word when you mixed our blood."

A blush crept up her neck. She nibbled her lip. "I didn't take you for a Celtic man."

"My mother was Welsh." He released her hands. "She had the same inkwell as you."

Her right hand rubbed the markings on her left wrist. Matthew had made sure her knot was tight. "That's a Celtic well."

"I know." His mother kept her inkwell on her person. "Her ink is different from my father's."

"It's how we know the truth."

"What do you mean?" Kenan had forgotten most of his mother's beliefs and myths.

"The ink from my well only works if what I write is true."

"We just signed my name to a parchment filled with lies." He stifled the groan. His mother once shared superstitions like Elyna but she no longer believed in myths. Her faith had abandoned her years before. "Elyna, he didn't just poison my men. He killed his friends, leaving only a handful for him to command. Life is not sacred to a man like him. Matthew won't back down because of a little ink."

"All men are led by fear or pride."

"Elyna." He placed a hand on hers. "When we're closer to Swansea, find the church on the eastern ridge. There's an elder couple there. Tell them I've sent you. They'll keep you safe until I return."

"You mean until Jowan returns and casts me out." She sighed and wrinkled her nose. "I am not naïve, Kenan. I know how the world works."

"Is that why you keep your secrets from me?" Kenan could feel the deception, an invisible current just below the surface. He didn't know if her secret was nefarious, only that she guarded it well.

"I promise, one day you, you will know." She looked him with a sobering gaze. "We're linked, you and I."

Her words pierced him. She *would* trust him, just not today. There was pride in that revelation. Kenan should be cautious but her confession had him leaning in. "Can you see everything I see?"

She shook her head. "No, it hurts too much."

"It pains you?"

"Not a lot." Elyna shrugged. "Jowan knows."

"That you can see inside my head?" Of course Jowan called her a witch. He'd have burned her at a stake if Kenan hadn't sworn an oath. Jowan was loyal, even if he hated the reasons.

She looked away. "He knows I can hear his thoughts."

"How does he know?" Kenan rubbed his neck. Jowan wouldn't keep a secret that big to himself.

"The same way you do."

"Can you hear everyone's thoughts?"

Elyna shook her head. "Only those close to you."

"Because of the blood oath?"

"Ay." She toyed with the ends of her hair. "Jowan was right. You shouldn't have taken the oath."

"I'll see you safely to Muiris." Kenan placed a hand over hers once more. "This pull or this bond will be broken."

"You think your tenderness toward me is because of the oath?"

Kenan felt the flush of his face. She knew of his feelings. There was a bond, one that only appeared once her grandmother pricked his finger.

Elyna slipped her hand from his. "I'll find my own way, Kenan."

✤ 25 ✤

S ienna
Lydcombe, England: Present Day

WALKING INTO GRANDAD'S HOUSE—EVEN WITH A LIMP—HAD BEEN
the most consistent feeling of my life, a promise that all would be
well. The moment I would walk into the kitchen, safety and warmth
would envelope me. Even as a kid with a broken arm or with a
bloody leg—or like now, with an annoying limp, Lydcombe was
home.

At least while Grandad still lived here.

Within minutes of being home, the doctor was called—Doris
insisted—and I was on the couch in the living room, my leg
propped up.

The doctor crinkled his eyes and squeezed my shoulder. "Keep the
compression sock on for a few weeks and you'll be right as rain."

Ioan stood quietly in the corner, a shoulder leaning into the wall.

The doctor chuckled while Doris banged the cupboards in the
kitchen. She'd shooed William the moment she saw me limp through

the door. She'd given Ioan the cold shoulder, something I didn't think was possible. He didn't cower, but gave her space.

"Sorry," I apologized to the physician. "She'll calm down."

"Doris is a touch protective." He winked. "How's your grandfather?"

"Good," I lied. Pity wasn't welcome. Not today.

Pots and pans were thrown about in the kitchen, Doris grumbling loudly about how irresponsible William was—and would always be. My pleas for his innocence went unheard. After another round of Doris' complaints, William and the doctor left with good-natured chuckles, promising to check in later.

In the corner, Ioan loomed. He was present and aloof all at the same time. Doris' fussing and fuming didn't scare him off. Even her chopping of vegetables sounded angry from where I sat in the living room—the same set up as Ioan's island home. The fact was screaming at me. I sat back silently both angry and grateful that Ioan wasn't speaking. He'd begun staring out of the window, his eyes on the swirling sea. His dark hair and broad shoulders against the gray and blue background of sky and sea made for a beautiful picture. I slipped the camera from its bag where Ioan had placed it next to me.

A few clicks of the button and he turned, eyebrow arched. "That's the second time you've stolen a picture."

"Stolen ..." Lowering the camera to my lap, I smiled, remembering Grandad's stories. "As in, stolen a piece of your soul?"

He gave an answering smile. "Yes."

A simple word. *Yes*. And yet, a warmth spread in my chest. An annoying feeling. Ioan was the same man who evaded my questions. He straightened no longer leaning into the wall. I tucked my chin, not knowing what he was doing. He came to my side. Doris must have seen the movement, the chopping became even angrier. From where I sat, she couldn't see me—only where Ioan had been. He sat on the other end of the couch, a crooked grin on his lips.

"What are you doing?" Hugging my camera, I sat up. My ankle no longer hurt with the compression sock on it. I was tempted to walk upstairs to my room. Or better yet, my grandfather.

Ioan slid a sketch book across the cushion toward me. It wasn't the one from his room but rather the one from the castle. Both were the same blue-gray shade of his eyes. "This might help."

The whispers began again, nipping at my ears and creeping into my mind. I reached for the book—but hesitated. He leaned over and placed the book on my lap, his hand touching mine—silencing the whispers. He pulled back his hand.

"Wait." I wasn't ready for the voices to begin again.

His gaze flicked to mine, his brow furrowing. Feeling foolish, I scooted back, away from his touch. This was silly. I wasn't a child. Ancient civilizations—according to my grandfather—had often spoken about the whispers of the sea. I wasn't crazy. There wasn't a curse.

Ignoring his stare, I opened the book, the spine complaining with a creak. Ioan stretched his arm and slipped a finger into the book, toward the back. "I drew this about a couple of weeks ago."

"I was getting arrested about that time," I murmured. My hands froze. In the center of the page was a woman on her back, an elbow propped up and her face toward the sky—a falcon circling above her. Above *me*. I was the girl. In the shaded background was the church's graveyard. The same graveyard I walked a few hours before. "Please tell me you have an explanation for this."

"I'm sorry you were hurt." Ioan let his head fall back, his eyes on the ceiling. "I see things, hear things. I'm not sure if they're happening right now or already happened. Or sometimes going to happen. I have no idea how it works or how to tell what's real and what's not."

"This is very real."

"My mom would say things that didn't make sense. Same with your grandfather." A hand over his face, he shook his head. "I can't help but think I'm going down the same path."

"It's not just you." My throat was dry. I didn't know who or what I was supposed to fear. Grandad spoke of legends from a faraway time— not today. Not with real people. "You can't be insane if you drew a picture of me before I'd even come."

His voice took on a husky quality. "I saw you getting arrested and texted Lacy."

"Does she know?" Did Lacy and my grandfather share secrets with Ioan as well—was I again, the lone Rothesay, kept to the periphery?

He frowned. "Unfortunately, yes."

"Of course." My heart sank. I didn't know Ioan that well, but I wanted at least *something* of my own. Grandad used to be my every-thing—or rather, I was his everything. His favorite grandchild—no, his favorite relative aside from his wife. But that was false. The proof lay in how much Ioan and Grandad shared together. And from the undeni-able recognition that my grandfather had with Ioan. And not me.

"I've sort of always seen you." He cleared his throat, the sheepish look appearing again. "Watched you in my mind."

"I don't know how to take that." The reason why my parents banned him became crystal clear. I'd never been the submissive type and being stalked wasn't on my list of things to achieve.

"You were young." Ioan squeezed the bridge of his nose, keeping his profile to me. "I saw you floundering in the sea. I ran to Liam—but your parents wouldn't listen." He sighed. "Why would anyone listen to a Morgannwg? So I ran to Lacy. I was frantic, but she believed me. I knew where you were. I pulled you out. Your brothers—" He eyed me. "Are idiots."

I laughed—and coughed—on the seriousness of his face. "You're not a fan of the Rothesay boys?"

"No." He scowled. "They had the audacity to lecture me when they let you nearly drown."

"Is that why my parents are leery of you?" A warmth began spreading in my veins. I'd thought my one connection in life was Grandad, but Ioan had been watching, looking out for me for years. No wonder Lacy trusted him—and didn't explain why.

"No, that has to do with my mother." He let his hand fall to his chest. "And the fact that your father is like William. There's bitterness that my parents outranked them."

"And now *you* outrank them?"

"In title only." He laid his head back, his eyes wide. "When has rank ever benefited our families?"

"I know next to nothing about my family history." I held up my hands when he shot me a doubtful look. "I am not your ordinary Rothesay."

"Neither was Lacy."

"Did she break your heart too?" I flipped the page of his sketch-book, not brave enough to see his expression. "Is it just one more reason why you and William don't get along?"

"Uh, no." Ioan chuckled. A glint of laughter sparked in his pale eyes. "Although, I'm sure William's heart was broken a few times."

The next sketch was of Grandad standing next to the window, a palm on the glass. With a finger, I traced the outline of my grandfather, a lump forming in my throat. This was the man I'd known all my life. His expression was thoughtful, as if he was about to relay another story he'd already told a dozen times before.

Ioan scooted closer. I turned, setting my feet on the coffee table. He sat next to me and tapped the page with his finger. "I have no idea when or where this is."

The drawing had a man slumped against a tree, a woman next to him. Both of them wore ancient clothing. "This could have been from a movie you've watched." Turning the page, I found my answer. In the center of an otherwise blank page was the sketch of a boy's face, his hair unruly and eyes wide. There was innocence in his face but a hint of mischief at the slight uptick of his lips. "I know him." This was the boy I'd seen in my head as a child—the boy I confessed to seeing in my mind. He was a secret I shared only with Grandad.

"Are you sure?" Ioan's shoulder was next to mine, his warmth spreading to me. "Do you know who it is?"

"Not a clue."

"Neither do I." He sat back, his fingers tapping a rhythm on his knee. "How do you know him?"

"Oh." I closed the book. Tossing out questions was easier than answering them. "I sort of see him. Or used to see him."

Ioan nodded. "As a child ... that's right."

My heart sunk. "Grandad told you, didn't he?"

He arched his eyebrow. "And that bothers you."

"Thank you for letting me look at this." Placing the book on the coffee table, I stood. There was only so much disappointment I could take. He shot to a stand. "I'm fine, Ioan. I'm just going to go lay down for awhile."

He slipped an arm under mine to steady me. "I'll help you."

"No," I snapped—then clapped a hand over my mouth. Defensive, obnoxious ... ungrateful—there were a million ways I could describe how I sounded. "I'm sorry."

"Liam loved you," he offered softly. He was being too generous. He should have told me off, not given me leniency.

"You've spent too much time with him."

"Is that why you're angry?" He inched closer, his hand grabbing mine. "Would it make you more comfortable if I stayed away?"

"Yes. No." I stared at my hand in his. "I don't know."

"I'm not trying to take your place, Sienna." He squeezed my hand. "He thought we were one and the same. That we were affected or bound together by the same myth." His voice sounded doubtful. He wasn't quite sold on my grandfather's stories.

We stood in silence for a beat before I whispered, "I used to believe every word he said."

"So did I." Ioan dropped my hand and stepped back.

A chill wrapped around me. He took another step backward—the temperature dropped once more. I hugged myself, completely confused by what I felt. I wanted him near but couldn't—*wouldn't* —admit it.

"Sienna?" There was an apology in his tone.

Doris burst into the living room from the kitchen, hands on her hips and a frown on her face. "Would you get Liam for dinner?" She pointed at me. "Get off that foot, darling."

Both Ioan and I scurried to obey our orders like guilty children. Doris grabbed a blanket from underneath the coffee table and wrapped it around me.

"Thank you," I mumbled, unsure if I was in trouble or if Ioan was still on her naughty list.

"Oh, Sienna. It's good to see you here." She smiled and patted my knee. Pausing, she tsked to herself. "I don't understand why Ioan does this."

"He wasn't there." I shrugged. "I fell and twisted my ankle all on my own."

"Why encourage you to go to the island at all?" She shook her head —completely forgetting that *she* was just as guilty of encouraging me to go. "He can see things." She groaned and shook her head again. "He knows you're going to get in a bit of trouble. Why not stop you? Why not help instead of swoop in afterwards ..." She took her one-sided conversation back to the kitchen.

I gripped the blanket and saw the image in my head—Ioan had heard every word she'd said.

❦ 2 6 ❦

S ienna
  Lydcombe, England: Present Day

GRANDAD WIPED HIS FACE WITH THE SLEEVE OF HIS CARDIGAN, THE
same old, navy fabric he'd worn for the last few decades. He'd slurped
his soup and struggled to pierce his vegetables on his plate. He'd
scooted to the very edge of his seat away from me, his eyes wary.
Without a word, I slid to the farthest chair, my fork moving the
chicken and potatoes around in circles. Doris peppered Ioan with
overly cheerful questions, leaving me to stare at my plate, blinking
away the tears.

Doris must have felt charitable; she'd let me keep my camera on
the table. I slid it into my lap, catching my grandfather's attention. His
eyes lit.

He pointed a shaky finger at my camera. "That's a pretty one."

"It is," I whispered and turned the screen toward him. The first
image to pop up was of Ioan staring out the living room window.

"That's interesting." Doris's grin was far too hopeful.

I quickly skipped to the next picture—Ioan's back in his kitchen on the island.

"Even more interesting." Doris chuckled.

"Katherine." Grandad's voice was strong. He reached for the camera. "That's Katherine's kitchen."

"You're right, Liam," Ioan cooed, a hand on Grandad's shoulder. He pointed to the kettle pictured on the counter. "You bought her that."

My grandfather's eyes cleared, his face sober. "I miss the sound of the waves."

I'd heard the same sounds despite the house being far too high on the cliff to hear any waves. Was Grandad like me—did he hear the whispers as well? Ioan's gaze flicked to mine before returning to the camera. He clicked the button. The falcon circling in the sky above the island appeared on the screen.

"*Hebog*," Grandad said with a soft smile. His eyes crinkled. He turned to Ioan. "Tell Katherine to come for a visit. Leave that silly island and come over."

A flicker of grief—so brief, I'd almost missed it—came over Ioan's face. He licked his lips and sighed. "Liam, Katherine is—"

"She'll be here tomorrow, love," Doris interrupted and cleared his plates.

"Good." Grandad nodded, his eyes losing the clarity. His shoulders slumped and he lost interest in the camera.

Doris patted my back and stacked my plate on top of Grandad's. She exchanged a knowing look with Ioan and tackled the dishes.

"Let's get you ready for bed, Liam." Ioan helped him to a stand.

With Doris busy with dishes, I snuck upstairs. Maybe I was still the foolish girl who fell in the water all those years ago, but Grandad was *my* grandfather. The person helping him into bed should be *me*. Not Ioan. But Grandad was scared of me—his own granddaughter.

The floor creaked in protest as I climbed the stairs. The house, the land, everyone seemed to love Ioan more than me. He could help Grandad up the stairs without a sound. At the last step, I gripped the railing. Even in my mind, I sounded like a spoiled child. I should be grateful for Ioan's help. Not jealous.

Light spilled into the hallway from Grandad's partially closed door.

His soft voice was singing bits and pieces of the same song he'd told when I was a child.

"Innocence was lost at sea..." Grandad mumbled the next few words—either that or he'd forgotten the lyrics. "Ink speaks the truth ..."

The words were wrong. He'd changed the lyrics. The story was supposed to be about a Welsh woman and a Cornish man. They meet as enemies but unite in forbidden love. One of them died, but for the life of me, I couldn't remember the exact words either.

I slipped inside his room, the lamp by his bed the only light on. He waved his hand in the air like a chorister leading a choir, humming the melody of the folksong. Only his profile was visible from where I stood by the door. He shook his head, his lips downturned. "All mixed up. Who is who and when is when?"

The bathroom faucet was turned on and then off. Ioan appeared with a glass in his hand. "I know, Liam."

Grandad continued to shake his head, his frown turning more severe. "Can't put it back together until—"

"The wrong has been righted—" Ioan stopped, his gaze on me. "Are you alright?"

"Yes," I lied. Nothing was alright with me. I felt turned around and twisted inside. The one place where I'd always belonged now made me feel like an outsider. The person I knew the most—and knew me the most was speaking gibberish. And Ioan, the most confusing person to me seemed to be the only one seeing me.

"Give me a minute." Ioan brushed past me. The scent of hay and sea followed him. He set the glass on Grandad's nightstand. He sat on the edge of the bed, his broad shoulders dwarfing my grandfather's shriveling frame in the bed. "Liam, do you remember Sienna?"

Grandad cocked his head to the side, his brow furrowed in confusion.

Ioan reached for me, pulling me into Grandad's line of sight. "Sienna."

Warmth spread from his touch. I'd never been a hugger—except for Doris—and should be pulling back from Ioan. Not stepping forward.

Grandad's eyes widened. "Elyna."

My heart sank. Blinking back tears, I stepped back. Ioan held my hand but kept his face on Grandad. "Who's Elyna?"

Grandad made a fist with the sheets. "Elyna."

Ioan pulled me forward. "This is Elyna."

"What are you doing?" I hissed.

Grandad's face smoothed. His hands relaxed. He peered up at me like a lost child. "Elyna, you made it to the cliffs."

"The cliffs?" Lacy had said I'd fallen into the water from the trail by the house. The ground was difficult and high about the water, but I wouldn't go so far as call it *the cliffs*.

"You made it out of the water." Grandad closed his eyes and smiled.

"I saw the falcon monument today." Even if he thought I was someone else, I could at least try to find common ground.

"Falcons hurt my arms." He kept his eyes closed.

"You don't like falcons?" I glanced at Ioan. He looked away.

"Ioan." Grandad pursed his lips and shook his head.

I pulled back from both of them. "He's calling for you, Ioan. Not me."

"Jowan," Ioan offered, placing a hand on Grandad's shoulder.

My grandfather calmed, repeating the name. "Jowan. Jowan."

Slipping from the room, I went to my bedroom, the *blue room* and sat on the bed. The same sea that Ioan had stared at a few hours earlier was framed in the windows I'd looked through as a child. But nothing was the same. Grandad had replaced me with some random person named Elyna. And instead of saying Ioan, the man who'd taken care of him for the last few years, Grandad had changed his name to Jowan.

The sound of the side door opening and closing marked Doris' departure. She would be back first thing in the morning. And Ioan would be here tonight, tomorrow, and every other day until Grandad passed. I'd only taken a handful of pictures of my grandfather despite coming to document him and all that made up Liam Rothesay. But sitting in the blue room made me wonder, was there truly any reason for me to stay?

Grandad's door shut. Ioan was leaving his room and probably placing the black half-circle outside the door. I wrapped the old Peruvian blanket around my shoulders. This was the closest I could feel to Grandad.

Ioan peeked into the room, letting my door swing open. He folded his arms and leaned against the doorframe. "You want to talk about it?"

"Which part?" I wrapped the blanket tighter around me. There was a part of me that wanted to talk about us—whatever *us* meant. Under the blanket, I flexed my right hand, the same one he'd touched earlier in the living room. And again in Grandad's room.

"Jowan. Elyna. All of it." He sat on the edge of the bed, making himself far too comfortable. "What Doris said."

I shot him a curious look. Doris wondered why Ioan had encouraged me to go to the island when he could see things. I didn't know what was more weird—the fact she was nonplussed about his ability or the fact that Ioan knew about the conversation. "Do you see her thoughts too?"

"No." Ioan folded his hands behind his head and leaned back. "I can see yours. Liam's. And sometimes William."

"Not all the time?"

He shook his head. "Only when he's near you."

"Why did you encourage me to go to the island with William?" My cheeks flushed and I didn't dare look at him, for fear he'd think my blushing had to do with William.

He crossed his ankles and sighed. "I don't always know if what I'm seeing is the past or present. Or another time."

"Won't the clothes tell?" There had to be rules for this sort of thing.

"It's not like a television screen," he said with a scoff. "I'm still not sure it's real."

"Do you know for a fact who Elyna was? Or Jowan?"

"For a fact? I'm not for sure on any of it." He arched an eyebrow. "She was the daughter of an earl. But records aren't what they are today. And Jowan, I can only speculate that he was part of the Wair family."

"Speculate on Jowan or speculate on Elyna?"

Ioan rubbed his tired eyes. "She's Elyna Morgannwg. That's the beginning and end of what I know."

"And Jowan?" If the records were subpar, the two could be related. Suspicion crept in. "You think I'm related to them both?" That must have been his true reason in getting me here.

He rolled his eyes. "No, that's not the reason."

"I didn't say that." I scooted away from him, my back against the wall. "Why can you see some things and not others?"

He held out his arms. "I don't know. That's what I'm trying to tell you. I have no idea why or what or how this is happening. I only know that it's connected to you. It's always been you."

"We're connected because of my grandfather." It came out defensive. I tucked my knees up against my chest. Groaning, I waved a hand in the air. "Pretend I didn't say that."

"Liam was the only one who could talk to my mom," he whispered. "She didn't recognize me."

Risking a glance, I peered over my knees. "What did you do?"

"When my own mother didn't know me?" He ran a hand through his hair, softening his features. A clump of hair flopped down his forehead. "She called me Jowan. Kenan. And some other name that I can't remember."

"How did Grandad help?" I patted the mattress next to me. Ioan being forgotten tugged at my heart strings. I wasn't exactly close with my parents but I couldn't imagine them not knowing me. I was the odd man out, but not an orphan.

Ioan didn't hesitate—making me second-guess my offer to sit next to me. He climbed up the bed and mirrored my position, back against the wall and legs out front. "He had a way of reminding her. Not of me. I was a far distant memory the last year of her life. But he could make her remember herself. Her life. My father."

"How?" I grabbed his arm. An electric hum danced up my arm. There was a power, some sort of connection between us.

His eyes flicked to my hand. "Liam would tell her old Welsh stories."

"He's not Welsh."

His lips quirked. "But he knew all the myths."

And there I was, the little girl again with my hand tucked into my grandfather's. The wind caressed our faces as we walked along the edge of his property, his voice singing ancient lullabies from both Cornwall and Wales. "I used to believe every word he spoke."

"What changed?" Ioan whispered, his eyes searching my face.

I shrugged. "Life, I guess."

"I suppose I'm the opposite." He playfully elbowed me. "The older I get, the more I wonder about our ancestors."

"You'd get along well in my family."

Ioan grinned and slid down, his head on my pillow. "Your family hates me."

"What are you doing?" I poked his chest.

He covered my finger with his hand. "Waiting for Liam to rearrange the furniture."

There was peace in the room with just the two of us. The curse and our families forgotten for a moment. A low hum sang to us, inviting confessions and secrets.

I whispered, "Why did you call my cousin?"

He laced our fingers together. My heart raced—I didn't know if I should run or stay. "She was the only one I knew would answer."

"Why?" I forced my voice to stay calm. It was hard to focus with his thumb making circles in my palm. "She said you texted back and forth for months."

He leaned over me, his scent enveloping me, and pulled open the drawer in the nightstand next to me. He pulled out three other sketchbooks and placed them on top. "Take a look."

I ran a finger down the spine. The cover was worn like my alpaca blanket. "How many of those do you have?"

He folded the pillow in half to prop his head. "What do you think I do at night?"

"Rearrange furniture with my grandfather. What else *is* there to do in Lydcombe?" I ignored his chuckle and opened the first book. The sketches were ink, not pencil. The first drawing was of the harbor of his island, but instead of the employee ship that we traveled on, there was another ship. The same one that was on stilts at the employee harbor.

"It's called a fluyt ship. They're light and narrow. Perfect for the island's harbor." Ioan inched closer. He apparently didn't know that I was not a cuddler. Or touchy-feely in any way. I'd shut down William as gently as possible. It was harder to reject Ioan—especially since he was assuming the sale—an old marketing tactic of assuming he'd get his way. "They were light and agile."

"Grandad said the currents made the island difficult to navigate."

"I wonder if these are the cliffs he talked about." Ioan sat up and tapped the paper. His cheek was inches from mine.

"Ioan ..." There was no easy way to say this. "Listen, I get that you feel a connection to me."

He leaned back. The chill was back. Even with the blanket around me, I could feel the draft from his withdrawal. "Do you want me to leave?"

"No." I should have said yes.

He smirked and closed his eyes. "Great. Let me know when Liam starts his routine."

Frozen next to him, I cradled his book and didn't dare move. Up until a few weeks ago, Ioan was a complete stranger to me. I'd been in this situation before—I'd run. Every time.

Ioan's breathing had steadied. His eyelids twitched. I placed the book on top of the others on the nightstand and debated leaving. One last glance at Ioan, I felt the pull. His face was relaxed, almost boyish. The temptation to touch his hair was there. He was asleep. He'd never know.

He sighed, contentment flowing from him. Another image, his arms around me—holding me. I'd spent my life being an outsider, never measuring up. Ioan admitted to watching me for years—he'd not judge me. Like Grandad, there was only soothing acceptance.

I lay back, my head against his arm, I touched his hair. My heart raced. He didn't move. I placed a palm against his chest, images flickered in my mind. Me—on the ferry next to William. Grandad holding my hand as we walked. Doris scolding my brothers. I didn't know if the memories were mine or Ioan's. He turned his head and shifted his arm, his hand on my head. Peace. I felt nothing but peace.

27

K enan
      Penyl, South Wales: 1606

WITH EVERY STEP TOWARD JOWAN, KENAN WAS TORN. HE'D SNUCK from the campsite after giving Elyna his knife. She would be blamed for his escape but was still protected by the simple fact that she was Rothesay's prize, the reason he'd launched the campaign. And if she was correct, Jowan needed Kenan more than she did. Kenan still didn't trust the woman, but he'd seen inside her head. Could she truly see that Jowan was injured?

Kenan's own head and sides ached with each breath. Elyna had tied a wrap around his chest, easing some of the pain, but his march toward Jowan set his injuries on fire. She'd grabbed his hand and let him see through his eyes to the tree where Jowan was tied. And that no other mercenary was left behind to guard Jowan. She'd not been able to show him the way, only the destination. Even now, he glanced back from where he'd come and wondered if he'd made the right choice. He'd left a lady in the hands of an enemy to search for a friend.

A familiar nicker echoed in the foggy night, followed by another. Their horses. Kenan dipped down into the enclave where dozens of tents still stood surrounding abandoned campfires. Hundreds of men were in the tents. Brothers, fathers and sons Kenan had fought alongside surrounded him, eternally asleep. Murmuring, he sang, "Whence the healing river doth flow, let the fire and the sword, lead me all my journey through ..." His voice broke. He began again, "Deliverer, deliverer be my strength and shield. Avenge my death and curse the traitor."

He kept his arms crossed, not able to touch the canvas of the tents, the frustration brewing inside. Passing his tent he'd shared with Elyna and Jowan, he closed his eyes, allowing his mind to remember where Jowan was held. The tree was split in half at the top, the trunk the width of a horse. Kenan retraced his steps from the night before—first to where Matthew's tent had stood. Slowly, he spun around and saw emerging from the fog a man slumped against a tree. *Jowan.*

Kenan rushed to his friend. Dried blood ran down Jowan's face below a large bump just above his temple. His left eye was swollen shut and his hand black and blue. Kenan kneeled before him, untying his hands and feet.

Jowan groaned, his right eye blinking. "Bloody man."

Kenan inspected both hands and face. "He's gone a bit mad on you."

"Blame your woman for that." Jowan winced as Kenan touched his injured hand. "Ay, don't touch it."

Nhwn. Kenan heard the word in his mind, Welsh for broken. Whispering, he repeated, "*Nhwn.*"

"She's got you speaking Welsh now?" Jowan cradled his hand against his chest. "You pledge your life and lose your men. Now you've forsaken your own tongue?"

"My mother's Welsh."

"I'm warning you, Kenan. That woman is no good." Jowan narrowed his gaze—as much as he could with his eye swollen. "She'd turn on us to save her own skin. She's hiding something."

"She's taking the brunt of Matthew's temper for my escape." Kenan felt her approval—as if she could hear his words. "Let's get you on your horse and to your family."

"My family? You'd abandon your friend for a witch?" He growled. "She's nothing but madness and ruin, Kenan. Let the fates decide. Let your father have her and all her witchcraft."

"I don't know if she's a witch—"

Jowan spat at the ground. "You don't know? Are you daft? Have you lost your senses? The woman can peer inside my mind. Can see in Matthew's as well. He blamed me for that." He pointed to the bump on his head. "He thought I'd given her information about what he'd done in the village. Things I hadn't even known."

"I'm not denying what she can see. Or hear." *But I can't leave her.*

"I can't believe my eyes." Jowan gingerly touched the bump on his head. "Or my ears. You've lost your mind. Can't you see that?"

"They didn't take your horse." Or Kenan's. They'd been forced to ride together—although Kenan hadn't been conscious enough to remember the journey. She'd been tasked with keeping him in the saddle.

Jowan whistled—then cursed, the sound hurting both their aching heads. His horse nickered. They followed the sound, coming upon both their horses. Jowan smiled wryly. "You don't think it strange that they took Elyna's horse but not yours?"

"Hers was a gift from Muiris."

"You still don't believe they're in league together?" Jowan spat again at the ground. "Are you blind?"

Kenan had watched his mother harden after his father had hit her. "Matthew struck her, Jowan. She'll not trust him."

"What if they were playing you false?" He waited while Kenan wrapped his hand. He cursed and winced under Kenan's ministrations.

"I don't think she is."

"You can't see what's in front of you." Jowan checked the saddle before mounting. "To hell with your father. And to her. It's not your fight."

Mounting his horse, Kenan said softly, "I gave an oath."

"And so you've sold your soul? Just like that, you'll give your life for a witch who'll see you to your enemy?"

"Matthew is only my enemy because of my father." Kenan couldn't blame the man. Rothesay wasn't known for honor. He'd cheat his wife and his men, anything to gain power. "He's not the first, nor the last, to hate me for a relative."

"Can't you ask your woman to curse Rothesay?" Jowan glanced down at his wrapped hand. "Or shove both of them over the cliffs at *Ynys Wair?* I think all of Cornwall will thank us."

"All of England." Kenan squinted at the early morning sky. He'd left his falcon on the island. One of many regrets. He didn't trust his father's men to keep that secret. The punishment for a having a royal animal was severe. He could have used his feathery friend to send word to Swansea. Jowan's parents could have rounded up reinforcements or at least been prepared to sneak their son away to their ship. *The ship.* Kenan would have a skeleton crew to navigate the waters to the island. He'd only left a handful of men in Swansea to guard his fluyt.

Jowan urged his horse alongside Kenan's. "I've sworn my life to serve you. Even if it means to free you of this woman."

"Why are you set against her?" Kenan gripped the saddle, the movement churning his stomach. His head was nowhere near healed, but he couldn't leave Elyna in Matthew's hands. "Is it fear? What is it that makes her the mark of your ill will?"

"It's not natural." Jowan kept his gaze forward, wind raking his hair. "I'm not a superstitious man but she's a witch, Kenan. The world doesn't take kindly to her sort."

"The world doesn't take kindly to our lot, either."

Jowan smiled, appearing the young boy who befriended Rothesay's second son years ago. "Ay, but a smuggler is a bit different than being a mad woman, now isn't it?"

"One skips out on taxes, the other—" An image stole Kenan's mind, erasing his words and thoughts. Elyna held a dagger in the palm of her hand, Matthew glaring at her with a split lip. Kenan could feel the panic in her chest as if it were his own. Matthew ripped a parchment into pieces and threw it at her, screaming, *You'll burn for this.* The image melted away, leaving Kenan hunched over his saddle, gasping for air.

"Kenan!" Jowan leaned over, grasping Kenan's reins. "Hold on."

For hours, Kenan let Jowan pony his horse, his hands gripping the saddle with the last of his strength. Neither man was strong enough to take on Matthew, if Jowan would even allow the battle. Images flickered in and out of Kenan's head, piecing together what Elyna faced. Matthew tore through her saddle bags, discovering sketches of him in the village, long before he'd ever laid eyes on her. There was something more, but Kenan wasn't sure. Fear was in Matthew's eyes—and Elyna had been the one to put it there.

Kenan needed strength. He must reach Elyna—some how. Some way.

Jowan had led them over the ridge instead of the lower trail, cutting their journey in half, the increased jarring from the uneven terrain weakened both men. They slipped into the barn on the outskirts of Swansea, tapping the barn's bell twice. Within minutes, the stocky form of Jowan's father silently took their horses with only a nod as a greeting. Jowan and Kenan took the hidden stairs behind the barn to the quarters above. Without a light, they waited in silence until the familiar footfalls of Jowan's mother made the trek. The windows were long ago boarded for privacy, offering little light. She lit a candle and gasped.

Jowan reached for his mother. "I'm fine, mum."

"Your eye." Her voice shook. "What happened?"

"Nothing, mum." Embracing his mother, Jowan whispered, "But we won't be if we don't let the boys know we're back. We need the ship ready to sail."

Kenan shook his head. "I'm not leaving until she's onboard."

☙ 28 ☜

S ienna
Lydcombe, England: Present Day

THE BATHROOM MIRROR WAS STILL FOGGY FROM MY SHOWER. WITH a quick swipe of the towel, I saw for myself the dark circles under my eyes. It'd been another long week with Grandad.

Last night, he'd muttered words I'd never heard before. Ioan would translate the few that he could understand. The morning didn't bring the hope I had expected. I'd waited for Doris to arrive. If anyone would know the languages my grandfather knew, it'd be her. She'd traveled with him the most, even before he fell in love with my grandmother.

I braided my wet hair and listened for sounds of Grandad waking. Ioan had already taken off to feed his horses. At least, that's what I assumed. He'd been inviting and strangely comfortable around me the last week, but he'd returned to the aloof man last night. No more than a nod and Ioan left for his room—leaving me confused and alone in the hallway. I should blame myself. When he'd lain on the bed a week before, I'd wanted him far away. But twelve hours ago, when he went to his room, I wanted him close.

None of it made sense.

My hand turned Grandad's doorknob—igniting an image in my mind. Ioan was shaking his head, facing a frustrated William. Saturday. I'd forgotten that William came home on the weekends. Ioan grunted and lifted a hay bale from the corner of the barn with William trailing behind him. *What are you doing, Ioan? She's not Lacy.*

Ioan moved another bale. I could feel the strain of his arms, the heaviness of the hay. He pulled a utility knife from his back pocket and sliced the twine.

William folded his arms, his eyes wild. *Quit ignoring me. This isn't a game.*

Ioan swallowed and tilted his head. He knew I was watching. I had zero proof but I could tell.

My stomach twisted. He was keeping information from me—and he was not William's enemy. They'd not come to blows, but they were most definitely not friends. At least, that's what I'd thought. A chill wrapped around my neck, settling in my chest. If William and Ioan were close, then William could have called Ioan when I'd hurt my ankle. Or texted him at the very least. William *had* come to pick me up from the train station. Ioan's sketches of me and the falcon, all of that information could have been given to Ioan from William. The question was *why?* What benefit would either of them gain from confusing me?

I'm telling her. The words faded from my head. I couldn't tell who'd spoken them, William or Ioan. Energy drained from me. I ran to my room and held my phone, not knowing how or what to text Lacy. Other than Grandad, she was the closest member of my family. And yet, she'd been just as determined as my parents to get me here. *Why* echoed in my head.

How's the wedding planning going? was all I could text, instead of *What the hell is going on* or *What aren't you telling me about Ioan?*

And William. What part did he play? He'd mentioned Lacy the first day I'd come. This was the first time in my life that my parents weren't pulling the strings. When my parents did their usual push and pull dance, there was always success involved—grad school, better job. Helping Grandad in Cornwall didn't fit that category.

Lacy and I were close—right? If we were, I shouldn't be scared to be honest. Taking a deep breath, I texted, *What aren't you telling me? What are William and Ioan hiding from me?*

The three bubbles indicating Lacy was typing started moving. And then nothing. She had to've read the text but not responded. I waited. Again, nothing.

I sat on the bed, the phone in my hand, my throat dry and pulse racing. The bubbles reappeared. Then disappeared.

The stack of sketchbooks was still on my nightstand where Ioan had left them. At this point, I now wondered if he'd even been the artist.

My head ached trying to understand what in the world was going on. Lydcombe was once my sanctuary. Tucking my phone in my back pocket, I grabbed my camera. Even if I didn't know the ins and outs of what was happening, there was one thing I could control.

The groans of the hallway welcomed me, reminding me that not everything had changed. I slipped inside Grandad's room. As quietly as I could, I opened the curtains. Soft morning light spilled into the room.

Grandad lay with his mouth open and face calm. Through the camera lens he looked like two different people, the grandfather and the stranger. His painting easel was folded, leaning against the wall. His brushes and paints were abandoned in a half-opened case. He'd not painted in a while. Even when he hadn't recognized me, he'd continued to paint.

After snapping a few pictures of his easel, I checked his closet. Not a canvas in sight, even the small four-by-six canvases. An old pair of my grandmother's boots was in the back. My heart melted. Grandad had given most of her things away when she'd died, insisting that she'd want her family to have a piece of her. I pulled a boot out but noticed a stack of sketchbooks. Grabbing one, my heart stopped. They were the same gray blue of Ioan's. Page after page were the sketches, the same simple charcoal strokes from his books. There were sketches of my grandmother. Of Grandad. And of a boy—*the* boy I imagined as a child. His hair was unkempt and his eyes searching. I'd always thought he was lost. I grabbed another book. And froze.

The first page was me on my back, the falcon in the sky, a near identical sketch to the one Ioan had shown me. The next drawing was of me holding a baby in my arms, my gaze to someone off the page. The next, a woman in medieval clothes writing into her skin. The falcon was after her, sitting on top of the falcon monument. The next drawing—me, placing a palm to Ioan's chest, his eyes closed. We were on the bed.

I dropped the book and scooted backward. Ioan and I hadn't been separated long enough for him to hurry and draw it. Or stuff the book in the back of my grandfather's closet. Cradling my head, I rocked back and forth. None of this was making any sense.

Grandad grumbled, his lips smacking. I grabbed my camera and placed it in front of the book. Someone was going to have to explain this. Grandad was sitting up. His eyes bulged at the sight of me.

I curtseyed—like an idiot. He wouldn't recognize me but I didn't want him to be scared. "Hi ... Grandad—I mean Liam. It's good to see you."

His brow furrowed. He held up a hand. I was too far away for him to touch me. He shook his head, as if to clear it. I stepped closer. He blinked and wiped his face.

"Did you sleep well...Liam?" His name didn't feel right on my tongue. He was *Grandad.* And would always be a simple grandfather to me.

"Is it time?" He looked down at his feet. "Have you come to collect me?"

"Sure. Doris should be here by now." I clutched the book and camera. This was the clearest he'd spoken to me. "Do you want to go down to breakfast together?"

"Breakfast?" He scoffed. "They serve breakfast?"

Grief pricked my heart. He might have spoken clearly, but his mind was anything but. "Yeah, they do."

He narrowed his gaze. "You're not Elyna."

"I'm Sienna Rothesay." A lump formed in my throat.

"Tell her she's late." He pursed his lips. "She never returned."

"Tell Sienna she's late?" This had taken a turn I'd not expected. "Why is she late?"

He made a fist with his hand. "She's late. Elyna's late. She should be here by now."

A thought wiggled in, inviting hope. This was the longest Grandad had talked with me in years. "Can you help me find her?"

"You don't know?" Grandad cocked his head to the side. He stood and slowly walked to the window. He pointed a shaking finger to the sea. "She's there."

The chill embraced me once more. A compulsion, from years of capturing moments, brought the camera to my eye. My grandfather kept his vigil, his eyes crinkling—as if the sea brought joy. My lips quirked. The man in front of me, for the briefest of moments, was Liam Rothesay, lover of the Bristol Sea—my grandfather once more.

✢ 29 ✢

S ienna
    Lydcombe, England: Present Day

ॐ

THE MORNING LIGHT IN MY GRANDFATHER'S ROOM PAINTED THE
truth in prettier colors. Ioan and William were lying to me, possibly
Lacy as well, but watching Grandad murmur the lullaby he once sang
to me made everything insignificant. A rush of memories came over
me, underlined by each click of the camera. Grandad walked to his
easel and without dipping the brushes in the paint, began creating a
work of art. He kept his eye on the sea, his hand massaging the
wooden easel. There was no paint. No canvas, but there was peace in
watching Grandad continue to create. At least in his mind.

    Pots and pans were clanking below. Doris must have arrived. Ioan
would be back from caring for his horses. And done talking to William
about me.

    My throat went dry. A day of uncomfortable questions was not how
I'd pictured today to be. Instead of descending toward the kitchen, I
took the back staircase, leading toward the sea. A few feet from the

house I turned around. Grandad was still at the window, his palm on the glass. A few clicks and I lowered my camera. These pictures were how Grandad would be remembered. It didn't seem fair or right. The jovial voice and color paintings, *that's* what should be remembered. Not the vacant stares and blank canvases.

The breeze picked up, combing my hair with whispers. Voices danced around me, singing and beckoning me to touch the water. I climbed on the wall at the edge of the front garden, the trail below me. Overgrown vines and grass covered the neglected path.

Behind me, I knew Doris was cooking breakfast and Ioan would be arriving any minute. I laid the camera on the wall, cracking open the book once more. This time I started at the back. The sketch was of me, my camera in front of my face but in the lens was the reflection of a police horse jumping a barricade. The picture I'd captured that day had snagged me a humanitarian award. I should run back inside and demand answers, one being who'd sketched this picture. It couldn't have been Grandad. He wasn't traveling when I was at the protest. He wasn't coherent enough and hadn't been for several years. If Ioan had drawn the image, why was it in my grandfather's closet?

The whispers grew louder, fluttering the pages of the book. The breeze stilled on a drawing toward the center. A man tying a woman's hands and feet up at the top right of the page. Both the man and the woman were dressed in ancient clothes. History wasn't my strong suite, leaving me to wonder what century. In the middle of the page a different man was embracing her, his frame shorter than the first. And finally, the woman staring at waves below—her bare feet on the cliffs above.

She's there. Grandad had pointed at the sea when he'd said it. I snapped the book shut. My mind was playing tricks on me. I rubbed my temples, feeling the fatigue of the last couple sleepless weeks. The voices started singing. Maybe my mind only knew how to trick me. I'd been playing tug-of-war with the water since I was a child. Maybe it was time to give in.

Leaving the book, my phone and the camera on the wall, I slid down the wall and carefully made my way down the path. The compression sock kept my ankle from throbbing. The uneven terrain sent sharp pains up my leg. The sock seemed to only work if I kept my foot level. The gorse became thicker, the yellow flowers nearly naked from the wind stealing their petals.

I heard shouting from up above. The voice sounded male—William or Ioan. The whispers grew louder. I covered my ears and took another step. Glancing up, the cliffs in the drawing were wrong. The edge of my grandfather's property wasn't high enough. The sketch had steep cliffs, the water swirling at its feet. The drawing of the ancient woman was of somewhere else.

The singing continued, wrapping around my wrist and gently leading me forward. My foot slid on the rocky step—my ankle screamed at me. The voices shouted in my head, refusing to be cast aside. Another step and they calmed. And another. The whispers became gentle. Alluring.

The waves crashed against the rocks, spraying me and the trail. Voices shouted—but not from the water. Another step.

The path turned to a cemetery of smooth rocks. My ankle struggled. To stay upright, I placed a palm on the rocky wall. A memory came to life. I was young and running after my brothers. They were betting each other to jump into the water. They were bolstered by the rare sunny day. Lacy wore a frilly summer dress, her strappy heels in her hand and her legs dangling over the edge. I'd been left behind again. I couldn't keep up because I'd lost the battle over my outfit with my mother. She'd wanted me to match Lacy but my legs were half her size. A tea length skirt on her trailed on the ground for me. The fabric would catch on the buckles of my dress shoes, tripping me. Twice, I'd been yelled at for hiking my skirt above my knees. I wasn't running toward them but the song. The whispers.

Like a snap, the memory disappeared.

The water swirled and splashed against the rocks. Closing my eyes, I felt the pull once more. With a hand on the wall, I hobbled closer to the water—with each step, the waves quieted.

The foaming of the water seemed to take on a shape, a form of a woman. Another wave and the form disappeared. I shivered. Glancing down, the water was up to my knees. I gripped the gorse on the wall to keep myself steady but the waves pulled me forward. Gently, like an embrace, I felt the waters envelope me. My body shook. The water was cold. Another step. The water up to my chest.

A woman swam nearby, her hair dark auburn. My footing slipped. A wave splashed my head. I wiped my face. The woman was gone. My hand was losing its grip. I looked around, the woman was farther away but she didn't seem to be swimming. She was too far away to see her expression. All I could see was her shape.

"Sienna!" Someone called from above.

The woman held out her hand, beckoning me.

"Sienna!" a man shouted.

She spoke, but I couldn't understand her. She was too far away. The woman started singing, the melody the same as my grandfather's lullaby. She pointed up, toward the house. Toward Grandad.

I let go of the gorse. The water rose. I started swimming. My foot caught. The woman started shouting. Hands grabbed my shoulders. I spun around—smack into Ioan's chest. "Let go."

He grunted and wrapped an arm around me, dragging me through the waters. His hands raked the gorse and pulled us toward the trail.

I struggled in his grasp. "I said, let go."

He didn't answer. Ioan's entire focus was on getting me out of the water. I pulled at his fingers. He tightened his grip, his bicep and forearm taut.

"Are you deaf?" I twisted—he spun me back around.

With a grunt, he heaved me up on the path. "No. I'm not."

"What are you doing?" My teeth chattered.

"We need to get you inside." He sat with his back against the wall, his breathing labored.

"Answer my question. What are you doing?" I wasn't going inside or anywhere with him.

He bent his knees and wiped his face. I wanted to scream at him— I didn't need him to rescue me. There was maybe a foot or two between the end of the trail and where I was.

"There was no reason for you to freak out and jump in."

He scowled. "I could say the same thing."

"I didn't jump in."

"Then what exactly were you doing?" he shouted, revealing a side of him I'd not yet seen. He was either aloof or comforting—or talking to William about me. But angry, this was new. "You promised me you wouldn't go alone."

"When?"

He held up a finger. "The first day you came back. I said to not go alone."

"Congratulations, you actually told me something." When he blanched, I added, "We both know I saw your conversation with William."

"No. You saw William talking."

Using the wall, I scrambled to my feet. "You lied to me."

He turned his face to me, whispering, "I've never lied to you. Not then and not now."

The tenderness of his voice caught me off guard. "What were you talking about? What don't I know?"

"It's about your family." Ioan swallowed hard. He rubbed his neck, grimacing.

"You mean Lacy."

He unfolded his legs and stood, his frame taking up most of the trail. "I mean your grandfather."

I folded my arms against the chill of the water. "I heard the name Lacy."

"There's a reason why your parents wanted you here."

"They didn't trust you." That was obvious.

He sighed and brushed past me. "And they shouldn't."

"What's that supposed to mean?" When he didn't answer, I ran up the steps—my ankle screaming at me. I pulled at his elbow. "Answer me."

He turned, his arm under mine. His touch warmed me—and I hated it. This wasn't natural. Or remotely normal.

"It means ..." He glanced out to the waters. Tucking his chin, he said, "Liam had said he didn't want the house to go to his children. He can't stop the barony from being passed on, but he can stop the house from going to your dad. And aunts and uncles."

"Grandad is disinheriting my family?" My family didn't always get along, but this was a whole new level of separation. "Are you telling me Lydcombe won't stay in the family?"

He didn't meet my gaze.

"Ioan, look at me." There was more going on. I hadn't known Ioan long, but his hesitation was all but shouting at me. I gripped his fore-arm. "Is this what William was talking about? That Lacy knows and I don't?"

He inhaled sharply. "It's worse than that."

"What could be worse?" My fingers dug into his sleeve, and my teeth chattered once more. The sun was out, but the cold sea water blocked the summer weather from warming me.

"Liam's giving me the house."

30

 enan
　　Swansea, South Wales: 1606

THE SHIP WAS FILLED WITH WINE AND WOOL BUT ONLY A FRACTION
of the men it normally carried. There wasn't the good-natured sparring
while loading, a sound Kenan cherished. His men were brothers, a
family forged on the water. The remaining crew said little after Kenan
had told of Matthew's mutiny and the poisoning of his men. More than
anything, Kenan had not told them he would be leaving them. The
silence weighed heavy on Kenan's shoulders, but nothing more than
the worry of what he must do. Kenan could not endanger his men
again, nor would he abandon Elyna.

"Everything's ready." He held out his hand to Jowan. "I'll meet you
at the island."

Jowan hesitated before accepting Kenan's hand. Neither man
looked fit to travel.

With a basket in one hand, his mother looped her other arm in
Jowan's, her head against his shoulder. "Be careful."

"He will be," Kenan promised. He avoided her gaze. She'd sided with Jowan last night, urging Kenan to leave Elyna behind. Kenan wouldn't. He knew Elyna was safe at the moment. He didn't trust Matthew's temper to hold much longer.

Jowan's mother crossed herself and shook her head. True to her role as a preacher's wife, she said, "Godspeed." She embraced her son. Stepping back, her hand lingered on Jowan's face, a thumb caressing just under his swollen eye.

"Ay, mum. I'll be fine." He enveloped her hand between his. "I'll be on the next ship over."

"Ay." She knew the lie but like the mum she was, didn't pierce the hope with the truth. The ship wouldn't return, the season too far gone. She would be separated from her son for the rest of the year. She turned to Kenan. "Please ... leave with Jowan."

"He won't mum," her son said softly. "Kenan's got too much of his mother in him. Not enough Rothesay."

Kenan clasped a hand over his chest and gasped. "You've hit your mark, Jowan."

Jowan grinned, his eyes twinkling. "I've never missed."

"Boys ..." His mother blinked back tears. "Done. 'Tis finally done. No more of Rothesay."

The weight in Kenan's chest lifted. For over a decade, Jowan had followed Kenan—on a ship, into battle, and now, into retirement. They would be their own masters now. No more of his father's demands. Their lives would play out on the island, leaving only to bring in a shipment from the continent or transferring to hidden ports in Cornwall.

"Godspeed." Mrs. Wair sniffed. She'd prayed for this day to come, her pleas vocal and consistent.

Kenan left the mother to speak with her son, drifting back toward the barn. He'd need another sip of willow bark to keep his head from throbbing. Elyna had given clues, a flicker of an image but nothing solid to help Kenan get ahead of Matthew. She'd given glimpses of her view, the direction of their journey.

With Jowan and his men safely aboard the fluyt, Kenan readied inside the barn. This was where he and Elyna would hide until they could safely get to the island. The timing wasn't right and they ran the risk of Muiris finding them, or worse, Rothesay. But Kenan's men would be hidden away, protected by powerful winds and mercurial currents.

The familiar stream of knocks sounded and Mrs. Wair entered the loft in a rush. "The butcher's son came running. A pair of men are circling the town. A ginger-haired woman is with them. They're headed north of town to the Severn ferry."

"It's too late in the year." But Matthew wouldn't know that. He was a Dover man. He wouldn't know the seasons of ferry or inner Bristol ports. Only a smuggler would memorize tides and currents. Not a mercenary.

She grinned. "The ferryman will have it cleaned and ready."

"It'll look like it's running." Bless the woman. "You've arranged for it?"

"Ay." The look of pride faltered, her face sobering. "Promise me you're done, Kenan."

"I'll owe nothing to my father."

She shook her head. "You never did. He made his own mess of things. Helping your mother leave that man is a blessing, not a debt."

"And yet, it's cost the lives of so many men." Kenan followed her out of the barn.

"You're a good man." Like she had hours before with Jowan, she raised her hand to Kenan's face. "You've treated us well. It's time to go live your life."

Kenan squeezed her hand and gave a sharp nod. "Tomorrow will be better."

"Only if you let it." She let her hand fall to her side. "You gave an oath to a worried grandmother and now promised a mother. Don't play me false."

"I wouldn't be in this mess if I could turncoat on my word." He felt the pull to Elyna. He needed silence to hear and see what she was experiencing. "I'll head to the graveyard."

"Keep to the outer brush. You're known in these parts," Mrs. Wair warned—a mother to her core.

"That used to be a good thing." Kenan paid a good wage and a portion of profits for those who'd worked with him for several years.

But coin in the hand could switch a man's loyalty, especially when war had drained so many pockets—from farmer to nobleman.

Only the worn graves near the church were true to their purpose. The monuments on the outer edge were filled with smuggled goods. Along the Severn River were dozens of graveyards just like this. Monuments filled with untaxed goods waiting to be sold under the king's nose. This church at least had a priest, Jowan's father. The man would walk from a room or cover his ears, a knowing smile on his lips. He could keep his word with God—and line his family's pockets. The eldest son was the priest on Kenan's island—his wife just as helpful to Kenan's cause as Jowan's mother.

Kenan hopped the fence, passing the empty monuments—the contraband already taken aboard the ship, safely on their way to *Ynes Wair* Island for storage. Bracing himself on the fence post, he felt for Elyna's sight. His view shifted, showing the back of Matthew's head. Her hands were tied and she sat on the saddle, her horse being led by Matthew. She glanced around—she knew Kenan was looking. Matthew was down to only one man. Something had happened to the other mercenaries. Before Kenan could wonder, Elyna asked Matthew, *What will you tell the parents of your men?*

Matthew scowled over his shoulder. *Hold your tongue. Or I'll remove it myself. Better yet, I'll have the boy do it.*

Rothesay won't pay for a marred woman.

He spun around. *I'll not warn you again.*

Warn? She giggled, the mischief false. Kenan could feel her pulse racing. She was playacting. Her gaze flicked to her wrists. Dried blood from repeated rope burns marked her tender skin. Bruises dotted her forearms. She'd not been treated well. Kenan's heart sank. His father would take her marks as an invitation for Rothesay to do the same. Her injuries announced her iron will—a temptation Rothesay could not withstand.

I believe it's you who was warned, Matthew. Her voice dipped.

Matthew clenched his jaw. He reached over and pulled on her wrists. She winced. His lips quirked to a smile at her pain. *I'll not be frightened by a witch. You've two destinies, woman. Either you're sold to Rothesay, or I'll light the match and burn you myself.*

Is that fear in your eyes? She whispered. *I should know, your men had the same look in their eye when they died.*

Matthew smacked a hand across her face. Kenan braced himself, the view dizzying. Matthew pulled her wrists toward him with one hand. Kenan felt her stiffen, trying to stay upright. Matthew gripped her throat with his other hand. Her heart beat wildly, her mind racing.

Kenan whispered, "Where are you?"

Matthew dropped his hands like he'd been burned. *What did you say?*

Elyna coughed and rubbed her neck. *You had your hand at my neck. I've said nothing.*

Your superstition will not work on me. He narrowed his gaze. *Rothesay will pay me for my two treasures. That I know.*

She grinned. *And yet you're hearing voices.*

He raised his hand. Kenan yelled, "No!" Matthew froze, glancing around. Elyna pulled her gaze to the sky. Off in the distance was the spire of the church. They were half a mile away. Too far for Matthew to've heard Kenan's yell.

Kenan stopped. Matthew had heard him. Elyna was in trouble—but she was very much a witch.

Matthew tossed Elyna's lead rope to the horse next to him—a boy, not more than ten or twelve years of age was on the horse. Elyna's heart calmed after Matthew had tossed the lead rope. She was fond of the boy.

Kenan shook Elyna from his mind and started down the smuggler's tunnel. If he hurried, the tunnel would spit him out just before Matthew could cross the last bridge toward the church. Down and around, Kenan ran, his pistol on his belt and his rifle strapped across his back. The willow bark crept through his veins, calming the throbbing of his head. He climbed the old yew tree, his heart in his throat. He looped a leg over the branch and braced the rifle against another, thicker branch. His vision blurred, his head aching. Kenan kept his body taut and his finger on the trigger.

For what seemed like hours, Matthew's bay horse stepped in line. Kenan felt Elyna searching. He swallowed hard, pushing her from his mind. He would save her but he didn't trust her. Not yet.

Matthew's horse snorted, tossing its head. Matthew turned the horse toward Elyna and pointed at her chest. He reached for the lead rope, ripping it from the boy's hand. Matthew's chest was too close to Elyna. If Kenan's aim was off, he'd injure her—or worse, kill the woman he'd sworn to protect.

Pointing at Kenan, the boy shouted and stepped in front of Elyna. She handed him something small and dark. Matthew pulled a pistol from his belt and followed the boy's finger—aiming the gun at Kenan. Matthew spurred his horse toward him. In a blur, Matthew was too close for the rifle. Kenan fired at the ground. The horse reared. Matthew fell. Kenan fired again, the horse bucked and ran, racing over the bridge. Matthew growled. He fired at the tree, his hand shaking. Kenan swung the rifle over his shoulder and cocked the pistol.

"You're hiding in a tree like a coward," Matthew taunted. "You can't stand and face me? You're a Rothesay to the core."

A horse neighed by the bridge. Kenan refused to take his eyes off Matthew and look. The sound of carriage wheels carried up to where Kenan perched in the tree.

"Sir, are you hurt?" a familiar voice asked Matthew.

Kenan froze, his heart racing—the voice belonged to Jowan's father.

Matthew ran toward the carriage, shouting, "Help me!"

Kenan scrambled down the tree. He couldn't warn Jowan's father without giving away their close relationship. Elyna and the boy were to Kenan's right, their horses behind them. They were too close for Kenan's comfort. Matthew could change his aim in an instant. He stood directly in front of Kenan, Mr. Wair at the other end of Matthew's gun.

"You're the spitting image of your son." Matthew's gun aimed at Mr. Wair's head. "The rumors are true. You've staked your claim in the smuggling business."

Mr. Wair spoke low and steady. "Son, I'm a priest. I've dedicated my soul to—"

"Save it." Matthew cocked the gun. "Kenan, drop the gun or your friend is gone."

Kenan's hand shook. He'd taken too much from Jowan. Kenan was failing, hurting those who'd surrounded him. Loved him.

"Kenan ..." Mr. Wair's cooed. "I'm at peace."

"Shut your mouth, priest," Matthew snapped, a vein on his neck bulging.

"Tell Jowan—"

A gun blew. Wair crumpled to the ground.

"No!" Kenan cried, firing his gun at Matthew. "No!"

Kenan fell back, his shoulder in pain. He sat up, blindly firing again. Elyna was at his side, the boy trailing her.

And then nothing.

✣ 31 ✣

S ienna
  Lydcombe, England: Present Day

❦

WITH MY HAND ON THE GARDEN WALL, I BALKED AT IOAN. "YOU'RE
lying." My voice cracked and my teeth chattered. The breeze chilled
me to the bone—my wet clothes not helping.

"I didn't believe it either," Ioan offered gently. "But Lacy found the
paperwork. Liam assigned Lydcome to my family's estate."

Of course Lacy had found the paperwork. Her stepfather—my
uncle—was a posh solicitor in London. "My parents would have said
something. Anything."

"They're hoping to change his mind."

"He doesn't have his own mind. How could he change it?" I pushed
Ioan out of the way and marched up the path, ignoring the whispers of
the sea. He was lying. It couldn't be true. "My parents wouldn't have let
you within an inch of this place if they knew."

"They don't have a choice." Regret filled his words.

"What do you mean?" I shot back.

"I'm the executor of his will."

"No." This was why Ioan was here. Grandad had given him the reins. A tear slid down my cheek. Grandad was giving Ioan the house. This was the real reason William was upset with Ioan. Lady Morgannwg's son was going to inherit *another* house. Fate had given him a castle and the barn near Grandad's house. And now Lydcombe.

My heart ached. Not only was Lydcombe no longer going to be my family's ancestral home, but Lacy had known. And never told me. Neither had my family. Was I thought of so little that I didn't deserve to be told the biggest secret of the family—did no one care about Lydcome? About me?

Ioan said nothing more, but I knew he was behind me. My body shivered, freezing from my impromptu water adventure. I opened the side door. Doris was aiming a finger at William who looked entirely too comfortable on the barstool. They turned at my entrance, both eyes wide.

"Sienna?" Doris rushed over. "You're cold as ice."

Shrinking from her touch, I blurted, "Did you know?"

"Know what?" She paused, her eyes scanning me. Worry filled her face, her lips taut. "You're soaked through. We need to get you out of these clothes."

"Did you know?" My voice cracked.

Ioan entered behind me. William slid off the barstool, a slow grin appearing on his face. "I volunteer as tribute. Taking one's clothes off is my expertise."

"Stop it," I snapped—halting William's progression. "Stop pretending to be interested in me. Is it true? Is Grandad leaving the house to Ioan?"

"What?" Doris's back straightened. She turned to Ioan. "That's not true, is it?"

"You threw him in the sea?" William chuckled nervously, his eyes flitting about, touching everything but me. "How can I not flirt with you now? Do y'know how many times I've wanted to do that?"

"Don't." The bite in my voice silenced the room. Without looking to my right, I knew Ioan stood there with shame in his hunched shoulders. I leveled William with a glare. "How did you find out?"

He shrugged and pulled on his collar. "It's Lydcombe. We know everything about everyone."

"It's true?" Doris shook her head and backed away. "Oh, love. I'm so sorry."

Backing away from them, I pointed to William. "You're lying. Doris didn't know."

William smiled, his eyes twinkling. "Hey now—"

"Get out." I refused to look at him. "Now."

"Sienna—"

"I said get out," I screamed, watching everyone wince at my tone.

Doris turned to William. "I think you should leave, my boy."

William's mouth fell open. He narrowed his gaze. "And of course Ioan stays. How is that fair? The man's conned you out of your inheritance." He side-stepped Doris. "Lacy reached out to me. She wanted to know just how involved Knight In Shining Armor is."

Ioan nodded sheepishly. "Liam did the will before his mind had declined."

"That's debatable." William scoffed. "The guy's been a half step from the mad hatter's residence for a decade."

"Sienna, you need to get out of your wet clothes." Doris held out her arms, ushering us toward the staircase. "You too, Ioan." Tossing over her shoulder to William, she said, "I'll send for you when they're dressed."

William rolled his eyes. "I won't hold my breath."

Without a word or even a glance to Ioan, I climbed the stairs, the compression sock no longer providing comfort to my throbbing ankle. The rocky terrain in my walk to the sea must have damaged it more. The long hot shower didn't lift my thoughts. A grief I didn't understand weighed on my shoulders. If Lydcombe was gone, everything that reminded me of my grandfather would be as well. I'd ridiculed my family for their obsessions with rank, title and material possessions. I guess I was just another Rothesay. Grandad dying was inevitable but not having Lydcombe, that was incomprehensible. My summers were spent here—a camera in my hand and a brush in his.

My phone lay discarded on the bed, several texts from Lacy, ranging from confusion to confession. The last one, *William just filled me in. In a mtg. Will call when done.*

She'd known about Grandad's estate giving the house to Ioan. My parents would be livid, although I doubted they believed my uncle. There was a weird friction between all the siblings. They were in competition with each other on who was the most enlightened. It was the most polite battle I'd ever witnessed. Their weapon of choice was paperwork and whispers. Or sending a daughter to the house—my heart sank. I was just a pawn.

Ioan knocked on the door and entered, wearing a hoodie with *Cardiff University: Prifysgol Caerdydd* emblazoned on the front. The sweatshirt was another reminder of Ioan's perspective, one foot in England, the other in Wales.

"Listen ..." He rubbed his jaw with his thumb. "You and Liam are the last people on this planet I would hurt. I'm not trying to steal your inheritance. I thought if you came. I thought if you were around Liam —you could change his mind. Put it in your name. Or at least convince him the curse was over."

"Lydcombe was never mine." My phone was in my hands, the text thread open. My stomach growled. The impromptu dip in the ocean had delayed breakfast. "It would have gone to my father or at least someone in the family." There would have been an opportunity to still visit, to still run a hand over the walls and hear the creak of the stairs.

"But it could be." He leaned against the wall, crossing one ankle over the other. "The stipulations are that I have to own it for several years before determining what to do with it."

"I can't afford to live here." My career as a photographer was not even remotely lucrative. The paltry income and low status I received was a stain on my family's stellar existence. "I just wish I was told."

"Would that have changed anything?" He held up his hands when my head shot up. "I'm not saying it's right. I'm just asking. Would you have still come if you knew before boarding that plane?"

"I don't know." And it didn't matter. I was here now. "Why have me come? It couldn't have just been about the house."

He broke our gaze, turning his head toward the sea. "Liam helped me uncover our shared past, but he wasn't the missing link." He turned back, leveling me with a sober expression. "You are."

"I hear whispers. That doesn't have anything to do with you and Grandad."

He frowned. "When I said *our shared past*, I wasn't referring to Liam. I meant you and me."

"Because you pulled me from the water?" That was a memory I still didn't have. I'd been told I was ten or twelve-ish, but Ioan wasn't in any childhood memories. "Because sometimes we have some weird ESP connection?"

He jutted his chin. "That's what you call it? A weird ESP connection?"

Groaning, I hung my head between my hands. "And now we're arguing over what to call it? Someone please tell me this is insane."

"Your grandfather knew that Elyna Morgannwg was born to an earl, one that lost his mind."

"To mercury. You already told me." That had no bearing on my life or Grandad's.

"She was pulled from the Bristol Sea as well." He came closer, sitting on the very edge of the bed. His eyes took on a fevered glint, a vein on his neck twitching. His arms were taut. "What I need to know is *who* pulled her, who saved her that day."

"What are you talking about?" I swallowed the growing suspicion. Tension radiated from him. "I don't know why this Elyna is important." *Elyna.* Grandad had called me by that name earlier. "That's a question for my grandfather."

"You don't understand." He came closer, his aftershave tickling my nose.

"Clearly."

"There's more to it than just the house." Ioan rubbed his jaw. "Liam didn't want to give me Lydcombe."

"Then why—"

"Every Rothesay son, except for the last born, met tragedy. They never inherit Lydcombe. And they won't, not until the curse is broken." He shook his head, sighing. "Liam is doing this to protect your father. To protect you."

"A curse?" I wanted to laugh, but Ioan's frown and downcast eyes made it impossible. He'd mentioned a curse a few times, but Doris had called my parents a curse on my grandfather. *Curse* was relative, literally. "You're kidding, right?"

He didn't meet my gaze. "Look at your ancestry. Only the youngest son is alive long enough to inherit."

Grandad was granted the barony after his older brother met tragedy. That wasn't enough to convince me. "Ioan—"

"It's true, Sienna." He stood and began pacing in front of me. "All of it. The connection ..." He waved his finger between us. "One of us has to be Welsh, the other has to be Cornish. But the connection is always the same."

"Because I was born here and you were born in Wales, that connects our minds?" A giggle escaped. I couldn't help it. There'd been too much in too short of a time. I'd arrived just a few weeks ago. There wasn't enough space for me to process the weirdness. I'd just discovered that the one place I'd called home was assigned to someone else. "There are other reasons for having a psychic experience. I had to photograph Madam—"

"The boy, Sienna." He stopped in front of me, his arms folded. "You and I see the same boy. Liam saw him too. Both Liam and I see things, sometimes it's the future. Sometimes it's the past. Liam's the reason I started drawing. It took years of him teaching me but he was right, it makes me feel less crazy."

"You're contradicting yourself." Leaning back against the bed, I sighed. "You were born in Wales. Grandad was born here in Cornwall. I was born in Cornwall. Aren't we missing another person born in Wales?"

Ioan swallowed hard. "My mother."

32

S ienna
 Lydcombe, England: Present Day

GRIEF HUMMED IN MY VEINS. THE IMPENDING CHAOS THAT WOULD happen once my parents accepted Ioan was in fact inheriting the house made me exhausted. No one could launch social warfare like a Rothesay. "What does your mother have to do with Grandad?"

"Everything." Whatever Ioan was about to confess, the worry in his eyes and the crack in his voice told me I would hate it. He hesitated, an apology in his tone. "Your grandfather visited the island the same year my mother visited for her grade school—"

"Don't." I covered my ears. My grandfather would not take advantage of a small child. Not the gentle man I'd known. "Don't even think—"

"They're the same age, Sienna." His voice came as a sigh. Fatigue hung on every word. I hated that it relaxed me, but he'd been here every day for years on end while I hid behind my camera in the states.

He cleared his throat nervously. "My mother gave birth to me months after her fiftieth birthday."

"That doesn't—"

"They would meet on the island every summer until Liam attended—"

"Swansea University." Grandad loved Wales. My family had assumed it was because of his Welsh university days. He even spoke a few phrases here and there.

"He brought home the woman he wanted to marry." Liam scratched his head, a nervous tick. "Liam's parents were angry that he wanted a Welsh wife, especially when her brother's in a mental hospital. Liam gave in and signed up to serve his country."

"He traveled the world until he found my grandmother." He'd loved her. By his own voice, he'd confessed his steady affection for my grandmother. They were different, I'd grant him that, but they loved each other. Deeply.

"Mum eventually married, giving up hope that Liam would return." Ioan shrugged and laid his head back against the wall. He closed his eyes for a brief moment. The temptation to reach out and touch him shocked me. He'd delivered horrible news. He was the reason my family would no longer have Lydcombe, and yet here I sat, my shoulder next to his as if I'd known him all my life. Ioan turned his head, his brow furrowed in worry. "Liam did return, but only after his brother passed away. That's when he realized the curse was still a thing and not some silly superstition."

"What curse?" I held up a finger. "Before you answer that. If he believed it was real, why not tell someone?"

"How many people have you told about hearing the whispers?" He smirked and covered my finger with his hand. "Or about me being in here ..." He tapped his forehead. "It doesn't roll off the tongue, now does it?"

"You're too comfortable with me." My voice shook.

A flicker of pain crossed his features. He dropped my hand but kept his gaze on mine. "Do you want me to leave?"

"No." I broke our gaze. This was madness. I should be furious with him—yelling, screaming. *Something.*

"Liam had the same connection with my mom. It would ebb and flow, sometimes grow stronger and sometimes weaker." He bent one knee and propped an arm over it. "When someone's in your head, even if it's not a steady stream or hit and miss, you get accustomed to it. You start thinking of it as yours. Unless you're William. He only craves what's mine."

I stiffened. "I'm not yours."

"I'm well aware." He chuckled, his finger tapping the top of his knee. Ioan vacillated between aloof and affectionate. The sound of his easy chuckle caught me off guard. "But William knows you've been on my mind. He doesn't know the specifics but he's chased Lacy whenever she's visiting her mum's family."

"That's maybe a handful of times a year." Not enough to form a strong attachment.

Ioan nodded. "We get together every time. William thinks Lacy and I have a thing." He shook his head. "But all I ever did was ask about you."

"You realize you sound like a stalker." I should leave.

He sobered. "Do I make you feel uncomfortable?"

"One-hundred percent, yes."

He moved to leave. I grabbed his shoulder. He turned, his face inches from mine. "I don't want to scare you."

"Being scared and being uncomfortable are two separate things," I whispered. We were inches from each other. I scooted back against the wall. It wasn't much but it made my pulse slow down. "You make me *very* uncomfortable. You see inside my head for crying out loud." I gave a nervous laugh. "And you have this bond with Grandad that I'm super jealous of. But..." I tucked my knees under my arms. "But I'm not scared of you. I don't know what this is between us and I don't understand or really believe in a curse."

Instead of returning to the wall next to me, he sat up and crossed his legs. "I don't know all the specifics. I just know the patterns. The youngest brother always inherits after all the older brothers die. And if you're"—he gave air quotes—"*lucky* and do live, you eventually lose your mind."

"Like your mom?" His theory was still hard to follow. "You said it was mercury poisoning." Pointing toward Grandad's room, I said, "And Grandad has Alzheimer's. That's not a curse."

"It doesn't matter how, it only matters that it happens." He sighed and returned to his earlier position, his back against the wall, careful to keep our shoulders from touching. I felt the draft from the lack of contact. I inched closer until our shoulders lightly touched. Warmth spread from his body, spreading from the touch down to my toes.

My pulse began racing. Lacy and my college friends were the ones who'd get excited over being next to a boy. They'd fantasize over their first kiss. I'd run from it—knowing I was just another toy to be gawked at. But Ioan had known me his whole life—and most of it without me acknowledging his existence. This was something completely new. If he'd peeked inside my brain or watched me, I wasn't a novelty. But a comfort. The idea of what my childhood or even my life was up to until this point seemed false or not whole, at the very least. I pulled the alpaca blanket over my legs. Not for warmth but for a reminder that at least some things were the same.

I whispered, "Neither of us are crazy, right?"

Ioan softly elbowed me. "You just walked into the sea."

"People have been going to the beach for generations." It was a weak defense, but I felt the need to fight against the idea of a curse. And of Ioan taking Lydcombe. I couldn't submit, not yet.

He leaned over, his eyes pleading. He believed in all of it. The curse. The connection. "And do they always see a woman with red hair when they go?"

"How did you know that?" My throat went dry.

"According to you, it's all just a simple ESP connection." He smirked, his eyes pale. Alluring. "And don't forget the sketchbooks. Ever wonder how they're all similar?"

An electric hum snapped between us, both a thrill and a fear. I searched for something to grasp onto, a lifeline to ground me. "You could have mimicked Grandad's drawings."

"I dare you to go through every last one of them. He has books stored in every nook and cranny of this house."

"So do you." And I should be scared. Suspicious. But with his shoulder touching mine, I couldn't truly doubt him.

"And how did the sketchbooks get that way? Did they just appear?" His eyes took on a knowing glint. I was no longer indifferent—to him or his idea of a curse.

The electric current crackled in the space between us. "You tell me."

"That's what I'm trying to do." Ioan scoffed. "You capture things just as they are, exactly how I do. Exactly how Elyna did."

"How would you know that?" I stiffened. The idea that an ancient woman was like me—a career photographer—made zero sense. "If we're so much alike, why does she appear in the sea? Why pull me into the waters?"

"Liam thought she was trying to save you. Or whoever the Rothesay is at that point. But somehow being on land causes us pain."

"What?" Pulling back, I coughed into my fist. "And you believe it? Wouldn't being in water cause more pain—as in death?"

He scooted closer. "And yet you still submit to her siren song."

I hadn't truly submitted. "Twice—once I remember, the other I don't—that's hardly submitting." The connection dulled, the electric feeling gone. "What does it matter? Even if everything you said was true, what does it change?"

"Your grandfather is going to give away your family's home to me if we don't do something." Groaning, he held out his hands in surrender. "I don't want to be the villain in this story."

"Who says you're the villain?"

He arched an eyebrow. "If there's a victim, there's always a villain."

"How do we know she's the victim?" A whisper wrapped around my neck—it wasn't a word but more of a feeling. Elyna—whoever she was —was pained. "If, and I mean a very big if, *if* what you said is true, what makes you think we can stop it? Give me one good reason we should do whatever it is you think we should be doing."

"I'd rather not go insane. And no matter how creepy or how much you think I'm a stalker, I've watched you. I've spent too much of my life watching yours to not care. I'd rather not see you lose it either." He pointed to my cell phone. "Do whatever you have to do for this to make sense to you. Call your parents. Ask about your ancestry. Every brother that lived eventually went insane."

"You're confusing genetic predisposition with a curse. Alzheimer's runs in my family." Even as I said the words, I felt the chill reappear. "And besides, your mom and Grandad were in love. There was a connection. There's nothing between us."

Ioan swallowed hard, his gaze flicked to my lips. My pulse raced. He turned from me, breaking the gaze. He whispered, "You're right. There's nothing between us."

✿ 33 ✿

K enan
Swansea, South Wales: 1606

✦

PAIN SHOT THROUGH KENAN'S SHOULDER. HE SAT UP, HIS PULSE
racing. He blinked in the darkened room. He was above the barn. His
shoulder was wrapped. And throbbing.

He licked his lips, his throat dry. The taste of bitter dwale, the
dulling agent. Details pierced him—Mr. Wair was injured. Kenan shot
to his feet, his head dizzy.

"Whoa, there soldier," Elyna cooed, her hands on his arm.

"Mr. Wair?" His voice cracked.

"He's..." She didn't wince. She didn't have to. "I'm sorry."

Kenan flinched, her memories flooding his mind. Mr. Wair's blank
stare—he'd died.

Another memory, Mrs. Wair stitching up Kenan and Matthew.
She'd not taken kindly to Elyna, throwing an icy glares and cutting
remarks. "Easy, Kenan."

230

He stilled. *Kenan.* His name on her lips dulled the pain. "Jowan ... does he know?"

Elyna nodded. "Ay, he does."

"It's my fault." Kenan gripped her shoulder to steady himself.

"I believe the blame lies with me." She pulled at the wrap to inspect the injury. "I can't see much in here. We'll need to get you downstairs."

"Where is he?" Kenan had failed Jowan deserved the truth. And quickly. "Jowan should be halfway to *Ynes Wair* by now."

"I couldn't reach him, if that's what you're asking. His mother flagged him down." Her pride at the mother was evident in her voice. "Never get between a mother and her child. She fired the rifle herself. Jowan knew it was her."

"Is he angry?" Kenan couldn't blame him. Jowan had every right to curse Kenan's name. "I can't make it right. I won't ever be able to do enough ..."

Elyna gently pulled him forward to the first step. "He's not angry with you. Only me."

"That's not right."

"There is nothing right about this." Squeezing his hand, she guided him to the next step. "We can't save everyone, Kenan."

"If you're asking me to abandon you now." Kenan felt the panic. He could no sooner leave Elyna behind than he could walk away from Jowan. One was a brother to him. The Wairs were the family he'd never had, aside from his mother. They were safety, and the reason he'd named the island after them. Only in the Wairs' embrace could Kenan have found himself and had the strength to leave his father's legacy.

"I'm afraid you might not have a choice in the matter."

"Elyna." He stiffened, his hand still in hers. "I'm a man of my word. Jowan knows that. He grew nervous at a spoken oath. But one marked by blood—even if my character could twist, I can't. My soul's bound to keep you safe."

"Ah, Kenan," she said and climbed the step to be eye level with him. "Please remember you're the good in this."

In the dimly lit staircase, Kenan was close to her. If he'd only lean forward, he could press his lips against hers. She'd never been this trusting. This soft. "Why are you bidding me farewell?"

She squeezed his hand once more. "There are some things you cannot control."

"I don't give up that easily." He wrapped an arm around her, as if he'd done it a hundred times before. The familiarity surprised him. The touch steadied him. His mind cleared and his pulse slowed.

Elyna smiled, her eyes welling with moisture. "It's tempting to believe ... to believe that by sheer will you can mend us."

"What has happened?" He gathered her against him, his heart yearning to be closer still. This pull couldn't be from the oath. It felt too raw to be anything but true.

She leaned her head on his chest and sighed. "It's not what has happened but what will."

She's a witch. Jowan was right. Kenan wrapped his other arm around her, his reserve melting away. The truth lay at his feet. She might've been a witch but Kenan didn't care. He leaned his head against hers. "Can you see what lies ahead?"

She lifted her head, her eyes searching his. "Are you not frightened?"

Kenan smiled and cradled her jaw with his hand. "Should I be?"

"Let me free you, Kenan," she whispered. "Let me break the blood oath."

"You know we can't." He leaned in. The dimly lit staircase welcomed his confession. "Even if I wanted to, and Elyna, I don't want to."

He leaned in, his lips brushing hers. Her breath hitched. He kissed her softly. His pulse soared. He would protect her. He would love her. Elyna was the keeper of his soul.

She gripped his shirt. He tightened his hold.

Elyna whimpered. "Kenan ... your feelings. They aren't real. It's the oath."

"Liar." He smiled against her lips. Peace. She could lie, but he knew the truth. "I can feel your emotions, your pulse racing."

"Don't, Kenan." She pulled away. A tear fell down her cheek. "Don't make it harder than it needs to be."

"You sound as if you're saying farewell." He wiped her tear with his thumb.

She leaned into his touch. "Because it is."

"It doesn't have to be." He placed his forehead against hers. He would not let her go so easily, his father be damned.

She stiffened and stepped down, away from his touch.

"Elyna—"

The door swung open, light spilling into the dim staircase. Jowan stood in the door of the barn. Elyna mumbled a greeting and left. The burst of light, the burgeoning of hope Kenan had felt—fled in an instant. He didn't deserve joy. Not when Jowan's father had been killed.

"Jowan ..." Kenan didn't have the words. Nothing he said could ever repay the debt, the hurt of losing Jowan's father.

"My mother is coming with us." With a grim frown, Jowan waited for Kenan to descend the stairs. "The tides are changing. We don't have much time."

Kenan placed a hand on Jowan's shoulder. "I've no words."

"I don't need your pity." He stiffened, retreating from Kenan's touch. "My mother won't stay here, and I can't blame her."

"I cannot deny her." Kenan stood dumbly, unable to comfort his friend—his brother in arms. He'd fought for years beside Jowan, only to fail him when Jowan needed him most. "I rushed from the tree the second I heard his voice."

Jowan held up a hand, his face stone. "I know who to blame."

Kenan whispered, "How can I make this right?"

"Do I have your word?" Jowan shifted his weight, his eyes dark with fury. "Will you do all that you can to make my family whole?"

Kenan retreated. "I cannot break the oath."

"So don't." Jowan scowled. "Send her with the boy to Rothesay. You promised she'd be safe. The boy can't harm her."

"She didn't shoot your father." Shame filled Kenan. He'd not protected a man of the cloth. A friend and a saint. "Matthew's to blame."

"Matthew's gun was cold."

"What?" Kenan's stomach churned. "What did you say?"

"Matthew didn't shoot my father."

Kenan's mouth fell open. "Did I misfire?" He gripped the hair on his head. His world shifted underneath him, his lungs refused to work. *Mathew's gun was cold.* Kenan bent to his knees, his injured shoulder screaming at him.

"I don't know who shot him." Jowan's voice came clipped.

"Jowan..." Kenan's tongue failed him. He glanced at his hands and held them out. Had he been the one to kill the priest? The one man who'd been more of a father than Rothesay ever would. "No, it can't be."

"We've sent post to your father, telling him of Matthew's treachery." Jowan turned from Kenan and said over his shoulder, "Elyna's horse will also be sent. A partial payment."

"I'll pay the debt." Kenan stood slowly. He couldn't heal Jowan's heartache, but at least he could save Elyna.

"You will not."

"I'll pay her debt." With each word, Kenan knew the truth. This was how he'd save her. Elyna would have her freedom. Her family would be out of Rothesay's reach. "I'll sell the island. Or the ships. I'll do what I have to."

"If you sell the island, where will we live?" Jowan growled. "That woman has—"

"Only my half."

"You know bloody well I can't own land," Jowan cried, his hands in the air. "Have you been so long without your father that you've forgotten? You and I are of different stars. Different ranks. I cannot own land. What you do affects us all."

Kenan circled Jowan, clapping a hand to his shoulder. "I'll make it right. Please. Let me make it right."

"You're the best of men." Jowan shook his head, retreating. "But you can't save everyone."

"Jowan—"

Jowan pulled away with his head hung low. His hunched shoulders pricked Kenan's heart. He followed Jowan to the hidden port, his body heavy with grief. Waves crashed against the hull of Kenan's ship. The tide was spinning. Jowan was right. Time was not their friend.

Elyna stood at the cockboat, her head bent. She lifted her head as

Kenan approached. The boy was at her side, fear in his eyes. He couldn't have been more than ten or twelve. He clung to her—his terror in the white of his knuckles and flitting glances.

"How did you convince Jowan to bring the boy?" Kenan knew his heart was good, but to harbor one of Matthew's men—even a boy— was a stretch Kenan couldn't make.

"This is Burke." Elyna wrapped an arm around the boy's shoulders. "Jowan knew you wouldn't board the ship if I wasn't on it."

"And you wouldn't board without the child?" There was little mystery as to why Jowan hated this woman. She'd strong-armed him once again.

"I'm not a child." Burke's soft voice said otherwise.

"And where is home?" Kenan couldn't discover his accent. The sooner the boy was shipped home the better. Kenan hadn't the slightest idea where the boy had come from, but Burke was once been in Matthew's possession. That fact alone would make him a target for Rothesay. Kenan's father would dig for truth—and hold it over all their heads. Burke being a child wasn't protection enough.

The boy hesitated, his hand gripping Elyna's. "My father was from Aberystwyth, sir."

"We're not going to Aberystwyth." Kenan could feel Jowan's stare from across the main deck. "We're headed to an island. I can't ask another favor of Jowan. He's suffered enough."

Burke exchanged a worried glance with Elyna, igniting Kenan's suspicion.

Elyna gathered the boy's hands. "Don't fret. This world is bound by the ink."

"If Jowan hears you, he'll begin railing against you," Kenan warned. Jowan was on the other side of the desk—not far enough for Kenan to comfortably have this conversation. "Fate cannot be controlled by a quill, woman. You'll not convince us otherwise."

Burke's lips quivered. "You promised."

"I did." She smiled, her eyes shining. Her gaze flicked to Kenan. "I never said a quill alone could control fate. By ink, by blood, and by sea. Fate cannot break that bond."

"Speak plainly," Kenan whispered. He didn't need Jowan's suspicions to grow. "The more men who hear you, the more they'll be eager to see you burn."

Burke winced. "She's not a witch, sir."

"I didn't say she was." Kenan softened his stance, his eye on the men bustling about the ship. "But I'm only one man on a boat of grieving men."

The boy reached for Elyna, his eyes full of fear once more. She wrapped him against her.

"Rothesay won't be as kind." Kenan knew his father would interrogate Burke. He'd want to know the truth. All of it.

"Rothesay won't know." With her eyes still on the boy, she smiled. "The story will be finished before he can lay a hand on him. Or me."

"Ah, woman," Kenan hissed. "You can't spout prophecies like that."

She lifted her gaze. "I know the power of sacrifice."

Kenan sighed and scratched his head. "You're speaking in riddles again."

She stepped forward, and placed a hand on his arm. In an instant, Kenan saw the boy at his side. Both were dressed in the clothes they now wore. They clung together on his island, sorrow in their stance. Rothesay was nowhere.

Kenan swallowed—neither was Elyna.

❦ 34 ❦

S ienna
Lydcombe, England: Present Day

WILLIAM DIDN'T COME OVER AFTER BREAKFAST, NOT THAT I HAD anything to say to him. I tried helping Grandad get ready for the day with Ioan but Grandad kept pointing at me, yelling, "Elyna!"

A few more agitated shouts and I slipped from his room. He'd not been this animated before. Ioan believed tragedy was inevitable with my family unless a curse was broken. My life was not a fairy tale. I'd spent the last decade capturing the truth, the raw humanity. I knew exactly what type of world I lived in. There was no happily ever after. There was grief and loss—and beauty.

With a sigh, I lay on the bed. My phone poked my back. Flipping over, I saw several missed texts from Lacy. The last one, *Call me. Now.*

My finger hovered over her profile. She'd lied to me. Maybe not outright but the sting of betrayal was very much alive. Other than Grandad, she was the only Rothesay I trusted. She wasn't my cousin by blood, but we were closer than sisters. At least, we used to be.

She answered on the first ring.

"Sienna?" Lacy's voice was worried and breathless.

Guilt crept in. I'd not given her the benefit of the doubt. Nor had I talked to her since her engagement party in her backyard. A text here and there didn't count. "Hi."

"How mad are you? Ten out of ten? Twenty out of ten?" Her words flooded through the phone. I'd watched Lacy turn combative police officers into purring kittens. If she was nervous about my feelings—did that mean Ioan was right? "It's not what you think."

"Explain it to me." I leaned against the window, my hand on the pane. Lacy hadn't a clue what I thought—about Ioan or the house. Or the safety I felt with both. They were home. I froze. Ioan shouldn't feel like home. He was a stranger. He might have affection for my grandfather, but the connection was between them. I wasn't—I *shouldn't* be a part of the equation.

"We still don't know for sure if it'll happen, but Dad swears the house is going to Ioan." Footsteps echoed. She must be pacing in her home office. She'd recently retiled the floors. She complained that her videoconference calls sounded tinny with the new acoustic feedback. "It looks that way. But let's be honest, none of us truly know until the will is read. And, I mean, that wouldn't happen until Grandad passes away. The only person who has access to it is the executor and that's—"

"Why did you encourage me to come?"

Lacy sighed. I pictured her closing her eyes and sitting in her over-sized leather chair. She would nervously run a hand through her hair before pasting a smile and sealing whatever deal she'd hatched. "I didn't mean for it to be like this. I did—I mean I *do* think it's a good idea for you to be there. To make peace with Grandad's Alzheimer's. But ..." She sighed once more. "I know Ioan needs to make peace too."

"The man believes in a curse, Lacy." I pinched the bridge of my nose. "Not hopes in it or kind of thinks about it. He thinks it's real. He thinks we're connected."

"Yeah..." Her voice trailed off. There was more going on here.

"What aren't you telling me?"

"Your father isn't the oldest." The footsteps began again. "We call it SIDS now—"

"I know what SIDS is, Lacy." I flinched. My tone was clipped. She could not do this now. My grandparents hadn't hid the tragedy of their family. They also didn't make up fairy tales to explain medical conditions. Things happened, good or bad. Life was pain. The image of the blonde little girl who watched her cousin die before threatening to shoot up the school came into my head. I'd won an award for capturing her grief. She didn't get a legend to explain why her cousin was bullied —and then tried to retaliate.

For a brief moment, I wished Ioan was here. I shook the thought. This was my family. And my life. "Whatever you're about to say, you should have said weeks ago. No, months ago. If you thought this was a real thing, you should have told me. Even if it wasn't true. How hard is it to say, *hey, Lydcombe is going to a neighbor you should probably go say goodbye?*"

"He's not just a neighbor," Lacy shot back. Her eyes would be glaring at me if we were in the same room. Her nostrils flared at the slightest provocation—something my brothers teased her endlessly about.

"Yeah, I know you two had a thing." It was a cheap shot, but I didn't care.

"He's a friend, Sienna. A really good friend." Her tone turned wistful. "And he cares for you."

"He doesn't even know me." Groaning, I started pacing. She'd missed the point. "For being such a good friend, you never mentioned him before."

"And what would I say?"

"Anything. Something." It was no secret I was the odd man out in my family. But Lacy—why had she kept pivotal information from me? My love for Grandad and Lydcombe was just as much a part of me as my *black sheep* position. "Why am I always left in the dark? Do my parents know?"

"About the house?"

I froze. The tone of her voice told something more. "Is there something else besides the house?"

"They don't believe my dad if that's what you're asking."

I braced myself against the window, my gaze on the gentle waves. "Lacy, is there *anything* else I should know?"

"My dad believes it," she said in a hushed whisper. "He's not the youngest son. He's scared."

"Both our dads are healthy." The hairs on my neck stood on end. Even if my father was sick, he'd hide it. Being ill would be a shot to his ego. He believed he was untouchable.

"Dad has early stages of dementia, Sienna." Her voice shook. My uncle might have been her stepdad but he'd taken the paternal role to heart.

"That ... that doesn't mean ..." Words failed me. My father was the oldest living son. He refused to retire. He believed the tech firms he consulted for needed him desperately. But even if he'd begun any form of treatment—cancer or otherwise, he'd hide it. He'd bury it. He couldn't handle the slow wrinkles appearing on his face. Mortality was not something my father would ever submit to.

"I know it doesn't make sense." The footsteps stopped. "To be honest, I'm jealous."

"Of what?"

"I wasn't lying when I told your parents you're the reason I'm getting married. I wanted a family of my own." She cleared her throat, a telltale sign of her fighting emotions. "I've watched Ioan for decades, Sienna. *Decades*. He's kept his distance. He knows your penchant for mishap. He searches for your work. He doesn't care what you did or did not accomplish. He just wants you to be okay. Whether that's here in the states or over there. I wanted that for me. I wanted someone who wants me to be content more than he wants me. I'm not Brian's trophy. I'm Lacy—a woman in my own right. And Brian loves that woman."

My throat tightened. "I just told Ioan there's nothing between us."

"You act like you've destroyed the boy."

"He's not a boy." At least not the one I'd seen in my mind. That was a child with sandy blonde hair and an impish grin.

Lacy sighed in the phone. "Then don't treat him like one."

I shook my head, even though I knew she couldn't see it. "It's not that simple."

"Yeah, I know." The sound of a chair swiveling carried through the phone. She must be sitting back down. "He's not going anywhere."

"If you ask him, his life is on the line."

"Sienna?" Her voice was shaky again. "I am worried about my dad."

"Alzheimer's runs in our family. It's not a—"

"Oh my gosh, Sienna. It's not just Alzheimer's."

The chill was back. Fear crept in. "Lacy, what are you—"

"I can't—I swore—I shouldn't ..." Footsteps paced again. And then the shutting of a door. She whispered, "Your father is being treated for melanoma. Skin cancer."

"No, he's not." My voice shook. This wasn't happening. Not now—not while I was half a world away. "He started doing chemical peels. I saw him at your engagement party."

"I'm sorry."

"He doesn't have cancer, Lacy." *Take it back.* "I would have noticed."

"Would you?"

"What did you say?" My ears rang. I was shouting. "What—what did you say?"

"I said ..." she sniffed. The footsteps again. "Would you have noticed? Would you have stopped long enough to pay attention?"

I balked and held the phone out in front of me, staring at the screen. This wasn't real. This conversation wasn't happening. *Would you have noticed?* He was my father. Of course, I would have. I slid to my knees, barely registering Lacy calling my name.

"Sienna?"

I picked up the phone and held it to my ear.

"Sienna, are you there?"

My throat went dry. "I am."

"I'm not trying to hurt you." Lacy sniffed and cleared her throat. "This is real, Sienna. This is happening. Whether you want to believe it or not."

"What am I supposed to do?" I cried out, my back against the wall. Taking a picture was the beginning and end of my talents. I wasn't a

CLARISSA KAE

doctor. Nor did I appear to be an attentive daughter. "You're making it sound like there's no hope."

"I know it's hard, but it's not hopeless. I mean ... we could still have a happy ending."

I squirmed. "This isn't a fairy tale, Lacy. There's no magical kiss that can bring Grandad back to me or stop Dad's cancer."

"Not for our parents but for you. And Ioan."

I clenched my fist. She'd crossed the line. "You're pushing for him too hard."

"Yeah, well, I'd like for you *not* to lose your mind, and although you might not care, *I* think Ioan's a good guy. It'd be nice if he didn't drop dead either. Or your brothers."

"Even if you're right, which you're not. But even if there is a curse, how would you solve it?" I hated the whine in my voice. And the worry in hers.

"Right the wrongs."

"I don't even know who was wronged."

"Oh, come on, Sienna. You and Grandad would sing that stupid song all the time. The Welsh woman who falls for the Cornish man. The whole Romeo and Juliet thing."

I scowled—even though she couldn't see me. "That doesn't help in the slightest. And I'm pretty sure the song wasn't about suicide."

"Whatever you want to call it, there was some sort of sacrifice involved."

"Sacrifice was never in the song." They loved each other and died. The end. "Nothing in the song portrayed that. It was just another tragic love story."

"Sienna—" Lacy cut herself off with a groan. "What do you think tragic means? Why is this so hard for you to grasp? You can march in the middle of a violent protest, but you're too scared to believe—no, to even think about the possibility that there's a link between our history and now? You've seen miracles. I know you have. You've told me of cancer patients who've defied the odds. Or last minute change of heart by a mob. Those are stories you've spent your life documenting. Why —just answer me—*why* can't you take a leap? Prove me wrong." Mumbled voices were in the background. She hurried, "Listen, Sienna.

I have to go. I'd love to be wrong on this. Please. Just please prove it. Or better yet, solve it."

The phone call ended. I tossed the phone to the bed and just stared at the sea, its waters beckoning me. Lacy was wrong. She had to be. I'd once believed in my grandfather's myths. Or maybe I once believed in Lydcombe and all its magic. But myths weren't real.

The whispers wrapped around my shoulders. For the first time, it felt more like an embrace, something to long for instead of avoid. A flash of red appeared on the water. Ioan's voice rang in my ear. *Do they always see a woman with red hair?*

Flicking my wrist, I checked the time. Twice I'd waded into the waters at Lydcombe without success, but there was another set of cliffs supposedly connected to this legend. The island. I needed to get back to *Ynys Wair*.

Grabbing my phone and purse, I scrambled down the stairs, texting William. I'd never been to his house. In truth I didn't want to go on my little adventure alone. Inviting Ioan would make me question my findings. He was too close—too involved—to keep an open mind. The proof of his belief was in several sketchbooks around the house.

I froze, a hand on the side door. I needed a sketchbook. Quick as I could, I raced around the house, collecting as many books as I could hold. Just as I slid outside, William stood with his hand up, ready to knock.

William grinned and began grabbing my books. "Are you going to tell me why we're headed to the island?"

"You'll laugh. So, no, I won't."

His lips quirked. "You do realize I've been friends with Lacy *and* Ioan for decades."

"Fantastic. You're officially vice president in charge of proving them wrong."

"Vice president?" He scoffed good-naturedly. "Why can't I be president?"

"You can be king and emperor for all I care."

"King William." He grinned and brushed his knuckles on his chest. "I'll take it."

"What are you doing?" Ioan barked.

His voice pierced me, forcing me to turn around. He stood with his arms folded, hurt in his eyes. His broad shoulders were hunched. I'd once laid my head against his chest. His shoulders promised to bear whatever burdens I'd offer up—his eyes begging the same.

"I'm ..." A lump formed in my throat. "I'm going to the island."

He raised an eyebrow. He'd not expected that answer. He jutted his chin. "With my books?"

"I want to prove Lacy wrong. To prove everyone wrong."

"You spoke to Lacy," Ioan whispered, his eye on William. "I'd have taken you to the island."

"Would you stand in my way?" My voice cracked. It was ridiculous. Silly and stupid. "What if I *do* prove you wrong?"

"I've perfected the art of standing by. I've not stopped you from entering the waters. Or from going to the island. I'll not stand in your way, but I'll stand by. I'll be ready to pull you to safety."

❧ 35 ❧

S ienna
Lydcombe, England: Present Day

WE MADE OUR WAY TO THE *HISTORICAL ROYAL SOCIETY* BUILDING
on the far end of the pier where the employee ship had dropped us off
the last time. We slipped in behind a group of young adult employees
giggling over some meme on the ringleader's phone. The captain
barked at everyone, complaining on how late the shift was running.

William and Ioan fidgeted the entire ride, both men eying me every
few minutes. I felt the tension between them. William's disappointment was written in his furrowed brow and heavy sighs. For once, he'd
thought he'd claimed a victory over Ioan.

A flash of red played peek-a-boo in the waves. My pulse raced and
the whispers shouted. Pretending to be bored, Willam yawned and
began pacing on the other side of the deck.

"Do you see her?" I didn't dare look at Ioan. He'd been hurt by my
earlier comment, *there's nothing between us.* It wasn't the right time to tell

him that I didn't fully believe in an *us*. But there was a feeling of safety that grew when I was around him. It wasn't the romantic love that Lacy used to talk about with her dozens of suitors. This was calm and quiet. Like Brian, her fiancé.

"Ay, I see her." He kept his profile to me.

We stood next to each other, our eyes on the water. The woman came and went. She wasn't swimming or floating, but when I looked, I saw that her hands were tied. And her dress was a blue-gray, the color of Ioan's eyes.

"Ioan?" I had to make one thing very clear. "I don't want it to be true. And that might mean that I prove there's no connection between us."

"Just the fact that we both see a woman in the sea." He smiled wryly. "I won't try to convince you. But I won't stand here and pretend that there's nothing that binds us."

The ship slowed, pulling into the hidden harbor tucked behind the dark cliffs below the castle.

William came over, his hands in his pockets, a fake smile on his face. "Alright, Sherlock. Where to now?"

"I'm not sure." My hands were sweaty. Instinctively, I reached for my camera—and cursed. I'd left it at the house. Life was less scary behind the lens. Stories began and ended with the click of my camera. I hadn't realized how dependent on that one little piece of equipment I'd become. "I guess the phone will have to do."

"Most of the world thinks they're good enough," Ioan offered, mischief in his eye. "I'm fairly certain that the photographer controls the outcome, not the camera."

"I spoke to Lacy."

"So you've said." He stretched, reminding me of his late nights with Grandad. He'd shouldered the weight of my grandfather and his own mother. It was tempting to add my own worries on his steady frame.

"She seems to believe you." I waved a hand in front of me, indicating all of us. "And everything else."

Ioan leaned against the railing, his eyes now on me. "I know what Lacy believes. She's not the one I'm worried about."

William slid in front of us and held out his hand. He was clearly done with Ioan's commentary. "Where shall we start? Better yet, what are we doing?"

"I told you." *Sort of.* There weren't a lot details to give. "Lacy thinks we can solve the family myth. There's hardly anything in Lydcombe. Except more of those." I motioned to the sketchbooks Ioan carried. He'd insisted on holding them, not that I could blame him. If I'd taken my camera, it'd be strapped to me and no one else.

The falcon circled above us, crying down at me.

"Your friend missed you." William shook his head. "I bet his family is part of the crew that poops all over my house."

I'd forgotten about William owning a home on the island. "Where is your house?"

Ioan dipped his head, the toe of his shoe digging at a pebble in the walkway. His smile was far too broad to be hidden.

William chuckled nervously. "That beautiful specimen right there." He pointed to the crumbling stone walls next to the castle, the roof long gone.

"I thought that was a barn."

"It might be now." He shrugged. "That's what happens when your ancestors are priests."

"Wait, you told me there were smugglers here." I grabbed his arm. The woman in red was back on the sea. The whispers buzzed around me. I caught Ioan's gaze. He nodded slightly. He could see her as well.

"Yeah, and?" William furrowed his brow. "I'd rather be accused of being a priest than a criminal."

"But you have a house here."

Ioan took a step back, his eyes on the falcon above us.

"Oh, yeah." William scratched his head. A sheepish look crossed his face. He stepped from me. "It's not that big of a deal."

"What aren't you telling me?" I was missing something. He'd talked about Ioan so often that I'd never asked him about his own ancestors.

He tugged on the collar of his jacket. "You'll think I'm an arse."

Ioan rolled his eyes. "She will if you don't tell her."

"The island was named after my ancestors."

Ioan fought a smile.

The details clicked together. "You're a Wair?" Retreating, I felt as if the ground shook from underneath me. "The first thing you said to me was how Ioan wasn't right in the head because he's a Morgannwg. If the island was named after the smugglers, that means your ancestors are just as guilty. Your idea that Ioan means bad, while William means good doesn't work."

William shot Ioan a nervous glance. "That's not exactly what I said."

"You said, Ioan gets everything. Life is granted to him. And yet an entire island is named after you."

William shot Ioan a nervous glance. "Well, yeah, but he owns it."

I rubbed the bridge of my nose. "That's why you're mad. You think you should have the island."

"You can't tell me you feel any different." William held out his hand to me. "He's stolen your inheritance too."

The red-haired woman shifted, now closer to the ancient fluyt ship on stilts in the harbor. The whispers pulled me forward. Ioan fell in line, following while William called after me, "What are you doing?"

Willam ran to us. He smirked, a hand on my arm. "We came out here to look at a ship?"

Pulling back, I shrugged. "I don't know what I'm looking for. I just feel ... I don't know if it's the right decision, but I think we should look in the ship."

"You've gone mad." William brushed a hand through his hair, his eyes wide. "You believe in this crap, don't you?" He turned to Ioan. "Did you drug her? How do you keep doing this?"

The hair on my neck stood on end. "What are you talking—"

"Lacy," Ioan answered gently. "He thinks I stole Lacy from him all those years ago. And Liam."

"Grandad?" The bite in my voice froze William to where he stood.

William held up his arms in surrender. "Okay, that's going a little too far. I just started visiting him, that's all."

"Only after he'd lost his mind." I brushed past William and marched to the ancient ship. William could have Lacy and any other conversation. I wanted answers. I wanted something to cling to. I

rounded the corner of the harbor. The ship's entire side was disman-
tled, the innards stripped to the studs.

"Sienna, let me explain." William ran after me, stopping at the
ramp. "That boat is a death trap."

"You don't have to come." My skin hummed, the same electric
feeling that came when Ioan was near. Behind me, I heard the heavy
footsteps of Ioan. He was staying true to his declaration. I felt—rather
than saw—he was right behind me. "There's something here."

"Ay, but I don't see the woman." Ioan's voice rolled over me like a
caress.

I reached for him. Without hesitation, his hand was in mine. His
touch was solid, steady. Nervous, I whispered, "I'm going to ask you
something—"

"Yes." Ioan circled me and entered the deck first, his eye on the
wood planks. "It's Elyna. Or at least, I think it is."

"This isn't safe." William was at the ramp, his arms folded. He
wasn't boarding the ship.

Ioan sighed softly. "My mother started the ship's restoration when
she was pregnant with me. It hasn't been touched in decades." He
kneeled in front of an old chest, the wood dented and warped from
exposure. "She thought something would happen if it was returned it
to its former glory. She must have given up." He cracked open the lid,
dust sliding off the top.

I peered into the chest. Only a small leather pouch lay in the
corner. Ioan palmed it and pulled out two quills—or what once were
quills.

Disappointment fell over me. "I felt something. I swear I did."

"I'm not doubting you." Ioan pierced me with a gaze. My stomach
fluttered. He kept his vigil, not turning to William's impatient
fidgeting or glancing to the sea.

"Thank you." A flash of red pulled my focus. In the water, just a few
feet from the ship was the woman, her dark ginger hair shimmering in
the water. The whispers rang in my ear, pulling me. Beckoning me. I
walked toward the railing, ignoring William behind me and Ioan at my
side.

"Sienna, what are you doing?" William whined.

Ioan said nothing. He didn't touch me. He calmly stayed at my side. With a hand on the railing, I scrambled over. Closing my eyes, I leapt into the water below.

⚘ 36 ⚘

K enan
      Bristol Sea, England: 1606

WITH GUT-WRENCHING FORCE, THE CHURNING TIDES HURTLED THE ship forward. Kenan was grateful for the quick passage. The brewing storm was setting an agitated Jowan further on edge. They'd made brilliant time and would be nearing the island soon.

Jowan paced in the tight captain's quarters, a hand on his hip and the other rubbing the back of his neck. "I just want the truth. Whatever it may be."

Elyna stared straight forward, facing the ocean. Her red hair complemented the emerald chair covering. She'd grown calm since boarding the ship. "You're wanting someone to punish."

"D'you see that I'm trying?" Jowan held out an arm, a plea to Kenan. "I'm trying to be fair. She won't even tell me where the boy came from."

Kenan reached for her. She didn't move. "Elyna, if you're trying to protect me. Please, don't. If I murdered my friend, I'll pay the price."

Elyna set her jaw and said nothing. Sorrow filled her eyes. She blinked back tears, clenching his heart.

"Jowan is grieving his father." Kenan felt the lump in his throat. "Even if I'm to blame, Jowan needs to know the truth. If I'd not passed out, I could tell him myself."

She winced and shook her head.

Kenan narrowed his gaze. She was protecting him. She had to be. "Jowan?"

Jowan stopped pacing, dark circles under his eyes. "Ay?"

"I should be the one to tell the men." It was the right thing to do—Kenan knew for certain. "I'll confess that I was the one who shot your father."

"I don't believe it. They won't believe it." Jowan shook his head. He'd not dismissed the idea, but he hadn't embraced it. The friendship was fractured, held together with a failing thread. "Her word is not trusted."

"The crew wasn't there." Kenan knew Jowan was right. They would blame Elyna for Mr. Wair's death *and* the murder of the company. Kenan could only protect them if he could keep their good opinion.

"I'll not speak a word against anyone." Elyna stood slowly and walked to the captain's desk, her hand trailing the edge of the desk. "But I'll sign whatever confession you put in front of me."

"Confession?" Kenan shot to his feet. "To what?"

She wouldn't look him in the eye. Jowan hadn't moved; he stood frozen in place. Elyna sat at the chair and carefully preened the quill. "I'm ready."

"There's no confession to be had." Kenan leaned over the desk. "If you state, by your own hand, that you killed Jowan's father"—he pointed to the door—"they'll be at your throat. I cannot help you."

"Who are you protecting?" Jowan's low voice carried in the small quarters. "Is it Kenan?"

Elyna cocked her head to the side. "How would you properly start a confession?"

"This is a cruel joke. Even for a witch." Jowan folded his arms. "But I have my answer." Without another word, he stormed from the room.

Kenan sank to his knees. "I did it, didn't I? I killed him. He was like a father to me."

"You did not." Elyna's hand made quick work.

"Then why are you doing this?" Kenan reached for the parchment. She held it back and continued to write. He tried again. "Elyna, what are you doing?"

"I'm doing what you did—what you would do." Deftly, she powdered the paper, tipping the surplus back in the tin. "I'll give this to Jowan."

"You will not."

She lifted her chin. "I have something for you as well."

"You can't save me, Elyna." Kenan had killed Jowan's father. A priest. He'd not meant to. "There is a price to be paid for sacrificing the innocent. Better to face the punishment now instead of the eternities. My die is cast."

Elyna took in the room, a tear running down her cheek. "Remember this, Kenan."

"He won't let you." Kenan had to intervene. Jowan hated Elyna, but not more than justice. Jowan knew—as did Kenan—that the guilty party was Kenan Rothesay, second son to the ruthless Baron of Lydcombe.

Elyna smiled sadly and left.

Kenan didn't chase her. Jowan's face was still fresh in Kenan's mind. Jowan was torn between loyalty of blood or brother-in-arms. Kenan mirrored Elyna's position earlier and sat at the desk. Jowan couldn't inherit the island, but Kenan would make it right. He would not hurt his oldest friend.

With a heavy sigh, Kenan left the captain's quarters. Elyna was in front of the boy, tears streaking down her face. They stood next to the railing, away from the men.

Burke shook his head. "No, no, no."

Elyna saw Kenan and wiped her cheek with the back of her hand. She gathered Burke against her.

"Elyna—"

"Promise me, Kenan. Promise me, you'll look after him?" Elyna grabbed Kenan's hand, the tears falling once more.

He opened his mouth to speak, but froze. His mind filled with her memories.

Elyna was in her childhood home, Morgannwg castle. Her grand-mother was coaxing her father to eat. A woman in worn servant clothes entered the dining hall, Burke at her side—his eyes wide with fear. Elyna rushed toward them, her arms outstretched. Burke clung to her.

Kenan could feel the boy's embrace, the arms around Elyna's neck. She kissed Burke's cheek, *It's just a little adventure. You'll be back in a few days.*

He nodded solemnly, *Yes, mother.*

The memory faded away. *Mother.* Kenan was once again standing on the deck of his ship. *Mother.*

Elyna was a mother—she was Burke's mother. Kenan had accused her of hiding something at the castle, of not being truthful. Jowan had not trusted her either. She was a mother. The thought echoed in Kenan's head. Before he could speak, his head filled with another memory.

Elyna's chest was heavy with worry. She'd watched the maid take her trembling son away. Burke looked so much like his father before the man had passed away. Neither wanted to leave her side. Elyna's decision to keep her son away from Rothesay's men and their prying eyes kept her warm at night. She would not let Rothesay have Burke or anyone else dear to her. Elyna had stood at the edge of the drawbridge long after she couldn't see him. Elyna had watched Burke glance back every few minutes as he walked from her arms. And now she stood in the tower, listening for the sound of an approaching army.

Kenan felt her love and panic—and the rush of another memory.

Elyna's hands were tied. The yard of the church was in the distance. Kenan recognized the walls and the gorse of Swansea. Elyna stood by her horse with Burke gripping her skirt. Matthew shouted and ran toward a tree.

Using her teeth, Elyna pulled at the rope, setting her hands free. A pistol fell from Matthew's belt. Elyna scrambled to pick it up, giving it to Burke. She stepped in front of him, whispering, *We'll run when he's not looking.*

Matthew aimed his rifle at an approaching cart—a priest sat at the front. Elyna covered her mouth. Her gaze flicked to Kenan jumping from a tree. Kenan was racing toward Matthew, his rifle perched, ready to aim.

No, cried Elyna.

Burke circled in front of her, his face determined like his father. He raised the pistol and fired—Kenan as well. Elyna screamed.

Burke's thin hands shook. His lip trembled. He kept the pistol aimed. The gun went off again. Matthew fell back. Burke yelled, the gun went off once more. The priest crumbled. Burke dropped the gun, his face white with panic. He killed the priest.

Elyna gathered Burke to her chest. Elyna slipped the gun in her pocket.

Kenan struggled to breathe as the image flashed forward to Elyna standing on the ship in Swansea. She watched Jowan and Kenan, their expression strained. She waited for their backs to turn before dropping the gun in the waters below.

The memories disappeared. Kenan stepped back, his heart in his throat. Burke—Burke was her son. Kenan swallowed hard. Burke had shot him. Fear tied Kenan's tongue. Burke had shot Jowan's father. The secrecy, the protection—Elyna had done it all for her son.

Kenan squeezed her hand, his heart heavy with grief. There was no easy path for her—or Kenan. He rubbed his thumb in circles on her hand. He'd given his word and a blood oath. He would protect her.

A tear slid down her cheek. She shook her head. "No, Kenan."

Kenan looked from her face to the boy's. Elyna was a widow—and Rothesay would love nothing more than a tool to dominate her. He would use the boy to force Elyna to do his bidding. Rothesay could steal her home, her son, and her will. And now Jowan would hate her for eternity. Her son had killed his father. Someone would pay the price.

Kenan fell to his knees. He would not let a boy carry the sin of a greedy baron. "Burke?"

The boy turned to him, his lip quivering. He was strong when he needed to be—Matthew was no longer a threat to Elyna.

Kenan saw the same strength and vulnerability in his own mother.

He saved her. He would save Elyna and Burke. They were his to protect.

"You, sir, did a very brave thing. You're safe now." Kenan held out a hand. Burke hesitated before taking it. "For now and forever."

Slowly, Kenan stood, wrapping Elyna against his chest. She clung to him, her hands gripping his shirt. He hadn't the slightest idea how to remedy this. But he would. He'd take whatever oath needed. Elyna would not be delivered to Rothesay and Jowan would be made whole.

She leaned forward.

Jowan came closer, his eyes narrowed.

Elyna leaned up on her toes. With dark eyes full of grief, she kissed Kenan's cheek. She stepped back and turned to Jowan. Jowan's eyes widened. Kenan wondered if she'd slipped into Jowan's mind.

Elyna gathered her skirts with both hands and said to Burke, "Remember what I said, love. Always and forever." With a nod to Kenan, she scrambled up the railing and fell backward to the swirling waters below.

Kenan lunged for her, his hand raking the hem of her skirt. Her eyes held his gaze. She hit the water and closed her eyes. The water swallowed her whole.

Kenan wrapped a leg over the rail. "Elyna!"

Jowan tackled him, pulling him to the ship's floor. Kenan fought, his injured shoulder screaming. She would drown with her heavy clothes. And the tides. He struggled against Jowan's grip. Elyna needed Kenan.

Jowan wrestled Kenan against the railing, pinning him in place. "She's gone."

"No!" Kenan gasped for air. "No!"

"Be strong," Jowan snapped. He sat back, revealing the broken boy clinging to the railing—tears streaming down his face. "Be strong for him."

Kenan stilled. Burke stared at the ocean, despair in his silence.

Jowan helped Kenan to his feet and held out an arm to the boy. "She'll return, Burke."

A falcon circled above. Kenan held out his arm. The falcon descended, flapping its wings—landing on Burke's shoulder.

Jowan nodded. "From one rescue to another."

37

S ienna
Ynys Wair Island, United Kingdom: Present Day

MY HAND BRUSHED AGAINST THE SHIP'S RAILING AS I FELL TO THE water below. The splash of cold took my breath away. I gasped. The water temperature felt colder here at the island than by Lydcombe. Or maybe I'd not yet warmed from my earlier dance with the sea. My lungs struggled to work. Sputtering, I beat my hands and legs to keep me upright. The woman turned to me, her eyes dark and her skin fair. She was older than me, closer to Lacy's age. The set of her jaw and shape of her eyes was eerily similar to what Ioan's mother must have looked like. The family resemblance was uncanny.

My teeth chattered. Fear threatened to take over.

A splash to my left. *Ioan.* He coughed, his eyes wide from the shock in temperature. He found my gaze and offered a hesitant nod. If he thought I was crazy, he kept it to himself.

The woman turned to Ioan and tilted her head, smiling. My heart skipped a beat. Her smile matched Ioan's, the curve of the lip, the lift of the cheek.

Ioan reached for me, questions in his eyes. The panic fled. He was here. I was safe.

The woman opened her mouth. *Elyna.* She was Elyna. Words didn't come but I somehow knew who she was. From faraway her hands had looked tied but she held out her hand, an inkwell in her palm. The same inkwell Ioan had shown me in his castle. She extended her hand to mine.

I grabbed the inkwell—in a flash, I was transported to another time. Another place.

A man with a pistol in his belt held a brunette woman by the throat. She was a maid. I somehow knew that detail. The man shouted at me—no, he was shouting at Elyna. This was a memory.

Matthew. The man's name was Matthew. A boy stood next to the brunette, yelling at Matthew. *Burke.* The boy's name was Burke. Memories came and went. The boy fired a gun. The priest was bleeding. Elyna's body trembled with grief. The priest was Jowan's father.

Another man lay on the road—Kenan. His name was Kenan. The memory shoved me forward in time. Elyna and Kenan are on the ship. The same boat that was behind us in the harbor. Elyna jumped to the sea, taking the blame of the boy.

Shivering, I pulled back. "You sacrificed yourself."

Elyna floated forward and closed my fingers around the inkwell, gently pushing it toward my chest. She grabbed Ioan's hand and placed it in mine.

She cocked her head to the side, a faraway look in her eye. *Right the wrong.*

"Who was wronged?" I asked, my teeth chattering. My hands and feet were numb, the water chilling me to the bone.

Elyna lifted her gaze, pointing to the ship where William stood. *Jowan.* She lowered her focus and smiled at me. *Kenan.* I felt the warmth of her love—not for me but for a man who would have done anything to protect her.

"Here." William called from up above. He waved his arms toward us. "They're down here."

To our right, a small row boat was making its way toward us from the other side of the employee harbor. William had called for help. Elyna faded, disappearing into the waves.

"Wait." I reached for her. Nothing. Only water surrounded us. "Elyna?" I spun around. "Where did she go?"

Ioan's hand found mine. "Hey, it's okay. She's gone."

I squeezed his hand—he was real. This wasn't some fairy tale that my grandfather sang about. Elyna was real. Kenan and Jowan. There was love and grief, just like the stories I'd captured with my camera.

Too soon, the security boat came, the men bright and cheery. They plucked us from the water. My hands and feet were numb. And trembling. My body ached but not from the cold, from being separated too soon from Elyna. I'd spent my life listening to the whispers of the water. I wasn't ready to end that chapter.

The security men peppered us with questions. I couldn't answer. Elyna was gone. It felt wrong to speak so soon of the dead—she'd been gone for centuries but she'd never truly left. Not until today.

The second we docked, William chatted to the security guards. Ioan stayed close by. He didn't touch or speak, only silent support. William held a one-sided conversation while Ioan and I changed into matching flannel pajamas. I swam in my borrowed pair while Ioan mirrored the American legend Paul Bunyan.

"You realize Doris is going to kill me?" William played host and poured tea for Ioan and I in the kitchen. "She's going to take the dullest knife in Liam's kitchen. She's going to gut me."

I couldn't focus on his words, my gaze staring out the window. There was a heaviness, both bitter and sweet in what had happened. Elyna wasn't the true victim. She'd sacrificed herself to save her son. Burke had accidentally wronged Jowan's family. And Kenan. The memory of Elyna's pain hurt my heart.

"She's not there, Sienna." Ioan's low voice pulled me back to the kitchen.

"Who is *she?*" William asked. "Have you both gone nutty?"

"Elyna." The name danced on my tongue. "Her name was Elyna Morgannwg." And she was gone. For most of my life, the sea had been a bond with my grandfather. And now it was gone.

"Another Morgannwg in the mix." William rolled his eyes.

Ioan gave a curt shake of his head. He seemed bothered by the loss of her as well, tension rolling off of him.

I cradled the mug. "Jowan was wronged. He should have had the island. It would have made him whole."

"Jowan?" William nodded his head dramatically. "Ah, Jowan. Love that guy. Sure wish he'd come around more often."

"Jowan Wair," I whispered. The inkwell was in the center of the counter. It was impossible for Elyna to have it, but there it was. She'd placed it in my hand and now it sat, staring at me, begging me to do the right thing. She'd given it back—just like the island should be given to the Wair family. "*Ynys Wair.*"

"Ioan, come on." William nodded to me. "She isn't making sense. What is she talking about? Please tell me this is a joke."

"I don't like it." Ioan frowned. "But she's right. We need to right the wrong."

"So that answers that." William sighed and shook his head. "Sienna was my last hope of sanity. Everyone's lost it."

Ioan rolled the quill on the counter with his finger. "I'm signing the island over to you. We'll do it officially with a solicitor, but we should do it here."

"With the inkwell." I placed the mug on the counter and flipped the hinge of the inkwell top. The inside seemed empty of ink, but I still wanted to try.

"Is anyone listening to me?" William held out his arms.

Ioan stuck the end of the quill in his mouth, then dipped the edge in the inkwell. He pulled a scrap piece of paper and scratched, *I, Ioan Morgannwg gift Ynys Wair to William Wair.* He signed his name at the bottom and slid the paper over to him.

"Not touching that with a ten foot pole." William made an X with his arms. "Not taking that trip to Crazy Town."

"Please, do me a favor and just sign it." I knew exactly what we sounded like. I'd accused Ioan of being insane as well. "What's the worst that could happen?"

William rolled his eyes and took the quill. "I can't believe I'm doing this." He signed his name and opened his mouth to crack a joke—and froze, his gaze on the window. "Did you see that?"

Just beyond the rocks was Elyna, her dark red hair and blue dress matching the pale blue-gray of the water. I slipped from the barstool and waited for the whispers. Nothing. No song. No pull toward the ocean.

Then she was gone. William shook his head. "Who was that?"

"Elyna. She's Elyna Morgannwg." I gripped the edge of the stool, wishing for just one more glimpse.

"If you can hang around Monday, I'll head into town and start the process." Ioan's gaze flicked from Williams to mine. His brow furrowed in frustration.

"You're not taking the mickey out of me are you?" William narrowed his gaze. "This is a joke, isn't it? You guys saw her right?" Before Ioan could answer, William laughed. He tapped his knuckles on the counter. "That's a good joke."

"I wasn't joking." Ioan stood and offered his hand to William.

William's mouth fell open. "I ... I ... I need some air." William backed away, disbelief in his face. He turned and marched out the door, a hand to his head.

Ioan chuckled and wiped his hands down his face. "That should shut him up." Ioan's eyes were back on me, his lips taut.

"Are you alright?" I asked.

His hands fell to his lap. "What happens now?"

"We go back to Lydcombe." I knew it was wishful thinking but maybe, just possibly Grandad was healed.

"Alzheimer's attacks the brain, Sienna." Ioan warned. "I'm not sure a curse can reverse the damage."

"Then why did we do it?" I scowled. "Don't answer that. I'm fully aware that I sound like a toddler."

He smirked but then his face sobered. He tilted his head. "If he doesn't get better. Will you stay?"

"I don't know." I forced my head to clear. Ioan's ability to look in my mind wasn't something I wanted right now. The decision to stay or go was something I needed to make alone.

"That's a no." He smiled softly. "And that's okay."

"Why?" I waited for the subtle dig. Instead, he offered his hand. Lacing our fingers together, I felt the lack—the void of what had been. There wasn't the hum or the electric snap. Maybe it was a sign—maybe it *was* time to go.

Ioan's gaze flicked from our hands to my eyes, then back again. He must have felt the change too. This was good-bye.

I slid from the barstool and stood before him, his legs on either side of me. "I've never been good at staying in once place. I don't know when I'll leave. That'll depend on Grandad."

Ioan didn't meet my gaze. He hunched his shoulders, worry in his eyes. "I don't want to cage you, but I need you to call me. To check in."

"And why is that?" I squeezed his fingers.

"Because I can't peek inside your mind anymore. I can't be there to save you." He sighed and looked toward the water.

"You're not forbidding me to go?" The electricity snapped alive at his confession, spreading from his touch. I felt the reassurance, the warmth and security of Ioan Morgannwg.

He raised an eyebrow. "I've spent my entire life with you in my head. I'd no sooner stop the rain than ask you to change."

"Do you think it'll pass, this independent streak?" A lump formed in my throat. My parents waited for me at every turn, hoping I would see the light and get my act together. "Do you hope that one day I'll give up the freedom?"

"When you flew in, I told you that sometimes it's not enough to feel the warmth of a fire. I only asked that you not go at it alone." Ioan pulled our intertwined hands to his mouth. He kissed my knuckle, sending my pulse racing. "I've known you longer than I've known myself. I will be here. I don't need your sacrifice. Or your will."

"What about my parents?" I felt the weight of their judgement. They'd hoped I would snag a surgeon or a millionaire. Not the supposedly insane neighbor who inherited Grandad's home.

"Give them time." Ioan wrapped an arm around my waist, drawing me close. He kissed my nose. Delightful shivers ran down my spine. "I'm going to miss seeing you."

"Seeing me or seeing inside my head?"

"Both." He kissed my cheek and whispered in my ear, "But that doesn't mean you should stay. If you feel the pull, give into it. I'll always be here."

❅ 38 ❅

S ienna
London, England: Present Day

THE LIGHTS OF THE CITY BLURRED AS THE TRAIN SPED TOWARD Lydcombe. I checked the time. Ioan would be pacing in the kitchen until I arrived. I'd texted him just before getting arrested, thinking I would be home in a matter of hours. The police had other ideas. Several hours later, I was finally on my way.

Grandad's routine hadn't changed, leaving Ioan with the majority of the work. The doctors believed my grandfather's fight with Alzheimer's was at an impasse. He'd not regressed, but not improved. The disease appeared to be frozen in time. The doctors were encouraged, but not shocked while Ioan was rejuvenated. He followed Grandad around like a harried mother. If a step was slightly less shaky, Ioan declared Grandad nearly cured. Last week, my grandfather ate soup without spilling, Ioan begged me to tell my family.

I called my father but not to talk about Grandad. It took two hours of coaxing before Dad admitted to skin cancer. He was quick to point out that his was improving—Mom butted in and corrected him. Like Grandad, my father's cancer was frozen. It hadn't shrunk but it'd not gained any ground.

Giving the island to William didn't reverse the course of history. It had only stopped the progress—and bought us time.

I'd hoped for a miracle, or at least, a moment of clarity with Grandad. With each passing day, the restlessness grew. Ioan encouraged me to continue my career. I'd flown to Los Angeles, New York and even Glasgow to document the world we lived in. My parents had made their frustrations clear. Not only had I failed the family in helping Grandad, but I'd continued bouncing from story to story.

I checked my phone. The last text I'd sent Ioan was filled with a dozen apologies. This was a crossroads and my pulse beat nervously in my veins. I never stuck around long enough for someone to worry— boyfriend or otherwise. Having someone at home pacing the kitchen wasn't something I was accustomed to.

My phone lit up with Ioan's text. *Please tell me you're in one piece.*

I am. Hugging my camera bag, I added, *But my camera is busted.*

Please tell me you didn't murder the person who ruined it.

A smile played on my lips. I could picture Ioan's smirk. There wasn't a hint of judgement.

I wished the train would hurry. I craved the security Ioan offered. *Are you worried I've become the wolf?*

Oh, the poor lamb. The police didn't stand a chance. The texting bubble appeared, only to disappear. He must be typing a novel. A GIF popped up—a lamb dancing around a wolf.

The early morning rays peeked above the black mountains. I rubbed my tired eyes. A quick trip to London had turned into an all night affair. If my camera's storage chip was still good, I would have amazing pictures of retired immigrants protesting against Brexit in their wheelchairs.

The train slowed and I opened the app to hire a driver. It was too early in the morning to rent a car. In just over a month, my family would be coming to Lydcombe. Lacy had convinced the entire Rothesay clan to give their respects to Grandad before it was too late. Her father—my uncle—was going to read the will. Ioan was against it.

He still didn't like the idea of inheriting Lydcombe. Having Ioan take care of the house and my grandfather had been a blessing. My pulse raced. He'd have to face my family's wrath.

Watching Grandad stare blankly at the windows was excruciating. But having Ioan by my side had been peaceful—no, there was something deeper there. He'd been home.

A thought wiggled in. After tonight, Ioan could very well ask me to walk away from photography. I knew he worried about me. The late nights and potential dangers were something that bothered him greatly, even if he didn't talk about it. Clutching my camera bag to my chest, I let the grief wash over me. I'd stubbornly refused to give up my independence. My parents wanted me to fit into a neat little box. But was my career worth more than Ioan's concern?

My stomach twisted and turned the entire ride to Lydcombe. As I exited the car, the sun stretched out along the sea. Morning was here. I should make my way to the house, but the sea was far too inviting. I walked to the garden wall at the edge of Grandad's property. Cornwall would always be home.

"So it's to be a sequel then?" A shadow fell across my view. *Ioan*. His presence was a thrilling comfort. Dark circles underlined his eyes and his hair hadn't been properly brushed.

Guilt nipped at my heart. "I'm sorry."

"For what?" He stood beside me with his distinct strange. Not English or Cornish enough. He was perfectly in between both countries.

"Because of me you were up all night."

"I was already up with Liam." Smirking, he wrapped an arm around my waist.

"You know what I mean." Warmth settled into my chest. Turning into his embrace, I toyed with the zipper on his jacket. "Are you mad?"

He stepped back, his brow furrowed. "I was worried. Not angry."

"Do you wish—do you want me to stop?" I couldn't meet his gaze. The truth would hurt too much.

"Is this because of your parents?" With a finger, he gently raised my chin. "Is that why you're acting funny? You think they'll pitch a fit when they come for the holidays?"

"Do you? I mean, honestly, do you want me to stop?"

He tucked a strand of my hair behind my ear. "I'd be lying if I said I didn't worry."

My heart sank. "I know—"

"Whoa, now." He brushed his hand along my cheek. "But I know how much it means to you—"

"You mean more," I whispered.

His eyes widened. A slow grin crept across his face. "Do I now?" He kissed my forehead, his lips lingering on my skin.

Home. Ioan was all that was home. He was the bridge from my ancestors to my future. I would never give him up.

"Ay, Sienna. I love you. But I won't be asking for you to sacrifice your joy for me." He took another step back. The electric hum I'd come to expect snapped alive—then grew. This was different. The whispers that had grown quiet swirled around me. Ioan didn't seem to notice, his gaze on me. "But in full disclosure, I'll be asking your father for his blessing. I'll be a true gent about it all."

"My father?" The wind caressed my skin. A song was carried in the breeze. Something had changed. I spun around, my eyes on the sea but there wasn't a flash of red. Elyna wasn't there.

"Are you alright?" Ioan's hand was on the small of my back. Steady. And strong.

"I thought I heard something." I reached for his hand, placing it between mine. "I swear to you, I heard it."

"I am not doubting you." His voice was tender, calling to me in a way the sea never had.

"Thank you." I squeezed his hand and turned to the house. Tossing over my shoulder, I said, "Are you sure you want to marry a wolf?"

He held out his arms. "I'll come willingly. A lamb to the slaughter."

With my arm looped through his, we walked to the house through the side door. The smell of Cornish potato cakes welcomed us into the kitchen. Doris was chuckling, a spatula in her hand. She waved it at the counter where my grandfather sat.

He smiled and turned to us. "Ah, you're home."

I froze. His eyes were clear—for the moment. His mind would cloud in a minute and my heart would break all over again. Doris' smile faded. She busied herself at the stove. Ioan didn't move, but I felt him glance at me.

"Sienna?" Grandad looked confused, his eyes scanning me. They lingered on my hand clasping Ioan's. His eyebrows raised and he stood, his movement slow. "It's done then."

"Sienna ..." I repeated. He'd called me by my name. *Sienna.* My throat tightened. It'd been years—*years*—since he knew who I was.

Ioan pulled me forward. "Ay, it's Sienna, your granddaughter."

Grandad's eyebrows knitted together, his mind confused once more.

Doris cleared her throat and set plates on the counter. She murmured, "He's been like that all mornin'. One minute he's the same Liam I've always known. The next, he's a man without a mind."

"He said my name." *Sienna.* Grandad had recognized me. "The whispers. I swear something happened."

"When?" Ioan wasn't looking at me, his focus on my grandfather.

"At the wall." I pointed in the direction of the sea. "When you talked about proposing."

"Proposing?" Doris dropped her spatula. She rushed to pick it up.

Ioan smiled, pride in his eyes. "Careful, Sienna. We don't need Doris having a heart attack."

"It's not *my* heart that needs mending." She gave a good-natured huff.

Grinning, Ioan cradled my jaw. "Promise me you won't give up photography."

"Are you sure?" I needed his tenderness, even at the price of my career.

"I'm not an ogre, Sienna." He leaned in—my breath hitched—our faces were inches from each other. "I've watched you. I know you." He kissed my forehead. "I understand you. But most of all, I love you."

The whispers whirled around me. My heart leapt to my throat. *I know you.* Like a hurricane, dozens of images flashed through my mind. The compulsion to jump in the heart of a violent protest, the curiosity of the homeless addicts—all of it—was a *need.* And now, the same pull wrapped around my waist, inviting me toward Ioan. Toward home.

I gripped the collar of his shirt and whispered, "I love you."

He brushed his lips against mine. He kissed me softly, smiling against my lips—settling the debate. I wouldn't give up photography and this was where I belonged. Lydcombe was my foundation. And so was Ioan.

Grandad's mind would come and go. Heartache and pain were a part of life. But Ioan was a part of me. Peace settled around my shoulders. Ioan was steady while I jumped from story to story. He knew his place in the world while I hadn't quite found my niche. Ioan pulled me closer, cutting through my thoughts. Maybe I did know where I belonged.

ABOUT THE AUTHOR

Clarissa Kae is a preeminent voice whose professional career began as a freelance editor in 2007. She's the former president of her local California Writers Club after spending several years as the Critique Director.

Since her first novel, she's explored different writing genres and created a loyal group of fans who eagerly await her upcoming release. With numerous awards to her name, Clarissa continues to honor the role of storyteller.

Aside from the writing community, she and her daughters founded Kind Girls Make Strong Women to help undervalued nonprofit organizations—from reuniting children with families to giving Junior Olympic athletes their shot at success.

She lives in the agricultural belly of California with her family and farm of horses, chickens, dogs and kittens aplenty.

www.clarissakae.com

facebook.com/AuthorClarissaKae
instagram.com/clarissa__kae

ALSO BY CLARISSA KAE

Pieces To Mend

Taming Christmas

Once And Future Wife Series

Once And Future Wife

Disorder In The Veins (Summer 2021)

Victorian Fairy Tales

A Dark Beauty, Beauty & the Beast